LITTLE GIRL LOST

When three-year-old Emilia Troy goes missing everyone knows that social worker Joshua Salem is the prime suspect. Although Emilia lived with her widowed and remarried father, Joshua was convinced that the child was at risk. Three days later a body is found in a shallow grave. Superintendent Gregory Summers has several suspects – and a new Chief Inspector sidelined with family problems. In the middle of a countryside riddled with foot and mouth disease, events move towards a chilling climax as he tries to trap an adversary who is cunning, ruthless and quite possibly insane...

LITTLE GIRL LOST

by

Susan Kelly

Magna Large Print Books
Long Preston, North Yorkshire,
BD23 4ND, England.

British Library Cataloguing in Publication Data.

Kelly, Susan
    Little girl lost.

    A catalogue record of this book is
    available from the British Library

    ISBN   0-7505-2001-9

First published in Great Britain in 2002
by Allison & Busby Limited

Copyright © 2002 by Susan Kelly

Cover illustration © Anthony Monaghan

The right of Susan Kelly to be identified as the author of this work has been asserted by her in accordance with the Copyright, Designs and Patents Act, 1988

Published in Large Print 2003 by arrangement with
Allison & Busby Limited

Magna Large Print is an imprint of Library Magna Books Ltd.

Printed and bound in Great Britain by
T.J. (International) Ltd., Cornwall, PL28 8RW

Prologue

By the evening of the first day of spring, three-year-old Emilia Troy had been missing for a day and a half and concern for her welfare was beginning to rumble into open hostility, even anger, among her neighbours.

The Peabody Estate, where the child lived with her father and stepmother, represented the more attractive face of Newbury's municipal housing. Councillor Mrs Maureen Peabody, the town's first female mayor, had opened it in person in 1978, wielding a silver trowel without skill and boasting openly that it was the finest council estate in the land. Onlookers, who had no idea who Mrs Peabody was and whom rumour had promised a minor royal, stood in the mud looking disappointed, as the photographs in the *Newbury Weekly News* testified the following Thursday.

The town's planners had learned from the high-rise, densely-packed mistakes of their predecessors. The small development was centred on a 'village green'. Four blocks of flats in mellow brick, each only four storeys high, stood as corner posts to Peabody

Green, right angles of a square, a row of cosy terraced cottages making up each side of the rectangle. Garages and hard standing were tucked discreetly round the back so as not to spoil the view, filling the half acre of land between Peabody Green and the Victorian-Gothic sprawlings of the Kennet Hospital.

All the cottages and half of the flats had passed into private ownership under right-to-buy legislation during the eighties, leaving something of an us-and-them atmosphere between the mortgaged and the unmortgaged, between those who had an inheritance to hand down to their offspring and those who did not. In the late nineties the dozen flats that remained in council ownership had been sold to a holding company named Peabody Enterprises, along with overall responsibility for the estate. Rents had risen steeply to cover the cost of repairs and soon only those eligible for housing benefit could be persuaded to take them on, to the annoyance of their home-owning neighbours.

The Troy family lived in a two-bedroomed flat on the top floor of Beaumont House at the north-west corner of the Green. Joshua Salem, the single man suspected of having abducted Emilia, also lived on the estate, but in one of the cottages, number four, on the south side.

Josh was one of the inheritors.

The clocks had not yet gone forward for daylight saving and it was full dark by seven-thirty that evening. All but three of the cottages showed lights, mostly the flickering of televisions behind thin curtains. Only number four south side had been dark since Monday, when Emilia had vanished at some time between the hours of eleven and two.

Although it was little more than twenty-four hours since the police had been called, rumour had spread round the estate where people knew their neighbours if only to say 'Good Morning' and a whispered 'Have you heard about the little Troy girl?' Emilia and her shabby father were a familiar sight to the residents, walking along the pathways, hand in hand, the father habitually silent but the child laughing and chattering with all the zeal of an infant for whom language is a brilliant new toy.

Roger Troy stood on his balcony looking out over the Green. He was barefoot and in his shirt sleeves but manifested no sign of cold, despite a stiff breeze which periodically spat sleet into his face and toyed with the prematurely grey hair which he wore loose about his bony shoulders.

As always, at least since his illness, he stood very still so that a casual observer might glance twice to check that he was a living, breathing human being and not a trick of the light. His sedated eyes, large in his thin, pale face, moved slowly up and down the asphalt path that bordered the Green, as if his daughter might materialise out of the night.

It was impossible to tell what he was thinking, or if he thought at all.

Roger usually slipped out to the balcony at this time of night to enjoy the single cigarette he allowed himself each day, keeping the smoke away from Emilia's little lungs. Tonight, although his daughter was in no danger from passive smoking, his craving for tobacco seemed to have gone with her and his smoking hand hung limply by his side.

Not all the lamps that edged the Green had come on at dusk. Two along the south side needed new bulbs. Peabody Enterprises had been informed of the fact five days ago but had yet to act on the information. If Roger Troy was staring at Salem's house, then he would see nothing but a dark shape, hidden among identical dark shapes.

If Roger saw movement outside that house a moment later, then he gave no reaction. If he heard the crash of breaking glass in the downstairs front room, then he made no response. If he saw the whoosh of yellow flame, first erupting noisily as the home-made petrol bomb exploded and later, encouraged by the wind, settling into a rapid devouring of curtains, carpets and upholstery, then he did not care.

If he saw, let alone recognised, the black-clad figure that was now sprinting silently past the garages into the refuge of the hospital grounds, then no one would ever know.

He went back inside as if nothing un-usual had occurred, drawing the curtains behind him, and wiped his feet carefully since the balcony was covered with a slick film of melted water. Now he shivered, despite the underfloor heating which was included in the rent and so was kept on all the time except for the most broiling summer's day.

He had promised Concepta that he would eat the fish pie she'd left for him but he had no appetite and it sat unregarded in the microwave. She had left the TV on when she went out to work on the night shift and he clicked it off with a tut of annoyance, unable to endure the gaudy colours and bright voices of the sort of brainless game show that she watched.

She had already worked a day shift today but her friend and colleague Alice had rung in sick and she had volunteered. They could do with the money and it wasn't as onerous as it sounded: the patients were asleep by nine and she could get some rest in the nurses' room, available in an emergency. As

11

she had said, there was little point in her sitting round the flat brooding – he did of enough of that for them both – and he had the ward number if he needed to call her urgently, if there was any news.

He was glad that his wife had a friend at last, perhaps the first she had ever made. Glad, even, for the refrain of 'Alice says this' and 'Alice thinks that' that had made up so much of her conversation these last few weeks.

By the time the wail of sirens became audible seven minutes later, called by the belatedly vigilant Digby Mercer, Roger Troy was absorbed in his project.

Oblivious.

Chapter 1

Earlier that day, on the morning of that same spring equinox, Superintendent Gregory Summers had been sitting in his office on the top floor of Newbury police station, contemplating retirement. This was something he did regularly, usually – though not exclusively – at the end of the month when his computerised payslip wound its way through the innards of Newbury police station and into his in-tray.

He had almost done his thirty years and could retire on two-thirds of his pay: an ample income for a man who had no dependants – unless you counted Angelica, who would not thank you for thus describing her – and had long paid off his mortgage. It seemed next to insane to put in the hours he worked, endure the strain of the things he heard and witnessed, when they would pay him good money to put his feet up by the fire when he was done with pottering round the garden or propping up the bar of the Blue Ball in Kintbury.

But how would Angie feel when her fellow students at Reading University asked casually, 'And what does your boyfriend do?' and she had to say, 'He's retired,' conjuring up an image of a white-haired man in slippers and elasticated trousers.

On the other hand, if Angie were ever to leave him, then he would need his work to keep him sane. He sang softly to himself: 'I've got my job to keep me sane' to the tune of 'I've got my love to keep me warm.'

He remembered Joey Snowy, one of his predecessors as head of Newbury CID, dead six months after retirement. Long time ago now. He had spent most of those months hanging pathetically round the local pubs, waiting for his former colleagues to come in, eagerly questioning them about the latest cases and being

13

politely but firmly rebuffed.

Out of the loop.

He reached the same conclusion he always reached on this subject and muttered, 'You'll have to carry me out in a box.'

'Sorry?'

'Eh?'

He hadn't noticed his secretary, Susan Habib, come into the room. She was standing in front of him, a look of mild exasperation on her face. He hoped that she hadn't heard the muffled singing.

'I thought you said something, Mr Summers.'

She always called him that and never 'sir', as if to underline the fact that she was a civilian.

'Just thinking aloud.'

'Only Chief Inspector Davies has arrived.'

'Then show her in.'

Greg had been without a chief inspector for the past three months, but that deficiency was about to be remedied. A cause for concern, although that was perhaps too strong a word.

Unease. Or merely embarrassment?

Megan Davies: it had been a long time ago, easily ten years. They'd shared a bed for three nights on a training course, both of them inspectors then, she based in the north of England somewhere. He could remember her appearance only dimly: dark hair, he thought, dark eyes; not a tall woman and quite thin, even wiry, a compact and demanding little body Nothing of the Welsh valleys in her voice, despite her name. Attractive without being pretty. Very clever.

He liked clever women. They had the power to surprise.

He'd merged his body repeatedly with hers over those three days and nights and yet he knew almost nothing about her. She was married, or had been then, a few years younger than he, now forty-two. What had brought her so suddenly to Newbury? Would she remember him, or had he been only one of a number of men opportunely enjoyed on such weekends, their faces – their bodies – blurring indistinguishably into each other?

He'd been thirty-eight, which now seemed such a young age, long divorced, free and – apparently – easy. He wouldn't do it now, not even if he were single himself, though he wasn't sure why, or why not.

Susan returned, accompanied by his new DCI.

'Mrs Davies.' He stood up as she came in and offered her his hand across the desk.

She shook it very firmly, looked him in the eye and said, 'Good to see you again, sir.'

His memory hadn't let him down for

once, he thought: definitely nothing of the valleys in her voice. So she remembered and she wanted him to know that she remembered. Fair enough. He would show that he, too, remembered. He said, 'Good to see you again after all these years.' He glanced at his watch: just gone ten. 'Susan, perhaps some coffee might be in order.'

'Decaff for me,' Megan said, 'black, no sugar.' She sat down, oblivious to the look Susan was giving her since she made plain, strong coffee out of a jar and offered nothing frilly.

Greg resumed his own seat and said, 'So what brings you to Newbury from ... Newcastle on Tyne, wasn't it?'

'*Upon* Tyne,' she corrected. 'We're very strict about that. But I come from round here originally.'

'I didn't know that.' That explained the lack of Welsh lilt.

'No real reason you should, sir. My parents still live here and they're getting on a bit. Dad had a stroke nine months ago and Mum's found it hard to cope with him since.'

'I'm sorry to hear that. Is he bedridden?'

'Far from it! That's part of the problem. He has these episodes in which he's inclined to wander off without telling her, often turning up miles away, not knowing how he got there and sometimes with no way of getting home. It's as if a switch in his brain is flicked on and off. The stroke also destroyed all the little daily inhibitions that keep society running smoothly: he'll strike up a conversation with anyone.'

'Well, that's nice, in its way.'

'Except that he'll suddenly become abusive, start railing at them, swearing, words he would never have dreamed of using a couple of years ago, words that would have made him wince.' She gave a thin smile, remembering. 'He sometimes used to ring up the BBC to complain if he heard what he called "bad language" on the television, now he's effing and blinding like a navvy.'

'It's strange,' Greg said, 'the way we all have it in us, however deep we repress it.' He wondered sometimes if we all had it in us to murder, to rape, to torture: the men he arrested for such crimes were invariably ordinary and not the monsters of popular imagining.

'He can be alarming,' Megan went on. 'He's a big man and the police have been called twice. Luckily, they've been sensible so far, smoothed things over, seen him safely home.'

'Has he been violent?'

'Not yet and I'd like to keep it that way.'

'I can see why you feel the need to come home.'

'When it became apparent a few months ago that there was no longer any hope of saving my marriage, I put in for a transfer here. It means I can keep an eye on the parents and, to be blunt, Mum can do some emergency childcare if necessary.'

'Oh, you have children?'

'Just one, a boy of nine, Gareth. I took three years off when he was born. That's why it's taken me so long to reach my present rank, in case you were wondering.'

'No.' He leafed through the file he'd been sent. 'Or do I mean yes? Your reports are excellent. I don't know when I last saw so many commendations.'

She went on with her story as Susan brought coffee and biscuits, plonking the tray noisily on the desk in mute protest, and they helped themselves. 'Initially they told me there was nothing suitable for a newly promoted DCI in the Thames Valley, then, quite out of the blue, a vacancy appeared.'

He sipped his coffee which was too hot. He couldn't tell from her face or her intonation if she knew why Harry Stratton had left the force so precipitately during the Jordan Abbot investigation the previous summer; or why his successor, acting DCI Timothy Monroe, had transferred back to Slough after only a few weeks, in the course of Operation Cuckoo at Christmas. There was no reason she should know and, at the same time, no reason she shouldn't.

There would be time for all that later.

'So where are you living?' he asked.

'I've rented a house while I sort out financial matters with my husband and look around to buy: a three-bedroomed semi on a modern estate up in Speen, easy to run and no more than a mile from the parents. It's plenty big enough for the two of us. Gareth spends quite a lot of time with Philip, his father: at least every other weekend and most of the school holidays. They're very close.'

'Was the divorce amicable, if that isn't too impertinent a question?'

'Yes, although we're not divorced, haven't got round to it. I expect we'll wait till we've been separated two years. Neither of us wants to start hurling accusations of adultery or unreasonable behaviour and it's not as if either of us wants to remarry.'

She had been unfaithful only once in all those years, when the temptation had proved too strong. Now she sat looking at the man who had tempted her and thinking how ordinary he was: medium height, thin build, brown hair greying round the temples but not yet receding. Lust was a strange beast. He was good looking in an unflashy way, she supposed, and there was something in his dark eyes ... something she remembered.

Greg said, 'I think I recall you telling me

'... once ... that your husband was – is – a barrister.'

She nodded, a wry smile curving her mouth. 'He does only defence work, usually for the most hopeless causes. A regular Rumpole of the Bailey – or of the Newcastle Central Criminal Court in this case.'

'Was that the trouble: that he was often on the other side, as it were?'

'We didn't bring our work home and he never defended any of my collars. No, we just drifted apart, as you do. A spirited difference of opinion is never the reason a marriage breaks up, or not in my experience.'

'No.'

'On the contrary: a brisk argument from time to time keeps it fresh.'

She was looking well on it, he thought. She hadn't gained an ounce in those ten years, still thin, still wiry, her neat cap of dark hair not needing chemical support, if he was any judge. Her beige trouser suit was practical and comfortable over a cream shirt thinly striped with brown, plain gold ear studs and an expensive-looking watch her sole ornaments. No wedding ring. She wore lace-up shoes in good leather and carried a briefcase instead of a handbag.

It had been she who'd taken the initiative, he remembered, all those years ago. He smiled at her, genuinely pleased to have her on board now that any initial awkwardness had passed. Their fling had been written on sand, he thought: the tide had washed it away and left no trace.

'Ready for work, Chief Inspector?'

She put down her empty coffee cup. 'Ready and willing, sir.'

'I was hoping that my sergeant, Barbara Carey, would be with us this morning so she could fill you in on the current cases, but uniform called her out first thing to a suspicious death in Woodhay.'

He could have sworn that her nose began to twitch at the words 'suspicious death', like a dog that's spotted a rat in the undergrowth.

He continued. 'No knowing how long she'll be, so I'd better fill you in on our main problem at the moment. We have a missing child: an infant girl who disappeared yesterday lunchtime. I'd like you to head up the case.'

'There was nothing about it on the local news this morning.' Megan looked puzzled. Child abductions were usually headline stories.

'We're keeping it low key at the moment, as we don't believe the little girl – Emilia Troy – to be in any danger.'

'Ah! Is it the estranged father who's taken her?'

Greg shook his head. 'Not a bad guess

but, as it happens, her mother's dead and she lives with her father. According to him, she's been abducted by her social worker.'

Megan puffed out her cheeks in a pantomime of surprise. 'That's a new one!'

'The social worker, Joshua Salem, has long been obsessed with the child, apparently, and has made several attempts to have her taken away from her father and stepmother by legal means, even doorstepping magistrates late at night demanding a Place of Safety Order.'

'Is she on the At Risk register?'

'No.'

'Then why has she even got a social worker?'

He leaned across the desk and refilled her coffee cup. 'That's a long story, so are you sitting comfortably?'

Chapter 2

Roger Troy and his first wife had been a golden couple: both scientists working at a government research centre called Mainstay House on the outskirts of Swindon. He was a chemist, a PhD by the age of twenty-three, she a brilliant applied mathematician.

They married a year to the day after their

first meeting at Mainstay when Joanna Mason, armed with her double first from Cambridge and all the enthusiasm in the world, was placed under the mentorship of Roger, a grand old man of twenty-five with two years service already under his belt.

Roger Troy wasn't handsome by ordinary criteria but the light of intelligence shone from his hazel eyes, making him compelling, mesmeric. Not merely intelligence, either, but a quest, a thirst for knowledge, for pure research. Tall and thin, there was nothing bookish about him: no stoop, no thick spectacles. He was a fit young man who spent his leisure time unwinding by rowing and hill walking.

A healthy mind in a healthy body.

Joanna had come a long way from a modest semi in Leicester. Pretty in a girl-next-door kind of way, she had a boundless appetite for life. She was petite and blonde, blue-eyed. She too was strong in mind and body.

At the end of her first day at Mainstay he invited her for a drink.

By the end of the second week they were lovers.

On their six-month anniversary he produced the diamond and sapphire engagement ring that had eaten up his salary for that month and begged to be allowed to spend the rest of his life with her.

They both knew that they had come home.

The Troys settled in a flat in Swindon. They did everything together: trips to the opera, strenuous activity holidays, cosy supper parties for their many friends. Both excelled at their work, enjoying regular promotions and salary increases. When Joanna announced after three years of marriage that a young Troy was on its way, the news crowned their happiness and they counted themselves truly blessed.

Three months into the pregnancy, a routine examination threw up an abnormality in one of Joanna's breasts and a swift biopsy confirmed the worse: a cancerous lump the size of a broad bean an inch short of her left armpit. But there was no sign that the cancer had spread to other organs and the prognosis was good: a small excision – no need for a full mastectomy – followed by a course of chemo- and radiotherapy.

The specialist looked pleased with himself as he told her the good news, using the grave smile he kept for such occasions so that the patient wouldn't think that he took her fears lightly. Naturally, he added, the foetus – he called it that: not 'your child' or 'the baby' – would have to be aborted, since it would not in any case survive the treatment without major damage.

'I know it's a pity,' he said, seeing her

dismay, his voice avuncular, 'but you're only twenty-six and have many good child-bearing years ahead of you, Joanna.' He added casually, 'We will freeze some of your eggs first, just to be on the safe side.'

She left the clinic in some sort of daze.

Roger was concerned when she was not home by six, but knew that hospital clinics often overran. By nine pm he was frantic and thinking of calling the police. Instead, he grabbed his overcoat and walked swiftly and methodically along the surrounding roads, examining the parks, the school yards, the alleyways. He peered into their favourite restaurants and pubs.

He found her at last, shivering on a bench outside the Railway Museum. He tore off his coat and wrapped it round her, sitting next to her, warming her with the heat of his own body, murmuring.

'Joanna. Joanna. My love, Joanna.'

She turned her face to him. It was streaked where tears had dried but there were no fresh tears. She told him dispassionately what the doctor had said, one scientist to another. She explained that she had thought the matter over and that there was no question of killing the child within her. Nor would she jeopardise it by going ahead with the therapy while its tiny body was so parasitically dependent on her own.

'It's only six months,' she concluded. 'I

can delay treatment that long. The tumour is small and the risk acceptable.'

He knew her well: she was his other self. He knew that there was no point in arguing.

What Gregory Summers told Megan Davies was, 'The child's parents were both scientists of some sort, a happy couple, by all accounts. The little girl's mother died of cancer shortly after she was born.'

It was the short version, the prosaic version. Greg hadn't known them; their tragedy didn't touch him.

'Sorry!'

Barbara Carey came swiftly into the room. Normally she would have taken a seat unbidden, but today she stood waiting for introductions.

'DCI Megan Davies,' Greg said simply, 'DS Barbara Carey.'

Megan rose and the two women shook hands. Greg watched with some amusement as they took time to size each other up, making no secret of their mutual scrutiny. Barbara was taller, fairer, stronger-looking, fifteen years the younger. Like the DCI, she favoured trouser suits in neutral colours with a minimum of fuss and shoes you could run in.

They were alike, he thought, which didn't mean that they would like each other. He gestured to Barbara to pull up a chair and she took the uncomfortable upright which he used when working at his computer and pulled it round to face her two superior officers.

'Sorry I wasn't here when you arrived, ma'am,' she said.

'I quite understand.'

'So what's the verdict on the suspicious?' Greg asked.

'Suicide. I've left SOCO there to go through the motions, just in case there was anything I missed, but there's no doubt in my mind. Farmer, name of Halfacre, sneaked out of bed some time in the small hours while his wife was asleep and took his own shotgun to himself in his barn.'

Greg winced. He had seen men with shotgun wounds, or what was left of them. It would not be the way he chose to do it, but it was quick and certain.

Barbara added, 'Farmers have been having a rough time of it these last few years and the foot-and-mouth outbreak was the last straw for David Halfacre. He hadn't set foot off his farm for a fortnight, maintaining a voluntary quarantine. He'd been watching his cattle grow older, eating their heads off, with him unable to sell them or send them for slaughter. Last week they passed the thirty-month deadline for BSE control and became worthless overnight.'

'It must have been like watching money wash down the drain,' Greg said. 'Did he leave a note?'

'No, I guess he thought the state of the farm said it all.'

Greg preferred it when suicides left a note; so much more considerate.

The Halfacres had come up in the world, he mused, since the medieval ancestor whose land, or scarcity of it, had been deemed worthy of note. They would have two or three hundred acres, the minimum for a viable farm these days, but would be coming down in the world again.

'I've spoken to his wife very briefly...' Barbara ground to a halt, lacking the words to express the woman's anguish. 'I called her GP out and I'll go and talk to her again later when she's in a more fit state.'

She turned to Megan. 'You're coming from an urban area, aren't you, ma'am?'

Megan nodded. 'Central Newcastle, but we've plenty of shotguns there too, even if it's not the weapon of choice for drug dealers. They prefer a nice Kalashnikov AK-47 assault rifle.'

'Well, it sounds as if this death is not our problem,' Greg said, aware that he might sound callous to a layman but knowing that his two colleagues would understand his relief at not having a murder investigation on his hands. 'I was telling DCI Davies,

Barbara, about the Troy case. Bit of background.'

The Troys' daughter was born on the third of March by elective Caesarean. Joanna had been weakened by her disease, which had progressed with virulent speed, and the obstetrician didn't want her straining after a natural birth. She was the image of her father, as if her mother had contributed nothing: black hair and eyes which, while initially baby blue, rapidly darkened into deep brown almonds.

They called her Emilia, for no particular reason, except that they liked the name: it was unusual without being outlandish; it somehow suited her. She was Emilia Joanna Troy.

At first, Joanna's specialist proposed to perform a double mastectomy, but as it became clear that the cancer had spread into the liver there seemed no point in putting her through that ordeal. Let her end her life intact, as nature had made her.

For what Joanna Troy had contributed to her daughter was her life.

She died four months later. In the last two weeks the drugs that kept her free of pain meant that she no longer knew Roger, nor their baby.

He buried her in the municipal graveyard in Swindon. They were neither of them religious, being scientists, and any lingering memories of Roger's childhood trips to Sunday school had died with his wife, but he had submitted to some sort of service out of deference to those to whom it mattered.

He had left the rings on her finger since he could not envisage either keeping them or selling them. The funeral had been almost unbearable and he wondered why people put themselves through this ritual. It was as if the mourners were saying, 'Today, I'm going to be as miserable as it is possible for a human being to be.'

Or perhaps they wanted to taste the dregs so that they could tell themselves that it could only get better after this.

A rite of passage, they called it, a necessary ceremony which allowed you to draw a line and move on. Rubbish, all of it. It was fine for those who didn't really care – their colleagues, old college friends whom she met for lunch twice a year – who were shocked but not devastated. They came to the funeral; they sang *Jerusalem* in their reedy little voices; and then they went home, putting the black tie back in the wardrobe, shaking the chilly atmosphere of the chapel from their hands and faces and shoes, saying 'That's that done and dusted. Now I can get on with my life.'

Dust to dust.

He knew because he'd felt that way himself when he'd attended the funeral of both her parents within a few months of each other. Sad, yes, solemn, but it had not *touched* him, not really. It could not break him.

He put her estate in the hands of her solicitors. She had made a simple will leaving everything to him and it went through quickly and smoothly. For two months Roger kept going, doing the necessary on automatic pilot. He fed Emilia from a bottle and tucked her up in her cot – on her back to avoid cot death – and cooed at her. He changed nappies, unappalled by the strange green, stinking excretions of her body as it learned the art of digestion. He sang half-remembered nursery rhymes. He washed her tiny clothes and ironed her minuscule frocks with the care of a Victorian nanny.

He informed bank managers and pension funds and the Inland Revenue of his wife's death. They commiserated with him by sending him complex forms to fill in. He replied to letters of condolence and stood immobile in the street before the kindness of neighbours as they enquired after his health and offered unspecified services. Normally it was the concerned friend who didn't know what to say to the bereaved; here, it was Roger who was the mute.

Then he had a massive nervous break-down.

Greg said, 'Then the father had some sort of breakdown and ended up in the loony bin.' He caught Barbara's eye. 'Sorry. I meant to say Edith Austin Ward, the psychiatric ward in the Kennet, here in Newbury.'

'I suppose I would give up my life to save my son's,' Megan remarked, 'but when he was a three-month foetus? Maybe not.'

Greg had sometimes wondered if he would have given his life to save that of his son Fred, dead of leukaemia at the age of twenty-two. If the offer had been made, a straight swap, what would his reaction have been? Hadn't Hercules gone to his elderly parents and asked if one of them would sacrifice their life for him and been told to bog off?

'That's a hell of a burden for a baby to bear,' Barbara remarked.

Roger Troy had spent two weeks in a bed in Swindon General before being transferred to the psychiatric ward at the Kennet Hospital in Newbury where the staff were accustomed to dealing with the long dark night of the soul. He had remained there for eighteen months.

Mainstay had tried to keep his job open for him but eighteen months was too long a time for patience and he had been replaced after three. It was in any case unlikely that he would ever be well enough again for the rigorous life of the scientist. And perhaps his colleagues were guiltily grateful that they wouldn't have to think what to say to a man who had had everything and had lost it in the space of a year, including his sanity.

His flat had been repossessed by some faceless bank when he was unable to keep up the mortgage payments, his and Joanna's modest savings being swallowed up by the accumulating compound interest. There had been no life insurance; who needed it at their age? He received the news with indifference as he could not have lived there again with all the reminders of Joanna, of the bliss that their life together had been.

Baby Emilia was taken into care and placed with foster parents, a couple named Fergusson who lived in a rambling Victorian house near Inkpen with an acre and a half of garden. There she grew strong and healthy and happy, accepting Annie Fergusson as her mother and Rupert as her father, knowing nothing of the haggard, drugged-up creature in the Kennet whose genes she carried and whose name she bore.

'Hence the social worker,' Megan said. 'Was there no family who could take her?'

33

'Apparently not.'

Barbara said, 'Joshua Salem was assigned to her case from the first and, when the Fergussons asked to be allowed to adopt the little girl a year into their fostering, he supported them all the way.'

Megan raised her eyebrows. 'Surely the real father could never be expected to consent to that.'

'He might have wanted rid of the child as too painful a memory of his loss,' Barbara suggested. Megan shook her head vehemently. 'But you're right,' the sergeant went on. 'His solicitor maintained that one day he would be well enough to be discharged from hospital and that he would then make a home for his daughter. Somehow.'

'The Court does, however, have the power to order an adoption without the consent of the natural parents,' Greg explained, 'in exceptional circumstances and if they're sure it's in the child's best interest. Joshua Salem applied for just such an order.'

'And was refused,' Barbara added.

Chapter 3

Concepta Tobin was a psychiatric nurse on Edith Austin Ward and Roger Troy's case interested her from the first. He was a romantically tragic figure, this bereaved lover who couldn't get over the death of his beloved, he was like something out of a novel.

To be loved like that, she thought, wasn't it what every girl dreamed of?

Concepta had never been loved like that, or at all. She had reached the age of thirty-five without having a serious relationship and, as a Catholic by upbringing, a serious relationship meant marriage to Concepta.

She was an almost aggressively plain woman, as if Nature had been in a bad mood on the day of her making; there was nothing wrong with her individual features but they added up to an undistinguished whole. She hadn't even the distinction of being ugly.

Her hair had been auburn in childhood but was already faded into a mousy nothing. Her blue eyes looked colourless, either side of a freckled nose that was too snub for her broad, flat face. She had a small mouth which gave the impression of too many teeth, crammed in any old how and faintly yellow in colour. Her skin was weather-beaten, a stranger to face cream, her figure shapeless, straight up and down, offering no curves beneath her graceless polycotton uniform, tunic and loose trousers in a pale green. She had thin legs, ending in clumsy white nursing shoes that looked too heavy for her to drag about.

They were not too heavy. Concepta was strong and had never had a day's illness in her life. Her work was who she was and she lived in the nurses' hostel, sharing a bathroom and kitchen with successive generations of girls who were, by now, almost young enough to be her daughters. These girls spent their salaries on make-up and fashion, CDs and mobile phones; they went 'clubbing' and smuggled boyfriends in. They kept the freakish older woman at arm's length, though not actively unkind.

It was a cheap way to live and allowed her to send money home to her widowed mother and her youngest brother Thomas.

Tommy had Down's Syndrome, born when their mother was forty-eight. Now twenty, he had a mental age of about twelve which meant that he was able to help around the house and garden. He and Mammy looked after each other, making a cosy and self-contained couple in their cottage in County Cork. Concepta sent a brief letter and a postal order every month but she rarely visited. Her other brothers and sisters were married with children of their own, houses and jobs, cars and holidays, too busy to ask after her.

Mammy replied to maybe one in four of her letters, cheerful accounts of trips she and Tommy had made to a local beauty spot or the seaside, gossip about people Concepta had never met but who formed a living soap opera. They ended always with a request to God to bless her oldest daughter and an injunction that she should be a good girl in the land of the heathen English.

Roger was heavily drugged for his first few months in Edith Austin. He would not have got out of bed at all if Concepta hadn't pulled him out each morning, moving him to an armchair in a fireman's lift, stripping the pyjamas from his unresisting body and clothing him in loose garments: a tracksuit bottom and sweatshirt, tartan slippers a size too big, left by some former inmate.

She sat with him at table, cutting his food for him and lifting it to his mouth on a spoon, saying, 'Open wide' like a dentist.

She read his post to him, knowing that he took in nothing.

She bathed him three times a week in the large white bath in the cold cubicle that gave the illusion of privacy but had no lock on the door. She took him to the lavatory, the final intimacy, but doubted that he could have picked her out from the rest of the staff in a line-up.

She was used to that and she was patient.

They began to reduce his dosage after six months and some light came back into his eyes. He was able to join in the occupational therapy sessions and sometimes Concepta would speak to him and get a coherent answer.

He had been there a year and a week when he asked after his daughter.

'Emilia,' he said one morning, eyeing the plate of rubber scrambled egg in front of him dubiously.

'I'm sorry?' Concepta sat down beside him.

'Emilia,' he repeated.

'I don't understand.' She picked up his fork and dug it into the tepid yellow heap.

'My daughter.'

'Ah!'

He took an obedient mouthful of egg, chewed it a dozen times and swallowed. He looked round the ward as if expecting to see his child, to find her sleeping peacefully in her cot in some quiet corner.

'I'll make enquiries,' Concepta said. 'I'll find out where she is and when you can see her.'

He turned his dull eyes onto her,

scrutinising her as if for the first time. She was used to men looking at her face with ill-disguised dislike, even contempt, but there was nothing of that in Roger Troy's gaze.

'I think you must be an angel,' he murmured and his lips curved into the semblance of a smile, the first that she had had from him.

'I take it the Fergussons have been interviewed over the abduction?' Megan said. 'These foster parents who took such a shine to her.'

'We've seen them certainly,' Greg said. 'They seem as baffled as everyone else, very concerned for Emilia's welfare.'

'I liked them,' Barbara put in. 'They came across as very straight.'

'Only it wouldn't be the first time that someone desperate to adopt a child has taken the law into their own hands,' Megan reminded them. 'There was that couple in Norfolk a year or two back. Did we search the place?'

'Not at this stage,' Greg said. 'I don't think I could have wangled a search warrant. Besides, Roger Troy is adamant that it was Salem who took Emilia and he should know – he was there.'

The first time Concepta met Joshua Salem, the augurs for a close and lasting friendship were not good.

He was waiting for her in the visitor's room on Edith Austin Ward, a cream box with two cheap brown armchairs and a walnut veneer coffee table with caravanning magazines. A watercolour of Hungerford Common hung on the wall. He wasn't sitting but stood with his back to the door, looking out of the window without seeing anything, his corduroy back bristling with unsuppressed anger.

He didn't hear her come in through the already open door and she had a moment to scrutinise him: a man of medium height, inclined to be tubby, his fair hair worn a little long, to the collar of his jacket, flecks of white scurf visible. The way he stood suggested a young man, maybe thirty, no aches or pains in the joints yet.

She said coolly, 'Are you Salem?'

He spun round and she saw that his cheeks were ruddy; a blond beard concealed his chin and upper lip, clipped short. He'd been nibbling at his thumbnail and snatched his hand away from his mouth like a guilty thing surprised. 'And you, I take it, are Miss Tobin.' She nodded, watching as his grey eyes took her in, dismissing her: an unattractive woman and probably a fool. *And you're no fecking oil painting either, mister,* she thought, apologising mentally to Mammy for the curse word.

Salem moved towards her, aggressive. 'I'm here to tell you that there's no way I'm going to let a vulnerable child like Emilia visit this...' Words seemed to fail him; his hands flailed wildly, taking in the room, the ward, the hospital in general. 'This *place*.'

'And who are you,' she asked, 'to make such grand decisions?'

The challenge disconcerted him. 'I'm Emilia's social worker.'

'And Roger Troy is her father, a good father. You would do well to remember that Emilia isn't in care because of abuse or neglect, but simply because the poor man has been ill.'

'Not only *ill*,' he pointed out. 'Not like it's cancer or some disease.'

'Ah!' she said. 'The stigma of mental illness, the fear that lives on, so vivid, into the third millennium after Christ. You a *Guardian* reader, Mr Salem?' He didn't reply, embarrassed by the word 'Christ' being used other than as an expletive. 'I bet you are. I bet you hate prejudice: prejudice against blacks and Jews and women, that is, Asians and Chinese. But the mad, the insane, the crazy, the deranged, the bonkers, the loonies, the tuppence-short-of-a-shillings – that's another matter, isn't it?'

Salem took a deep breath, winded, perhaps half aware that he was in the wrong but

41

determined not to be chastened. 'I'm sorry for all that Mr Troy's been through – obviously I am – but my first responsibility is to Emilia, her well-being and happiness.'

'Then you'll be hearing from Dr Troy's solicitor.' Concepta turned away, dismissive, the interview at an end. 'Very soon.'

Salem didn't want to come up against Roger Troy's solicitor again, not after the beating the woman had given him over the adoption order. Legal-aid solicitors were not usually the best lawyers available, but Deirdre Washowski was an exception: an idealist who could have been earning hundreds of thousands a year in some city firm doing commercial law but instead chose to defend the weak, the hopeless and the incurably criminal.

At Newbury police station when the words 'Who's the solicitor?' were answered by 'Old Deirdre Washbasin' the response was invariably a groan and an extra two hours spent making sure the case was watertight.

Salem had gone to court confident of the righteousness of his cause, certain that the family judge would see why Emilia's future lay with the Fergussons: this nice, stable, middle-class couple with their detached home in the country, their gardens and paddocks, their Persian rugs. The Fergussons, who loved her like their own, who could offer ponies and private schools and holidays abroad.

Deirdre had demolished him in less than a minute. She wasted no words; she never did. She wasn't over fond of her own voice like so many advocates. Leaning back in her chair at the informal hearing, her big face framed by the halo of white hair that was her trademark, adjusting the wire-framed spectacles which she used more as a theatrical prop than anything else, speaking without notes, she began.

'Joanna Troy died that her daughter Emilia might live. She gave her life so that her child could be with its father, her husband, Roger Troy. Is that all to have been for nothing? Is Joanna to have sacrificed herself in vain?'

There was a silence when she stopped. Salem was aware of the Fergussons looking at each other, then at him, and avoided their gaze.

Finally, the judge cleared his throat and said that he would give them his decision in writing in a few days.

They went home, no one in any doubt as to what that decision would be.

Concepta had called Salem's bluff but it took him ten days to admit it. In the middle of the following week he brought Emilia Troy to visit the father she didn't remember.

She took all day getting Roger ready. She reminded him to bathe – which he now did by himself – and shave, and ensured that he washed his hair. She stood over him while he brushed his teeth. She dressed him in his neatest clothes, which she had cleaned and pressed. Perhaps most importantly, she persuaded Dr Peach to halve the dosage of his medication, just for today, and he was more lively than usual, if also more anxious. He was like a teenage boy on his first date.

'I might not recognise her,' he said more than once. 'She will have changed.'

'She'll be the only little girl there,' Concepta said, half humorously. 'Or the only one with yer man Salem.'

She'd arranged to meet Salem and the child in the hospital cafeteria, aware that some of the inmates of Edith Austin could be alarming to adults, let alone a small child. At three o'clock that afternoon she led Roger there, taking him across the bedraggled gardens, the muddy lawns.

It was early December, too late for flowers, too early for Christmas festivity. She thought the hospital had never looked worse than it did now, but she saw her patient gazing about him in wonder and realised that it had been well over a year since he had set foot off the ward.

The cafeteria was past its busiest period,

lunch over. A huddle of nurses sat in one corner eating pasta or hugging warm mugs of tea. Visitors sat conversing in anxious murmurs, speculating.

'Prognosis?' one old man said in a thick Polish accent. 'What is *prognosis?* Why can't they speak English?'

Emilia was also dressed to impress, the Fergussons anxious to demonstrate to her stricken father that she was getting the best of care. Three months shy of her second birthday, she sat in a high chair next to Salem in her cream cotton dress with red rosebuds, her white woollen tights. The little red anorak that kept out the autumn cold was draped over a nearby chair. Her feet in their good leather shoes stuck out in front of her, emitting an exuberant kick from time to time. She was too young to understand the purpose of this outing but any trip to a strange place was a joyous thing to an intelligent child who was just starting to make sense of the world.

She still had her baby plumpness, her fat cheeks glowing pink.

Concepta did the introductions since Roger had not been well enough to attend the court proceedings that had rejected Salem's attempt at a forcible adoption. The social worker got to his feet and offered his hand with its nibbled thumbnails, making a visible effort. Roger looked at it in surprise

45

then, remembering the daily decencies of his former life, took it and waved it limply up and down.

'I'll wait outside, Roger,' Concepta said, but he shot her a frightened look and said, 'Can't you stay?'

'If you like.' She glanced at the table. Emilia had a cardboard cup of orange juice, almost empty, Salem a polystyrene mug with a dark brown smudge in the bottom. 'Can I get anyone refreshments?'

'No,' Salem said quickly. 'We're fine.'

'Roger?'

'Yes?'

'Tea?' Gently.

'Thank you.'

When Concepta came back with tea for them both, Emilia was chattering away incoherently about her latest acquisition: her pet hamster, who was called Desmond. She was too young to have preconceived ideas about mental illness, too inexperienced to be afraid of the clouded eyes of this benign stranger. Indeed, she found him fascinating, the way a child will gravitate towards a smelly tramp.

Roger sat listening to her, rapt; despite the scarcity of her vocabulary and her idiosyncratic grammar, to him it was the purest poetry. His tea grew cold in front of him during the course of the meeting.

He made a great effort of will to respond

to his daughter in kind. 'When I was a boy I had a... I forget.' He stopped in frustration. 'It was bigger than a hamster.'

He looked helplessly at the other two adults.

'Guinea pig?' Concepta suggested.

He repeated the words to re-imprint them on his brain. 'Guinea pig.'

'And what was it called?'

Roger thought hard for a moment. 'Einstein!'

Concepta laughed. 'Always the scientist, Roger.'

Even Salem let a little smile escape him.

Roger looked about him, taking in the unknown faces, the bustle of the hospital, almost contented. He beamed at his daughter and said, 'I have been ill for a long time, Emilia, but I'm getting better now.'

As they were leaving, Roger wandered a little way ahead, swinging his daughter up on his shoulders, clasping her white woolly legs firmly while she seized his hair for balance, giggling with pleasure.

Salem grabbed Concepta roughly by the arm.

'You see,' he hissed. 'You see how well and happy she is with her foster parents. Bright and confident. Don't ruin that. Don't take all that away from her for the sake of some misguided, sentimental principle.'

Concepta shook him off. 'She's his reason to live – can't *you* see *that?* – his reason to get well, to get out of here and start again.'

'And you'll sacrifice *her* for that!' With a final, darting, hostile look, Salem took off after his charge.

Last thing that night Concepta looked in on Roger. She was not on duty but it took only a few minutes to pay the goodnight call on what the other nurses laughingly called her pet patient. She found him sitting by the open window of the television room, smoking a low-tar cigarette.

'And what did we agree about you smoking?' she asked.

He didn't look at her. 'Don't talk to me that way, Concepta, that *nurse* way. It's patronising.'

She sat down heavily on an armchair and looked at him thoughtfully. 'You're a lot better, aren't you?'

'I will be. I have to be, if I'm to get my daughter back.' He turned to look at her, blowing a stream of smoke out through his nostrils. 'I'll do anything I have to do to make that happen.'

'I just don't believe it!'

Josh Salem paced up and down in front of Caitlin Kramer's desk three months later, angrily gnawing at the rough skin around his right thumb where there was no nail left to bite, bringing the bitter taste of blood to his mouth.

She said mildly, 'You know that Social Services' policy is to keep a child with the birth family, if at all possible.'

Caitlin looked at her junior without enthusiasm. She was a world-weary woman in her mid-forties, long divorced, long hardened to the cases she and her team dealt with day by day. She wished that Joshua would bring a little more reason and a little less emotion to the job. No one doubted his dedication but she often found him more trouble than he was worth and now was set to be one of those times.

'He's mentally ill.' Joshua leaned over the desk, thrusting his face into hers.

She did not retreat, despite the not altogether freshness of his breath. 'He's being discharged from the psychiatric ward. They wouldn't do that if he couldn't look after himself.'

'After *himself*, maybe, just about, but you're talking about a single man with no experience of kids looking after a girl who's only just turned two.'

'Didn't you hear?' Caitlin flicked open the case folder on her desk. 'I was talking to Dr Peach from the Kennet this morning. It seems that Roger Troy is getting married, to a nurse from the hospital.'

Salem was shocked. 'Not that hatchet-faced Irish bitch?'

His boss glanced at her own blunt handwriting, her lips pressed together in disapproval. 'A Miss Concepta Tobin. It certainly sounds like a good Irish name, although Sarah Peach didn't see fit to mention the shape of her face. It seems that she'll be able to look after Roger, make sure he takes his medication and–' she held up her hand to pre-empt Salem's interruption '–she's the eldest of seven children so she has the child-care experience.'

Salem, defeated, sat down heavily on the hard chair in front of the desk.

'I can't win,' he said bleakly. 'If I try to keep a child from its birth parents then I'm some sort of monster and when a child comes to harm at the hands of those same parents, who gets the blame? Who gets vilified in the press as a heartless incompetent?' He struck himself hard on the chest. 'That's who!'

'I've taken legal advice,' Caitlin said, 'and that advice was that an application through the courts for care and control of Emilia Troy by her father and stepmother will succeed, especially with Dee Washowski batting for their side.'

She snapped the file shut. 'So get used to it!'

As Roger Troy was officially homeless on his

discharge from hospital and unlikely to be able to undertake paid work for the foreseeable future, the council housed him and his bride in Beaumont Tower on the Peabody Estate, not much more than a stone's throw from the hospital.

Roger didn't object in the least to being able to see the place of his former incarceration and it would be handy for Concepta.

He had no idea, at that stage, that Joshua Salem lived across the Green.

It wasn't the wedding of Concepta's girlhood dreams. They were married in the hospital chapel with Dr Peach and another nurse as witnesses. She wore a cream suit that she had bought for the occasion. She had her hair set into an unyielding helmet, the style of a much older woman, and powdered her face. A gash of red lipstick only drew attention to her plainness and the thinness of her lips.

Roger wore his best suit which was too large for him as he'd grown skinny during his eighteen months of illness. He was calm, much calmer than she was, speaking the brief responses in a clear voice while she could manage no more than a mumble.

It took less than five minutes. The handful of inmates from Edith Austin who had been well enough to attend gave them

51

a round of applause.

There was no reception and there could be no honeymoon. They must prepare the flat for the coming of Emilia and Desmond the hamster, must make it into a family home. Money was short; she had not told Mammy of her marriage, didn't want a fuss, couldn't explain about Roger and why he was so odd, so very much not the sort of man they might imagine for her. Nor would Mammy understand why there had not been a church wedding and a nuptial mass.

She would have to go on sending the money each month; Mammy and Tommy relied on her.

That night, they were alone together in the flat, each a little uncertain, a little lost. It had all happened so quickly. As yet they had nothing but a second-hand sofa standing square in the middle of the uncurtained living room, two adult beds – a single and a double, one in each bedroom – and a cot which was in the same room as the single bed. Concepta had a few days off and would spend them combing the furniture warehouses of Newbury for tables, sideboards, chairs, a desk for Roger. She would buy plates and forks and mugs, saucepans and frying pans.

She'd brought her teapot from the hostel and it stood proudly on the breakfast bar with its matching jug and sugar bowl, a blue and white pattern of flowers and birds, delicate, even beautiful.

She went out for fish and chips for their supper. When she returned Roger had made up both beds with the polycotton sheets she had so lovingly chosen, a flowered pattern in pink and green.

After supper he said, 'It's been a long day. Do you mind if I turn in?'

She didn't reply, watching as he made for the smaller bedroom, for the single bed, closing the door behind him. She cleared away the chip papers and washed her sticky hands in plain hot water, adding washing-up liquid to her mental list.

She hesitated before the closed door then went in without knocking. It wasn't as if she had never seen him naked. He was already in bed, lying on his side but with his eyes open. His bottles of tablets stood neatly lined up on the hard chair by the bed with a glass of water.

'You've taken your pills?' she asked.

'Yes. I'll say goodnight, then.'

'So ... you're sleeping here.' She bent over and dropped a faint kiss on his cheek. 'Goodnight, darling.'

It wasn't the marriage she'd dreamed of.

Greg said, 'Have you got that photo of Emilia, Babs?'

Barbara took out her wallet and produced a snapshot which she handed to Megan. The Chief Inspector examined the picture. She saw a girl with dark ringlets cascading round her shoulders, dark eyes to match. She wasn't smiling at the camera but looked almost solemn – as if she thought that having her photo taken was a serious business.

She promised to be pretty when she grew up and Megan made a sudden internal vow to make sure that happened.

'Nice kid,' she said neutrally

Greg said, 'Well, I'll leave you to it...'

He almost added *ladies*, but thought better of it. According to Angie, a lady was a woman who behaved the way men thought women ought to behave, which meant no swearing or hard drinking.

Chapter 4

'I don't want to tread on your toes,' Megan told Barbara, 'but if I'm to head up this investigation–'

'You want to go over it from scratch,' Barbara concluded for her. 'That's fine, ma'am. I'd do the same in your position, coming in after the start of the movie.'

And she would be in that position one day, she was sure of it.

They were in Megan's office, as yet unlived-in. It was little more than a cubicle, cut out of one corner of the empty CID room. Megan was sitting on her functional desk, one leg swinging rhythmically, while Barbara perched on a chair as if poised for sudden flight.

'Only it seems a bit low key at the moment,' Megan went on. 'I mean, after all, a missing child. Why no hue and cry?'

'The thing is that nobody thinks Salem is a danger to Emilia,' Barbara explained, 'not even the Troys. On the contrary, he seems to think he's acting in her best interests, *protecting* her. Emilia knows him well and isn't afraid of him and the full panoply of the law with screeching sirens and shouting police officers is more likely than anything to traumatise her.'

'I get the point.'

'So, where do you want to start?' Barbara asked. 'I'm at your disposal.'

'Tell me where we are so far.'

'Right. Mrs Troy called the police when she got home from work at five last night. I was there by six and took their statements. Having established that Salem's whereabouts were unknown, I obtained a search warrant for his house and we made a forcible entry at 7:30 am.'

'He lives alone?'

'Yes, since his mother died about a year ago.'

'Mummy's boy?'

'Looks that way. We've also got a warrant for his garage although his next-door neighbour says he doesn't use it, except maybe for storage. His car is provided by Social Services so he's not fussy about it.'

'Lucky it's only public money!'

'The car registration has been passed to all UK forces with a request to stop and hold. Ferry ports and the Channel Tunnel ditto. Airport security will be checking the passports of any single men travelling with infant girls. So there's a good chance he'll be picked up today. Either that or he'll use his bank card or credit card and we'll be alerted to his location that way.'

That was the nature of police work: that much of it petered out before it really got going, minimum excitement.

'Has he got a mobile phone?' Megan asked.

'Yes, I'm glad you reminded me. It's supplied by his office and I've alerted the service provider, a small company called Airways. They say it's switched off but they'll contact us the moment he uses it, tell us where he is. I've been calling it at intervals but no joy.'

'You have been busy. Is he stupid enough

to use it?'

'He probably doesn't realise how sophisticated modern technology is. I doubt if the average mobile phone user grasps that they might as well be electronically tagged. He doesn't even have to use it, only switch it on.'

'Lucky for us.'

'Meanwhile, I've made an appointment with Salem's immediate boss at 1:30 pm today,' Barbara went on, 'a woman called Caitlin Kramer, but I can call and re-schedule that if you like.'

'No.' Megan examined her watch. 'We'll squeeze it in somehow. Is anyone checking Salem's office, assuming he has one?'

'I thought we could do that after we see Ms Kramer.'

'I suppose it can wait till then.'

'And we've another appointment at three with Dr Sarah Peach who's in charge of Edith Austin Ward at the Kennet, the psychiatric ward where Roger Troy was being treated until a year ago.'

'What's her connection with Joshua Salem?'

'None, but I've been keeping my options open. It's Roger's word against Salem's at the moment.'

'Except that Salem's the one who's done a bunk.'

'I haven't forgotten.'

'So, who've we got on board?'

'There's DC Andy Whittaker. I've left him in charge of searching the house with a handful of uniformed officers. I was going to look in on him first thing but then I got called to that suspicious death. When I rang him he said everything was under control.'

'Is he good, this Whittaker?'

'He's new to CID,' Barbara explained, 'but he's passed all the courses with flying colours and he's been an excellent uniformed copper for several years. He needs training on the job now, of course, but I think he'll be a real asset to the team. Then there's George "The Bubble" Nicolaides.'

'As in bubble and squeak – Greek?'

'That's right, though he also answers to Nick. About the one thing he doesn't answer to is George, which is what Mr Summers keeps calling him. I haven't worked out yet what sort of mindedness that is: absent or bloody.' Megan laughed. 'He's an experienced DC, recently joined us from the Metropolitan Police,' Barbara added.

'Do you get a lot of officers coming out from London?'

'What with the price of housing there, we pick up quite a few good men looking for somewhere cheaper to live that's still within reach of the flesh pots. They get more variety of work here too. I mean, you could be twenty years in the Met without ever being seconded to a murder squad. Nick seems like a decent enough bloke, bit full of himself at first, like all the ex-Met lot, thinks we're a bunch of provincial plods, but we soon knock that out of them. He's older, early thirties.'

'Can't get promoted?'

'Passed the sergeant's exams four years back but fails the board each time. Bit chippy.'

'And what's Nick the Bubble up to?'

'Organising house to house on Peabody Green. We did a lot of them last night, of course, but he's checking back over the rest.'

'Okay, we'll catch up with him and Whittaker later but first I'd like to meet the Troys.'

Roger Troy nodded recognition at Barbara, barely acknowledging her introduction of DCI Davies.

'May we come in?' Megan asked. She spoke gently. There was something about Roger that was appealing, like a puppy that had been often kicked but still came optimistically to sniff your shoes. He wore his grey hair tied back with an elastic band this morning and it looked as if a squirrel had perched on his head.

It was hard to believe that he was only thirty-two.

He looked doubtful. 'Concepta's at work. She said there was no point in hanging round the flat brooding.' He looked embarrassed at the need to explain his wife's apparent lack of interest in her step-daughter's disappearance. 'She said I could do enough of that for both of us.'

'I'm sure you can answer my questions, Mr Troy.'

Megan moved slightly forward so that he automatically took a step back, allowing her to enter the hall. She took in at a glance the grey and white vinyl tiling on the floor, provided by the council when the flats were built and wearing well after all these years, warm underfoot, soft enough for a child to fall on and rise up laughing.

The hallway had no source of natural light and magnolia walls reflected the little that filtered in from open doors to other rooms. An unframed mirror fooled the eye into making the passageway bigger and a solitary radiator was the only other feature.

Barbara, who had been here before, led the way into the sitting room to the left. Megan caught a glimpse of a compact kitchen across the way. She crossed to the balcony window and looked out.

'Nice view,' she remarked. It was a clear spring morning and she could see the front of Salem's house with her excellent eyesight, a uniformed police woman, slightly bored, standing at the gate to deter nosy parkers. She turned back to the householder, who stood uncertainly in the doorway.

'May I sit, Mr Troy? Thank you.'

Without waiting for his answer, she selected a chintz armchair and gestured to Roger to take the one opposite, which he did. Between them, an electric fire with fake coals stood set into an equally fake chimney breast with a mahogany surround. A china doll, garish in its blue frilled dress and pink bonnet, danced a solo waltz on the mantel.

Barbara sat at one end of the sofa which was of a different pattern to the armchairs and draped with a cotton throw in a ginger brown. She took a notepad and pencil from her pockets, a silent observer, alert for discrepancies in Troy's tale.

'Will you tell me what happened when Emilia disappeared yesterday morning?' Megan said.

'I told her.' Troy nodded at Barbara. 'All of it. Last night.'

'I know, but I'm new to this case so I'd be grateful if you'd be patient with me.'

Roger looked down, examining his bare feet, the unusual length of his toes. All through the interview, he never spoke without a preceding silence of ten or twenty seconds while he framed his thoughts but his speech, when it came, was coherent, logical and organised.

'He used to come often.'

'Joshua Salem?'

He nodded. '"Drop by", as if he was a friend. Because he lived just across the way he acted like it was all right to do that.'

'You could have turned him away.'

'I didn't want him to think I had anything to hide. Besides, Millie liked him.' He had balked when Concepta had started calling her that, protesting that her name was Emilia, but his wife had scorned that as a pretentious name, as if Concepta was one you came across every day. Gradually he had stopped arguing, grown used to it and, one day, found himself using it too.

'He knew that I was home all day,' Roger went on, 'with Millie.'

'You never went out?' Megan asked. She wondered if Troy was agoraphobic. Eighteen months shut up in a mental hospital might do that to anybody.

But he merely shrugged and said, 'We went for a walk every day, round the Green, or even to the park, but the door to the block faces the Green and Salem could always see us coming and going and I felt as if I were being constantly spied on. Once we walked past his house and I could see him staring out at us. Millie waved at him and he waved back but it made me uncomfortable.'

'But didn't he have work to go to?' Megan asked.

'Sure, but it's not an office-bound job. They're out all day, visiting clients, going to court. He has a car and a mobile phone. I'm sure his superiors don't know what he's up to half the time.'

'And the day Emilia disappeared?' Megan prompted.

'He came by about eleven. Yesterday was one of my bad days.' He looked apologetic. 'He asked if he could take her out as it was a lovely morning – suddenly, like that, in the middle of all this wind and rain – but I said no. I didn't want him to get into the habit of it.'

'Did Emilia want to go with him?'

His smile was sweet at the thought of his child. 'She's such a kind girl, so protective of me. She wanted to stay here in case I might be lonely.' He looked at the ceiling, blinking back a tear. 'I have been lonely since she left, lonely all last night, all morning.'

'But Salem didn't go?'

'Millie wanted to show "Uncle Josh" her new teddy bear.'

Megan glanced up sharply. She knew that this sort of intimacy was discouraged among social workers: the pretence of family, of a relationship that was not strictly professional. Joshua Salem had been bending more than a few rules by the sound of it.

'They started playing with it together on the sitting room floor. I was feeling … my head was fuzzy. It happens. I went to lie down. I fell asleep. It was half past two when I woke up and they were gone, teddy and all. At first I thought he'd just taken her out to the park without my permission, but they still weren't back when Concepta came home from the hospital just after five and she called the police immediately. She was cross with me for not calling them at once. She said it might be the chance to get Salem into trouble, to get him out of our hair once and for all.'

'Are you afraid for her safety?'

He looked surprised by the question. 'He wouldn't hurt her. He adores her. That's been part of the problem. I sometimes think he wanted her for himself, not for the Fergussons.'

Megan looked round the room. It was oblong in shape, about fifteen feet by ten; the sofa and armchairs grouped round the fireplace filled a ten-foot square while the far end was taken up by a deal table covered with papers and two overflowing bookcases.

'May I take a look round,' she said. 'Get the feel of the place?' He gestured after the usual pause for consideration. 'Be my guest.'

She walked up to the table and stood looking at its burden without touching anything. There were scientific journals, many ragged and torn, and reams of A4 paper with small, neat handwriting on it in black ink.

'Keeping up your research?' she asked.

His eyes lit with enthusiasm. 'My project!'

'Oh?'

Troy joined her by the table and Barbara rose and came to look too. He pushed aside a layer of papers to reveal a set of blueprints with the same neat, black hand. Megan looked at Barbara and raised her eyebrows. Barbara shrugged.

'I'm looking for new ways to achieve cold fusion,' Troy explained.

'I'm sorry?' Megan said.

Suddenly all the hesitancy in his speech was gone. 'Cold fusion. They said it couldn't be done but it *was* done, in Utah, more than ten years ago, only nobody's been able to repeat the phenomenon and so they make out it was never done at all, that it was a hoax. But there are still scientists all over the world working on it, especially in Japan. It's like the ... the Holy Grail of science.'

'But what does it do?'

'Creates almost infinite amounts of energy. It could replace fossil fuels and solve the world's energy problems. It's cleaner, cheaper, safer than any known fuel source. Look.' He began to point out aspects of the blueprints but he might as well have been

65

speaking Swahili as far as the two women were concerned. Seeing their vacant looks, he soon ground to a halt. 'Sorry. Concepta says I could bore for England on the subject.' He flushed and pulled a copy of the *British Journal of Science* over the plans.

'And how are you getting on?' Barbara asked politely.

'Slowly.'

'Has there been any word from Alice today?' Concepta asked her junior colleague.

Brian Andrews paused for thought. He was a good-looking man in his late twenties, tall and strong, but not the brightest bulb in the box. She felt a surge of pride at having such a brilliant husband for her own, then a sagging of that pride as she wondered what good it did her when he was too sick for work.

She knew what her mother would think of a man who was supported financially by his wife: that he was no man at all.

Brian had collected his thoughts. 'She said it was the flu and we shouldn't expect her back for a few days.'

'Flu? In March?'

'Bad cold probably. Dr Peach always says you can't beat healthcare professionals for hypochondria. Can you help me get Mr Aimory out of bed?'

She followed him, her mind elsewhere,

mulling over the events of the previous day. She had come home and been surprised to find Roger alone in the kitchen with a mug of tea.

'Where's Millie?' she'd asked and a frown had crossed his face.

'Josh Salem took her out earlier. I thought they'd be back by now.'

She stood with her hands on her hips. 'Why did you let him take her at all? I thought we agreed.'

'I didn't exactly *let* him.'

She had got the story out of him, word by lingering word, then gone straight to call the police. He had followed her into the hall, protesting that she was over-reacting and that Millie would surely be home any minute.

People would think it strange, she thought, his attitude, people who didn't know him as she did. It would bother them.

There was only his word for it as to what exactly had happened.

And that bothered *her* a little.

But then Salem was missing, which proved Roger's story. Didn't it? She wished Alice was there so that she had someone to talk it over with, to share her fears with.

'Concepta?' Brian said.

'What? Sorry! I was miles away.'

'That's okay.' The young man's face was all gentle concern. 'I understand.'

She stationed herself on the other side of

67

the bed from Brian and waited for him to make a move. Mr Aimory weighed eighteen stone and it certainly needed two of them. Brian braced himself under one shoulder while she took the other and they both heaved. Once he was sitting up she moved his legs off the bed onto the floor and inserted his feet into his slippers. Brian came round to help pull him into a standing position and she wrapped his flannel dressing gown round his blue cotton pyjamas and knotted the belt.

'Where are we going?' she thought to ask.

'Bathroom.' Brian wrinkled his nose. 'We need a bath.'

The man stood swaying back and forth on his heels moaning, 'Sorry. Sorry. Sorry. Sorry.'

'It's all right, mate,' Brian said. 'Could happen to anyone.'

Concepta became aware that Mr Aimory had wet the bed.

She sighed.

'Will I be punished?' the old man said with a note of hope in his voice.

'Nobody's being punished,' Concepta said. 'Not on my ward.'

A card, she thought, as she went to fetch fresh sheets. A get-well card for Alice. That was the thing. It was what friends did. It was not something she had ever done but it was a simple matter of popping out at lunchtime and buying one. They would have them in the shop in the hospital foyer. Then she could drop it round after work and see if Alice needed anything.

She remembered that she didn't know where Alice lived. She would have to ask Dr Peach. Surely she would give her Alice's address in the circumstances. Alice had been oddly cagey about her home situation and Concepta feared that there was a man in the picture, not a very nice man perhaps. Somebody else's husband, a criminal, a madman. She didn't like to think of her friend in an unhappy relationship.

Or a woman even? She paused in the unfolding of a crisp white sheet as this idea came into her head, not for the first time. She didn't know what she thought about that. Six months ago she'd have known what to think but how could anything her dear friend did be wrong?

She understood a desire for privacy, even secrecy. She respected it.

Since Alice had been promoted to Charge Nurse, like herself, they were usually on different shifts and had to snatch moments together in cafés and wine bars. The last time had been on Friday.

They'd met in the café by the canal bridge in Northbrook Street. Alice had introduced her over the past weeks to the pleasures of cappuccino and latte in their seemingly endless permutations. Today she'd ordered a long, skinny, decaff, almond latte, just for the pleasure of letting the words roll off her tongue, so much indulgence, so much choice, and at such a modest cost. Crushed into a corner table they'd giggled and confided although it seemed in retrospect that the confidences were only hers.

'Sometimes I feel like that woman in Rebecca. What was her name?'

'She didn't have a name. That was the point. She was nobody.'

'Even better!'

'She was just the second Mrs Maxim de Winter.'

'And I'm the second Mrs Roger Troy.'

Alice stirred her latte vigorously and licked foam from the long-handled spoon, her pretty mouth turning up at the corners into a knowing smile. 'You're not suggesting that Joanna will turn out to have been an adulteress, a total bitch, and that Roger secretly murdered her?'

'Of course not.' Concepta smirked guiltily. 'Joanna was perfect.'

'Oh, I don't suppose for a moment that she was.'

It had been a twenty minute oasis before she went home to the pressures of the silent Roger and the loquacious child.

The child. Emilia. She should be fretting about her, not about Alice with a mild dose of flu.

70

She missed Alice.

When Dr Peach stopped by that afternoon she readily agreed to look Alice's address up for Concepta in her files.

'Send her my love too,' she said.

Send your own card, Concepta thought.

The address was the other side of town, so in the end she posted the card. She would try to get round in a day or two.

Roger led the way along the corridor, past the kitchen, the adjacent bathroom and into the smaller of the two bedrooms on the right hand side.

'My room,' he explained.

It was decorated as a child's room: banana yellow ceiling, blue wallpaper with yellow balloons on it. Megan took in the single bed and the cot tucked into the corner. 'You don't share with your wife?'

'What with her shift work,' he said, 'she needs to get a good night's rest, or a good *day's* rest. And I talk in my sleep sometimes, disturb her.'

'And Emilia?'

He pointed to the cot.

A scrabbling noise drew Megan's attention and she noticed the wire cage by the bed. An inquisitive nose quivered out of a wooden box with a hole in it, stiff whiskers. A hamster, she thought, nothing but a rat who knew who his ancestors were.

'I think we woke Desmond up,' Roger said. 'He's Millie's pet. She'll be missing him. I'm surprised he didn't go too.'

Megan noticed that the hamster had methodically chewed through the yellow candlewick bedspread on Roger's bed, pulling the little hanks of wool out to line his nest, leaving only cloth with a pattern of regular holes in it. She tried to remember when she had last seen a candlewick bedspread. It had been the fashion in her girlhood, long forgotten, though not here.

A child-sized chest of drawers was squeezed next to the cot, painted white with a black cat stencilled on it. It contained Emilia's clothes, carefully washed, ironed and folded.

'It doesn't disturb Emilia when you talk in your sleep?' she asked.

'Oh, she sleeps like the dead,' he said.

They crossed the hall into the bigger bedroom. A double bed stood plumb in the middle of the far wall, its quilted satin counterpane matching the mauve roses of the curtains but clashing with the wallpaper of red poppies. There were built-in wardrobes along the wall opposite, one sliding door slightly ajar, a wad of woollen sweater poking out, scarlet.

Megan slid the door further open and examined the inside: hanging rails with a meagre collection of blouses, dresses and skirts; shelves with pullovers, trousers and tee shirts.

Roger silently picked up the scarlet sweater and poked it back into its allotted place.

A heavy oak chest, its polish scarred in places, stood in the corner. On top were a hairbrush and a glass vase containing three yellow tulips, their tired heads drooping to brush the wood, so that Megan longed to offer them fresh water. The drawers contained underwear, socks and vests, utilitarian and much washed.

Barbara examined a photograph in a papier maché frame without picking it up. She saw a woman of indeterminate age, but not young, somewhere in her sixties or seventies, probably, with the same coarse hair that Mrs Troy had but a lot more flesh on her bones, comfortable in a floral dress with flip-flops on blue-veined feet. Beside her, stood a boy in his late teens with the characteristic flat features and slanted eyes of those born with the genetic disorder of Down's Syndrome.

They looked happy, grinning into the camera.

It struck Megan that the flat had been decorated by someone who had no conception of style, and who had never opened a decorating magazine or watched *Changing Rooms*. It reminded her of how working class homes had been when she was a girl in the early sixties, with the ethos of make-do and mend still fresh in people's minds from the war.

Furniture was handed down from generation to generation, as were kitchenware, ornaments, even clothes and shoes. These were no antiques, no heirlooms, only second-hand tat. The notion of getting rid of an article because it did not match the rest of your decor was laughable, if not immoral. How gladly had her mother replaced it all as manners began to change and wealth to accumulate.

It had been not merely a sexual revolution.

All the beds had been neatly made that morning, presumably by Roger, who acted as househusband. The floors were freshly swept and no dust rested on the chest of drawers. She was suspicious of possible crime scenes that had been recently scrubbed.

'You're on the top floor.' Megan went back into the hall and scrutinised the ceiling. 'Do you have access to the roof space?'

'It's in the bathroom.' Roger indicated a hatch in the centre of the room, between bath and wash basin.

'Is there a ladder?'

'It'll come down if you open the hatch,' he explained. 'I've never been up there and I'm sure Concepta hasn't. She's not fond of ladders, heights. Millie and I can hardly persuade her onto the balcony on a warm night.'

The two women exchanged glances and the junior officer silently volunteered. She produced a torch from her bag and, swinging the ladder easily down, climbed it. She stood on the second-to-top rung, her head and torso in the attic.

'Nothing here,' her muffled voice reported. Megan could see the flashes of her torch as it swept the area. After a few minutes Barbara descended, a sprinkling of dust on her hair and shoulders, and Megan closed the hatch while she brushed herself down.

'I'd like to speak to your wife,' Megan told Troy. 'What time will she be home?'

Roger thought before answering. 'Her shift finishes at five today,' he said finally, 'so she'll be back by ten past.'

'Then we'll come back later,' Megan said. She headed for the door but Barbara hesitated.

'This cold fusion. Is that what you were working on at Mainstay?'

'I can't talk about my work at Mainstay. Official Secrets Act.'

Chapter 5

'A new source of fuel,' Megan mused as they left the block of flats and strolled onto the Green in a brief burst of sunlight. 'Cheap, clean and inexhaustible. I'm no scientist but it sounds too good to be true.'

'It does to me too,' Barbara said, 'so I won't be buying shares in Roger Troy Ltd just yet. It's clearly all theoretical, anyway, nothing but papers.'

'I suppose it's something for him to do, letting him think he might still have a useful role to play in society – looking for the Holy Grail!'

'He was brilliant by all accounts,' Barbara said, shaking her head sadly. 'I spoke to his old boss at Mainstay House on the phone.'

'That's the government research facility near Swindon?'

'Mmm. Top-secret, hush-hush, whatever else you want to call it. I had quite a job getting them to speak to me and then they were no help, hadn't seen Roger since the day he locked up his desk, as usual, went home and went quietly bonkers.'

'What made you ask him about it just now?'

'It struck me that if there was anything in this cold fusion theory then it would be worth billions of pounds to whoever patented the process. The country that controlled it would virtually rule the world. If Mr Troy was working on it for the government and is now taking his knowledge and expertise freelance...'

'Then Special Branch have kidnapped his daughter to put pressure on him to hand over his research?'

Barbara laughed. 'Oh, well, if you're going to say it out loud, then obviously it sounds ludicrous. What now, ma'am?'

'Let's see how the search is going on at Salem's house.'

As they crossed the Green, Megan said, 'What's Mr Summers like to work for?'

'One of the best. He listens to your ideas and he doesn't try to pass them off as his own. He gives us a lot of rope.'

'Good, because if there's one thing I hate it's some desk jockey interfering with my investigation.'

'I wouldn't call him that. He likes to get out in the field, especially on a murder case. He's also not afraid to admit it if he's wrong.'

'That takes a lot of strength.' Megan hated to admit when she was wrong. Apologies came out of her mouth like pebbles steeped in acid, burning her lips in their progress.

'And he likes women,' Barbara added, 'actually *likes* them, I mean, not just sniffing round them like a randy Alsatian.'

Barbara had recently been told that there was a place for her in the National Crime Squad if she wanted it, based in London. She'd thought about it carefully for twenty-four hours then turned it down without regret. The NCS dealt with big and glamorous crimes but it would mean working in squads of literally dozens of officers and she didn't think she would be happy without the freedom and respons-ibility that Gregory Summers gave her as a matter of routine.

'He's changed these past couple of years, though,' she added, 'since his son died.'

Megan stopped walking and stared at the younger woman. 'His son died?'

'Of leukaemia. He was twenty-two.'

'Jesus! That's enough to change anybody.'

The women walked on in silence, both steeped in thought. Barbara was remember-ing how Gregory Summers had changed.

He used to smoke, she recalled with surprise, not like a madman, but twenty a day, regular. And drink a bit too much a bit too often, hitting the scotch, like so many men in stressful jobs. Now he confined himself to a couple of glasses of beer at a session in the pub after they'd got a result, a drop of wine with his dinner.

He was less conventional too, more willing to take a risk. If anyone had told her three years ago that Gregory Summers would pal up with a gay man like Piers Hamilton, the young photographer from Hungerford, she'd have laughed in their faces, but now the two men were like brothers.

Or maybe the charming Piers had become a substitute son.

If Gareth were to die, Megan was thinking meanwhile, I couldn't bear it. I wouldn't be able to go on. I should just curl up in a corner... I should end up like Roger Troy. She forced herself to stop thinking the unthinkable – the way she would sometimes wake from a nightmare and make herself forget the details – and set her face determinedly towards her new case.

'Fred was his only son too,' Barbara added. 'Makes it worse, somehow.'

Megan said crisply, 'Yes,' and the sergeant looked at her in surprise. She was still trying to figure the new DCI out, waiting patiently for the invitation to call her something other than 'ma'am'.

The woman on duty outside Salem's house was Jill Christie, a young blonde who stood very straight by the front gate, her hat exactly square on her head, her hands folded behind her back, feet eighteen inches apart. She looked like a younger and prettier version of the Duke of Edinburgh. Three or four times an hour she would walk up and down a few paces to ease the strain on her legs. She saw Barbara coming and managed to stand even straighter, a feat Megan would not previously have thought possible.

'Sarge!'

'Hello, Jill. This is Constable Christie, ma'am. Jill, this is Mrs Davies, the new chief inspector in CID.'

'How do you do, ma'am.'

Megan acknowledged the greeting with a nod and a smile and the two CID officers walked up the short path to the open front door. They could hear movement in various parts of the house and, as their eyes grew accustomed to the gloom, Andy Whittaker came bounding down the stairs. A tall man and powerfully built, he gave the impression of a rottweiler coming to give burglars a very special welcome.

'Sarge! Any news?'

'Not yet.' Barbara did the introductions again. 'Anything useful?'

'Nothing.' Whittaker looked disappointed, standing with his hands in the pockets of his chinos. He had been desperate to get into CID for a long time, puzzled by Super-intendent Summers' reluctance even to discuss it. This was his first case as a detective and he longed to be the one who made the breakthrough, so that he could show Nick the Bubble that he didn't know everything after all.

'Any messages on his answering machine?' Barbara asked.

'None and I did a 1471 which said he was last called on Friday afternoon. I checked the number and it was Social Services – his office trying to locate him.'

'Okay, we'll ask them about that.'

'Get on to Telecom,' Megan said. 'I want a list of all calls in and out of this number for the last six weeks.'

'It's in hand,' Barbara said. She asked Whittaker, 'How much longer do you estimate?'

'We're nearly finished with the house,' he said. 'I've sent Tom and Sharon over to make a start on the garage.' He addressed Barbara, accustomed to her authority. 'Do you want someone left here on guard after we're done?'

'It might be best,' Barbara began but Megan broke in, vexed at not having her rank recognised.

'I don't think it'd be the best use of manpower, Sergeant.'

Barbara bit back her retort, unwilling to argue with her superior in front of a constable. 'No, ma'am.'

'He's not going to sneak back here, not unless he's an idiot and there's no indication of that.'

'He might find he's forgotten something vital.'

'Are we overmanned?'

'Hardly!'

'Okay. Is there a Neighbourhood Watch, or something like that?'

Barbara looked at Whittaker who said, 'I'll say! Old bloke, two doors down, number six, came round the minute we set up last night to ask what we were up to. Jill had to stop him bodily from coming in but I went out for a chat. His name's Digby Mercer, he's seventy-eight and he served in the Western Desert with Monty in '44.'

'Blimey,' Barbara said. 'Has he adopted you or something?'

'You know the type, Sarge. His wife died two years ago. He's lonely and he'll chat to anyone. He runs the Neighbourhood Watch. Correction: he *is* the Neighbourhood Watch, and not much goes on on Peabody Green without him knowing about it.'

'Good,' Megan said. 'Then he's got a job. He'll love it. Give him plenty of numbers to contact CID if he gets a whiff of Salem, but remind him to dial 999 in an emergency and not to try any heroics.'

'Yes, ma'am,' Whittaker said.

She added to Barbara under her breath, 'I'm not as convinced as everyone else seems to be that this Salem is a harmless buffoon.'

They took a quick look round the place, moving easily among the working police officers. It was a smart little house, the front door solid oak with gilt fittings, a carriage lamp on the wall at head height. It was carpeted throughout in beige with a solidly upholstered three-piece suite in the through lounge, floral chintz, matching curtains. A chess board was set up there, abandoned in the middle of a game.

Barbara moved a few pieces at random. 'Serve him right,' she said.

The front bedroom was Salem's, untidy but not chaotically so. He clearly used the back room as a study and a young male officer was sorting patiently through his papers while the computer stood packed up ready to be taken back to the station where the contents could be examined at their leisure.

Whittaker came in as they were there and hefted the computer into his strong arms.

'Any sign he left in a hurry?' Barbara asked.

'No, Sarge. On the contrary, he'd emptied the fridge and it looks like he cancelled the milk and papers.'

'Send someone up to the newsagent to check about that.'

'Okay.'

'Do you know how Nick's getting on?'

'Last saw him coming out of Middleton House,' Andy said, bringing one knee up to hump the bulky computer more effectively into his arms.

'I'm assuming he's a bachelor,' Megan said. 'It's not exactly a "bachelor pad", is it? No expensive hi-fi, not all decorated in black and chrome.'

'And no black silk sheets,' Barbara agreed. 'No, he's never been married. He inherited the house from his parents who bought it from the council in '84. My guess is that the carriage lamp and the three-piece suite were Mum's taste. I doubt he changed much after her death.'

'So what do we know about him? Is he straight?'

'As far as anyone knows.'

'Find any pornography. Whittaker?'

Andy looked surprised. 'Er, no, ma'am!'

'Pity. Still, maybe he's got a few interesting websites among his favourites.'

'You think he might be a paedophile?' Barbara asked, dismissing Whittaker with a nod of her head. He moved thankfully and awkwardly towards the door.

Megan said, 'Just not ruling it out. Close friends?'

'I think his boss is the best person to ask about that,' Barbara said. 'She must have known him better than anyone.'

Megan checked the time. '12:25. Let's get some lunch before seeing her, somewhere quiet where we can talk some more.'

'There's a pub the other side of the main

road, the Greyhound.'

'Then lead me to it.'

As it was still early, the Greyhound was quiet. Barbara and Megan found a corner by the fireside with their half pints of orange juice and soda, their cheese sandwiches. By tacit agreement they turned away from the case for a few minutes to establish a more personal acquaintance. In police work you made friends quickly or not at all and Megan's overriding of her sergeant's decision at the house had not been a good start.

'You married, Barbara?' Megan asked.

Barbara shook her head, removing slivers of pallid tomato from between the layers of soapy cheese and eating them separately. 'Not planning it either. I mean, what's in it for me?'

'Regular boyfriend?'

'No one special. There's a doctor in Hungerford I see sometimes and an inspector from the National Crime Squad who scoops me up and takes me out for dinner whenever he's in the area.'

'And Gregory Summers is divorced, isn't he?' Megan said.

'God, for about a hundred years. He lives with someone, though,' Barbara added hastily. 'Angelica. They make a good couple.'

Megan grinned. 'Oh, don't worry. I

haven't got my eye on him.'

'Have you two met before?'

'At a training course about ten years ago.'

Barbara pricked up her ears; she knew what police courses were like.

'On DNA testing, I think it was.' Megan took a long swig of orange juice. 'It was before your time, I suppose, but we were only just starting to use it then and it took about three weeks to get a result back from the lab. There were people on the course who thought it'd take all the fun out of policing.'

'Imagine if we had a DNA database of everyone in the country,' Barbara mused. 'We could run the evidence through the computer, make an arrest and be home in time for lunch.'

'Now, that *would* take the fun out of it!' Megan finished her sandwich and looked doubtfully at her empty plate, wondering whether to order another. Gourmet food it was not, but it filled a hole and she sometimes had to remind herself to eat these past few weeks. 'I'm getting used to being on my own,' she said. 'Well, me and my son Gareth.'

It was not an apology for her high-handed behaviour at Salem's house, nor was it a request to call her Megan, but it was an offer of intimacy which Barbara seized. 'Your marriage has broken up?' she asked with sympathy.

'Yes, but we had fourteen good years and he's still the first person I'd turn to if I were in trouble. I can't understand people who talk as if divorce nullifies the whole marriage, even the good times.'

'It seems to be the trend, though,' Barbara said. 'Women and children on their own, I mean, now that we don't need men to bring home the bacon. Friend of mine did it recently: had a quick fling, got the baby she wanted, never even knew the man's surname, let alone told him he'd become a father.'

'Do I detect a note of disapproval?' Megan asked.

'Just that if I was a bloke I'd insist on condoms. I wouldn't like the idea of someone stealing my seed.'

'They seem to have plenty of it, though, and they're pretty careless with it. I mean, half the time they just–' Megan joined the thumb and forefingers of her right hand into a circle and made and up-and-down motion '–toss it away'

Both women snorted with laughter, glad to have established that they were on the same wavelength. Two middle-aged men at the bar looked nervously in their direction.

'And I don't see what difference it makes,' Megan said, 'if the man never learns of the deception. I mean, if the woman makes no demands, emotional or financial...'

Barbara shrugged. The two men at the bar now seemed to be engaged in a heated debate. Finally, one broke away, saying, 'They can only say no.' He walked across to the two women and stood awkwardly with his hands thrust into the belt loops of his jeans. 'My friend and I were wondering if you two ladies would like to join us for a drink.'

In chorus, they said, 'No.'

He reddened and rejoined his friend. 'You were right,' he said loudly, 'couple of lesbians.'

'Far too old to wear jeans,' Barbara said in an equally loud stage whisper. 'And with that beer belly.'

Megan lowered her voice, personal bonding over. 'So where is Joshua Salem?'

'He had it carefully planned, it seems to me. If he'd cancelled the milk and papers and so on.'

'Maybe he doesn't have milk and papers delivered. Not everyone does.'

'True.' Barbara didn't actually know *anyone* who got their milk delivered these days, and yet the roads were clogged up with milk floats, pootling along at ten miles an hour. Perhaps they were a front for the CIA.

'And he couldn't have known that the opportunity to snatch Emilia would present itself in such a timely manner,' Megan was saying, 'that Roger Troy would fall asleep while he was there.'

'Oh, I don't know. Roger says he was having *one* of his bad days, which implies that he had them regularly and I suspect Salem knew that. He only had to engineer a visit at the right time. Or keep visiting until the right time turned up.'

The bar door swung open and Andy Whittaker entered, scanning the lounge. He spotted the two women and made for their corner but stopped abruptly half way across the room. Megan watched in alarm as his tall figure tensed, then seemed to go into an uncontrollable spasm. She half rose from her seat, ready to offer first aid.

'Atishoo!' His eyes closed and his whole body shook.

Barbara sighed. Andy had this disconcerting habit of sneezing, without warning, at immense velocity and volume. It was like an explosion in a snot factory. The two men at the bar turned to stare while Megan sank back onto her seat and Whittaker, not at all disconcerted, continued his interrupted progress across the room.

'Sarge– Sorry.' He turned his attention to Megan. 'Ma'am, I mean. You know we put out a general alert on Salem's car?'

'Dark blue Ford Escort with white trim,' Barbara said, 'sun roof.' She recited the number plate from memory.

'That's right. Sharon's just pointed out that it's only sitting there in the bloody Peabody Estate car park.'

Lunch was over. Both women sprang to their feet.

'Andy sent us over to make a start on Salem's garage,' PC Sharon Moore explained. 'And I just glanced round the car park and it struck me that we'd been told to look out for a dark blue Escort and here was one just sitting here, so I checked the registration.'

Barbara sighed. 'Get someone here to open it up for us and go over it the same as the garage and the house.'

'Sarge.'

'And tell the station to put out a call to other forces telling them they're still looking for Salem and the kid but not in *this* car.'

'Right on it.' She began to walk away, talking into her radio. Barbara called after her, 'Well done, Shaz,' and got a wave of acknowledgement.

The two women stood looking at the car, an innocuous lump of metal, no different from millions of others. Megan peered in at the driver's window, although condensation on the glass from the spring night made it difficult. A coat lay flat on the back seat, road maps unfolded on the passenger side.

'No fool, our Mr Salem,' she said. 'Has he hired a car?'

Barbara shook her head. 'Too easy to trace. He'd have had to show his driving licence so the hire company would have his correct name and address. My guess is he's bought an old banger for cash – somewhere outside the area, most likely. Which confirms my view that he'd planned the whole thing in meticulous detail.'

Megan straightened up. 'And is holed up – where?'

'A rented cottage, something like that. Lake District, Devon or Cornwall. A harmless father on a spring break with his little girl.'

'And what are we doing about that?'

'Checking bookings with the main holiday companies, then trawling through the papers, looking for cottage owners who don't use an agency.'

'Haven't a lot of people cancelled holidays because of foot-and-mouth?' Barbara nodded. 'Which means it's all a bit chaotic,' Megan said, 'and records may be out of date.'

'It's a long job all right, but the chances are he used his real name as he'd have had to send a cheque, and it's hard to open a bank account in a false name these days.'

'Unless you're a money-launderer,' Megan pointed out. 'Let's get over to Social Services.'

Caitlin Kramer waved the two police officers in as soon as they appeared at the open door of her office. Both women displayed their warrant cards but Caitlin didn't bother to look at them. She had a paper plate with a half-eaten sandwich on her desk and a can of coke. Beside her a computer was switched on, the screen saver showing a haunted house with a full moon moving slowly across the night sky.

'Thought you'd be in uniform,' she said.

'We're CID,' Barbara explained.

'Something about Josh Salem. What's he done now?'

'Is he in the habit of doing things that get the police called?' Megan asked mildly.

'I didn't mean it like that,' Caitlin said. 'In fact, it's the nature of the work that we usually have to call the cops for our own protection.'

'It's about Emilia Troy,' Barbara said.

Caitlin nodded. 'I had a nasty feeling it might be. Go on.' She took a bite out of her sandwich. It was egg salad, and mayonnaise dripped onto the plate. She scooped it up with her finger and sucked it greedily.

'Emilia disappeared from her parents' flat yesterday lunchtime,' Barbara said. 'Her father says that Mr Salem abducted her and there's been no sign of him or the child since.'

Caitlin didn't speak for a moment, cramming the rest of her sandwich into her wide mouth and chewing vigorously. She sipped some Coke. As a delaying tactic it was unassailable. The screen saver suddenly made a creaking noise and an owl hooted. The two police officers looked at it in surprise. The full moon began its progress across the sky once more.

'Joshua Salem is a very dedicated social worker,' Caitlin said at last, 'sometimes too dedicated. Ever since he was put on the Emilia Troy case when she was a baby, he's been ... *obsessed* is not too strong a word, with her welfare. But I never dreamed that he would go this far.'

'Have you seen Mr Salem in the last couple of days?' Megan asked.

'No, but I wouldn't expect to.' Caitlin swivelled round in her chair to stare at a year planner on the wall behind her. 'He's had two weeks' leave booked since last autumn.' She pointed. 'Those brown dots are Josh.' The other two women followed her finger to where that week and the following one were a continuous line of brown. 'He said he was going walking in Scotland.'

'In the middle of a foot-and-mouth outbreak?' Barbara queried.

'I asked him about that last week and he said he'd still go up to Scotland but visit the towns and cities, museums, art galleries and

93

so forth.'

'When did you last speak to him?' Barbara asked.

'I tried to phone him Friday afternoon but his mobile was switched off, so I called his home number – just to say "Have a good holiday", really – but I got the machine so I didn't leave a message.'

'What form did this obsession take?' Megan asked.

'He was very anxious that the foster parents should be allowed to adopt Emilia, which is not the usual procedure. It's true that the Fergussons had been accepted as possible adopters but they were by no means top of the list and, even assuming that Emilia had been available for adoption, which she wasn't, I would have recommended placing her with another couple.'

'So, how did it even get to court?' Barbara asked.

'Mr Fergusson's well connected. He's a merchant banker in London, went to a "good"–' her fingers mimed quotation marks '–school, knows the right people. It helps. The Fergussons had the best solicitor money could buy but Deirdre Washowski crucified him.'

She grinned, amused by the memory. The visit of the two policewomen did not disturb her. Indeed, it was starting to look as if she'd seen the last of Joshua Salem and that made

94

this a red-letter day.

'Were you annoyed with Salem over the attempted adoption?' Megan asked.

'The whole thing was portrayed as emanating from the Fergussons so I couldn't reasonably blame Josh.'

'How did Salem react when he lost the case?'

'Blind fury. Then the Troys applied for care and control of Emilia and he fought that tooth and nail but was defeated again. Josh isn't used to defeat. He likes to get his own way, but then don't we all?'

'Anything else?' Megan asked.

'Yes, the most troublesome incident of all, really, took place a month or so ago when Emilia had been with her father and stepmother for almost a year. Josh found out that she was sleeping in the same room as her father and got all worked up about that. He doorstepped a magistrate late at night demanding a POSO. The JP sent him packing.'

'Why was that more troubling?' Megan asked.

'Because he'd been playing things by the book up till then, following office procedures, but he didn't get anyone's authority to go to the JP and she clearly thought he was crazy, rang me to express concern the following morning.'

'Which JP was it?' Barbara asked.

'Sunita Lawson. Do you know her?'

Barbara nodded. 'One of our more sensible magistrates.'

'Amen. Comes from a Hindu family of six where the youngest invariably slept in the parents' bedroom till they started school, so she had no idea what Josh was complaining about.'

'And what did you do about it?' Megan asked.

'I paid a visit to the Troys myself at that point. I met Emilia and saw a happy, normal kid – well fed and dressed, obviously much loved, confident and chatty. I also gave her some elementary intelligence tests and she scored very highly: excellent vocabulary for her age. I told Josh that if there was one more incident like that one then he'd be off the case and facing disciplinary action.'

'I'm surprised you didn't take him off it anyway,' Megan said, 'to be on the safe side.'

A door creaked on the computer as Caitlin thought about it and there was a surge of organ music. She tutted and leaned across to switch off the speaker. 'Emilia really was – is – fond of him and I thought she'd had enough upheaval in her little life.'

'What is Salem like,' Barbara asked, 'as a person, as a man?'

Caitlin thought about it. 'Average

intelligence, not much charm. Could have been more attractive if he'd made a bit of effort. His heart was in the right place but he was disorganised, even shambolic, and you know what office life is like these days, even in the public sector.'

'Bureaucratic.'

'That's the polite word.'

'Did he have friends in the office?'

'Not what you would call friends, no. We're all colleagues but we don't tend to socialise; we keep sane by getting away from it at the end of the day.'

'Do you know if he had close friends outside work?' Caitlin shrugged a negative. 'Girlfriend?' Caitlin laughed at the idea.

'One thing that puzzles me,' Megan said, 'was why Emilia had to go into care at all when her father had his breakdown. Was there really no family on either side?'

'Apparently not. Let me see.' Caitlin touched her computer mouse, causing the haunted house to disappear in favour of a list of files. She tapped a few keys and brought up a lengthy file on the screen. She swivelled the screen slightly towards her so that the two visitors could no longer see it.

'Ah, yes,' she said. 'I remember now. Both sets of parents were dead. Joanna had had a kid sister but she'd vanished.'

'Vanished!' Barbara echoed.

'Oh, not police business. She ran away from home at the age of fifteen and hasn't been heard of since. We had no idea where she was and she wouldn't, in any case, have been deemed a suitable guardian for a vulnerable child. Then there was a Troy aunt but she'd quarrelled with Roger's father in 1973 and didn't want to know. She was getting on a bit, anyway. You need energy to care for young children.'

'Roger doesn't strike me as full of energy,' Megan remarked.

'No, but his patience seems boundless.'

'I'd like to take a look at Salem's desk,' Megan said.

'Search it, you mean?'

'Yes, that is what I mean. And I assume he has a computer here?'

'Yes, but we're talking confidential files.'

'I'm only interested in anything personal he keeps on there. I can get a warrant if you like.'

Caitlin looked for a moment as if she was going to be difficult then changed her mind. 'I'll show you the way.'

Concepta stood clenching and unclenching her fists in the kitchen, her cheeks flushed with fear or shame. She could hear the hum of talk from the sitting room – the child's shrill babble, the older woman's calm tones – but couldn't make out any of the words.

She turned her anger and frustration on her husband, furious at his unruffled demeanour as he sat at the breakfast bar sipping orange juice.

'You're taking this very calmly, Roger, I must say.'

'It's just routine. She said.'

'And you believe that?'

'Why not?'

'Because she's the head of Social Services, Roger. She spends her days sitting in an office, not coming to visit cases herself.'

'Perhaps she's dissatisfied with the way Salem is handling the case,' he said hopefully. 'Perhaps we can even cease to be a case.'

Concepta snorted. 'Finding reasons to take Millie into care, the way he wants, you mean.'

Roger said serenely, 'I'm sure Millie will give a good account of herself.'

'I'm going to offer her some tea, see what she's up to.'

'Concepta—'

She had already left the room.

She returned almost at once and he heard the sitting room door shut firmly behind her from inside. He was reminded of the phrase 'a flea in her ear' and suppressed a smile at his wife's grumpy expression.

'They're just playing games,' she said in disgust. 'She more or less threw me out.'

'What sort of games?'

'Fitting blocks into holes, that sort of thing.'

'A standard intelligence test, in other words.'

'I suppose.'

Caitlin Kramer emerged a few minutes later, holding Emilia by the hand. 'That's one very bright little girl you have there, Mr Troy,' she said with a big grin. 'Shouldn't be surprised if she grows up a genius.'

She shook hands with them both and left.

Roger said, 'See. You shouldn't get so worked up.'

'You never know what a child will say that could be damaging. I was reading her a fairy story at bedtime the other night about a girl with a wicked stepmother and she kept saying it – "Wicked stepmother" – over and over.'

'So she liked the sound of the phrase.'

He had heard Concepta's efforts at bedtime stories, the laboured delivery, the lack of inflection. It did not come naturally to her but that didn't stop her from trying, bless her.

'Until she says it to a social worker,' his wife went on. 'They live in a fantasy world at that age.'

'Don't we all?'

'This is going to take too long,' Barbara said. 'We'll have to put somebody else on it if we're going to see Dr Peach this afternoon.'

She took out her mobile and punched in a speed-dial number as Megan began to open the drawers of Salem's desk, using a pencil

100

to move the crammed upper layers aside.

'Nick?' Barbara said. 'DS Carey. How's the house to house going? Yeah, I know.' She placed a palm over the handset and said, 'Mostly at work,' to Megan. 'Can you get over to Social Services? I need Salem's desk gone over... Yes, I do mean now. Well ask one of your lads for directions. Okay.'

As she disconnected, Megan straightened up. 'Well, I can't see anything at first glance unless you count about a year's supply of extra strong mints. He's left no obvious clues here.'

'Why do I get the feeling he's always one step ahead of us?' Barbara said. 'It's bizarre.'

'Especially for a man his boss describes as shambolic.'

'There's still his credit and debit cards,' Barbara remarked as they drove away from Social Services, heading for Peabody Green en route for the Kennet Hospital and their appointment with Dr Peach.

'But it looks as if he thought of everything so he's probably been stockpiling cash.'

'What about Scotland?' Barbara said.

'The last place he'll have gone.'

'I agree.'

Chapter 6

The day Salem came to inspect the flat Concepta acted like the Queen was coming for tea.

They'd been in less than a month and things were still not straight. The paintwork had grown dingy and needed a fresh coat but there had been no time. The ready-made curtains were not a perfect fit, sagging below the sills. The picture window that led onto the balcony had no drapes at all, although Roger was fitting a childproof lock to them, demonstrating something of the man who had once been a scientist and a householder.

She rushed about the house, tidying, vacuuming, polishing, wiping.

He told her to calm down. 'They know our circumstances. They know we don't live in a palace.'

'Not like the Fergussons,' she grumbled. 'I bet their place is a palace.'

'Am I doing the right thing?' he asked, sitting on his haunches as he fiddled with the bolt on the window. 'Am I being selfish in taking her away from a better life?'

'Children are happier with their parents,' she said, although she had enough experience of the world to know that that was not always true. 'Blood,' she added, 'is thicker than water.' If only literally.

She'd bought biscuits and cakes, much as it galled her to entertain Salem. She put them all out on the new plates, white with a blue rim, from Tesco, then put half away again. It mustn't be thought that she had no care for her stepdaughter's health or her teeth, that she would ply her with junk food to pacify her.

'But Emilia isn't coming today,' Roger said patiently when she voiced these thoughts aloud because she was so full of them that she was afraid they might burst out.

'No, but he'll judge us. Salem. Roger, let me show him round, okay?'

'If you like,' he said.

'Let me do most of the talking.'

He shrugged. Talking was still an effort, mostly because he was out of practice, but he was getting the hang of it again.

Salem was more than half an hour late: deliberately, she was sure, reminding them of their insignificance. He did not apologise. He glanced at the plates and refused her offer of food or even a cup of tea.

'Let's get this done, shall we?'

He looked round the flat with a critical eye, remarking on the smallness of the kitchen and bathroom. Concepta showed him the childproof lock but he didn't look at it, glancing instead out of the window and saying, 'You can see my

103

house from here.'

'What!' The news had stunned her.

'I live just across the Green.' He gave her a big smile with no warmth in it. 'Didn't you know?'

She said grimly, 'I did not know.'

'So, we're neighbours. Isn't that convenient?'

She took him into the bedroom with the double bed. 'This is our room,' she said firmly. He made no response but walked across the hall to the second bedroom.

'Cramped,' he remarked.

'Big enough for a child,' she responded sharply. 'My parents raised seven of us in a two-up-two-down.'

'But that was in Ireland,' he said, as if the mere fact of being Irish meant that one could expect no better. 'And she won't always be an infant.'

'By the time she's older we'll be on our feet,' she said. 'Roger'll be back at work and we'll get somewhere nicer. With a garden.'

He gave her a steady, sceptical look. 'Mr Troy is to be the primary carer, I understand.'

'For the time being.'

He walked round the room. It didn't take long. 'Bed and cot?' he said.

'The bed's for when she's older.'

'Uh, huh. At the moment she has a big room, three times the size of this. Plenty of space for her toys and she's got lots of toys. Lovely garden. A swing, paddling pool.'

Concepta was tiring of his manner. 'Well, are

you satisfied?'

'Hardly that!'

'Is there any good reason we shouldn't bring a child up here, perfectly decently, like millions of other people? Since when has poverty excluded people from the pleasures of parenthood?'

He had no answer for her. It annoyed him that this ugly woman debated with him so skilfully. You could trust the Irish to have an answer to everything. Nurse bloody Ratchet, he thought. As with many unimaginative people, mental illness was one of his greatest fears and those who chose freely to work with the insane were beyond comprehension, living daily with a fate worse than death.

'I shall make my report,' he said, and left.

A week later they had a letter from Caitlin Kramer telling them that weekend visits could begin at once, with a view to Emilia moving in as soon as she was used to their company.

'We should have champagne,' Roger said gleefully and Concepta said, 'Don't be silly, Roger.'

Aled knew where he was. He just didn't know how he'd got there, let alone why. He'd been brought up chapel and looked in disgust at the gaudy trappings of the church of Rome that surrounded him: the saccharine virgin in her blue gown, the sinister confessional, the bleeding hearts.

Bleeding hearts; too many of them in the

world. Who needed them? Not Aled. Blame their upbringing, blame society. God forbid that anyone should take responsibility for his own actions.

He felt tired, as so often these days, exhausted by his internal rant. His heart was beating too fast and he needed to sit down. There was sweat, clammy in the armpits of his well-pressed shirt, in the small of his back. He squeezed himself with difficulty into the nearest pew. He was a large man, a good six foot four, and had filled out since his retirement seven years ago: not enough activity, too much of Matilda's good cooking.

The silence of the church was welcome, the darkness and the cool, and he closed his eyes and sighed. He felt no prayer in him and this was the wrong place for it if he had. He tried to remember the last time he had been to chapel but couldn't. He wondered why his wilful feet had brought him here today, to this alien god.

He squeezed his eyes shut till he saw white stars and red whorls, like thumbprints, on the inside of his eyelids. He made an effort. 'Oh, God,' he began. 'Please... Oh, God. Oh, God. Help me! Oh, God!'

No answer.

The heavy wooden door creaked open and a woman came in. Aled gave up his futile pleas, opened his eyes and glanced round.

She either didn't see him or considered him not worth acknowledging. Or maybe there was an etiquette about such things among the Papists. That was fine by him.

Ugly cow, he thought resentfully. He liked pretty women. Ugly women were an affront, useless. Matilda had been pretty forty, fifty years ago, dainty. Knew it too and had made him run after her, made him beg. He had respected her for that. Women nowadays didn't understand the rules of the game: they made it too easy, then they wondered why a man didn't stick around. Matilda was still a handsome woman.

The ugly woman dipped her hand in the trough of water by the door and crossed herself, up and down and left and right, her hand finally coming to rest briefly against her lips. What was the point of that? Popish rubbish. She moved along the aisle, took a pew about half way down on the other side from Aled and knelt, burying her head in her hands.

He lumbered to his feet and left the church, marching across the wooden floorboards, deliberately noisy, but she didn't look up. He let the door bang behind him, inhaling the spring air, the damp grass, convincing himself that he had left behind an odour of stale incense, although there was none.

No churchyard; the Catholics seldom had

churchyards. Pity: he liked to read the names on the gravestones, the dates, the trite verses. Not dead, only sleeping. That was a mean trick to play on anybody. He laughed out loud at the old joke. A few daffodils grew by the path as he strode to the road, past their best.

He stopped at the gap where the gate should be, nothing but a rusted iron fitting to testify to its sometime existence. Vandals. He knew what he would do with vandals if he was in charge. He felt his heartbeat quicken again and a fresh patch of perspiration dampened his woollen shirt under his tweed jacket.

Another bloody ugly woman and this one in uniform! A black woman of about fifty, standing at the front of his car as it stood brazen on the double yellow line, copying down the registration number onto her clumsy electronic pad, probably getting everything there was to know about him from some central government computer, down to the hernia operation fifteen years back.

He staggered slightly and it was if a red mist flooded his brain. Then he moved toward her as fast as his unsteady feet would take him.

She glanced up, smiling, her voice rich and sweet with the faintest trace of West Indian accent. 'Your tax disc's out of date too, I'm afraid, love.'

Smiling? Bloody smiling at someone else's misfortune!

Love!

'No ID?' Dick Maybey, the custody sergeant, said.

'Can't find anything, Sarge.'

'She stole my wallet,' Aled said. 'That black bitch.'

PC Chris Clements looked at the ceiling as he gathered the remnants of his temper. 'I don't think so, sir.'

'Name?' the sergeant said, pulling a fresh form towards him and readying his biro.

'Aled Davies.'

'Is that Davies with an e or Davis without?'

'With, and you can't treat me like this because my daughter's a police officer.' He poked his finger in Maybey's face. 'A very senior police officer. She'll soon sort you out, sonny.'

The sergeant and constable exchanged glances. Clements pulled a face of caricatured dismay.

'I don't seem to have a mobile number for the new DCI,' Maybey said, fussing papers in his filing cabinet.

'She's out with Babs this morning,' Clements offered. 'I saw them going off about eleven.'

Maybey reached for the phone.

Barbara's mobile rang just as she pulled up at Peabody Green again. She took the tiny thing from her pocket, flicked it open, looked at the incoming number and said, 'Uniform. Let's hope they haven't got another dead farmer.' She pressed the on button. 'DS Carey. Yeah. Yes, she's here with me. Hold on.' She passed the handset to Megan. 'It's for you.'

Surprised, Megan said, 'DCI Davies.' She said nothing more for the space of at least a minute, listening, then, 'I'll be right there.' She disconnected and handed the mobile back to Barbara. 'Can you drive me back to the station? Then I'm afraid you're going to have to see Dr Peach on your own.'

'Is that her?' Megan murmured to Maybey. 'The West Indian woman.'

He nodded. 'There was some racist abuse, ma'am,' he said apologetically. 'The arresting officer heard it too.'

'He's not a racist!' Megan said.

The sergeant shrugged. 'People of his generation ... it's practically bred in the bone.'

'No,' she said firmly. 'Dad's got no problem with black people.'

'Whatever you say, ma'am.'

'Where is he?'

'I put him in the cell for a bit to calm down.'

'He's not been charged with anything?'

'Not yet, ma'am, but the warden's very upset and she's not going to let it go easily.'

'I'd like the doctor to take a look at him.'

'You're in luck,' Maybey said. 'Dr MacDonald is in the station just now, checking out a bloke we brought in who twisted his ankle resisting arrest. No really,' he added, although Megan hadn't queried the statement. 'Jumped over a stairwell, landed awkwardly.'

'Then ask him to look at ... my father please.'

'Her, ma'am. Tessa MacDonald. Right away.'

'Meanwhile I'll have a word with the traffic warden.' Megan winked at Maybey. 'Hope my charm's in full flow today.'

'I'm sure it is, ma'am,' Maybey said without a trace of audible sarcasm.

The traffic warden was standing uneasily in the front office, trying to maintain a look of affront and disgruntlement, which wasn't easy to do for the lengthy period of time that the law took to grind its way through an arrest.

'Mrs Heston? I'm Chief Inspector Megan Davies. I'm sorry you've been left standing around like this. Shall we go to the canteen for a cup of tea?'

111

Slightly mollified, the woman followed her and soon they were settled with two steaming mugs.

'About the man who frightened you–' Megan began.

'Frightened!' She bridled, offended. 'I wasn't frightened of that old man, but he can't go around treating people like that, assaulting them–'

'Did he hit you?'

'Don't need to touch me for it to be an assault,' the woman said triumphantly. 'You should know that.'

'Of course.'

'Wagged his finger at me.' She demonstrated. 'Poked it in my face. And the language!' Her brown cheeks darkened into a flush. 'He used the N word, if you must know.'

'I'm really sorry.'

'I've lived in this country since I was five years old and it's been fifteen years or more since anyone called me–' she lowered her voice and glanced round the canteen to make sure no one was listening '–a *nigger*. And me a traffic warden, as puts up with all sorts of abuse. I been called a fat cow and a fascist and a bloodsucking bitch, and that's just in the last month, but I thought the days of being called a nigger were gone.'

'Look.' Megan leaned forward across the table, confidential. 'I'm sorry to tell you that

112

that old man is my father–'

'Oh, I get it!' Mrs Heston's face was hostile now and she leaned back in her seat, pushing her half-full mug away from her, rejecting the comforting beverage and the woman who had paid for it. 'Cover-up.'

'No, I assure you. If you want him charged with assault and threatening behaviour and conduct likely to cause a breach of the peace, then he will be, but if you'll hear me out, I hope you'll take pity on a sick old man who is, I promise you, no racist.'

She explained about her father's illness, about the stroke which had changed his personality, turning a gentle, polite man into a bully, even a bigot. Mrs Heston's look of indignation faded as Megan told her story and, when she came to an end, she murmured, 'Poor old man.'

'It's hard on him, even harder on my mother.'

'I'll bet! My own father was getting a bit cranky towards the end, sometimes came out with stuff you wouldn't think he had in him.' Mrs Heston drained the last of her tea. 'And hard on you too, sugar. But I can't accept your apology, not on his behalf.'

'Oh.'

'Gotta hear it from him.'

Gregory Summers poked his head round the door of the CID office and saw Andy

113

Whittaker tapping away at the keys of a computer, every bit as fast as Susan Habib could do, though using fewer fingers.

He hesitated, then went in.

He'd opposed Whittaker's desire to join CID for a long time, making excuses not to discuss it with the young man, to his hurt and bewilderment. He could hardly tell him that his wife, Tina, was the block over which he stumbled in his quest for advancement. Whittaker had not been aware that she'd had any connection with the Jordan Abbot case and he and Barbara had agreed that there was nothing to be gained by bringing charges against her.

Where ignorance was bliss...

Barbara, however, had been determined that Whittaker was just the sort of constable she needed – bright, hard working and conscientious – and had nagged him about it incessantly. The news that Tina had packed her bags and headed north to Yorkshire to live with a man who owned a string of prize-winning show jumpers had tipped the balance.

Greg hoped she got foot-and-mouth.

At least he was an improvement on Nicolaides who seemed not to hear when Greg spoke to him, before jumping like a startled rabbit and saying, 'Sorry, sir. Were you talking to me?'

Whittaker was so absorbed in his work

that he didn't hear his superior officer's approach.

Greg said, 'Is that Salem's computer?'

'Sir! Yes, sir.'

Greg took a seat next to him. 'Checking his Internet activity?'

'DCI Davies asked me to, sir,' Whittaker said, a little defensively.

'Of course, of course.' He had a lot of ground to make up with the boy, he knew. 'Anything interesting?'

'He's got quite a long list of favourite websites.' Whittaker pointed at the screen. 'He hasn't organised them in any way so I've just been working through them from the top but I've found nothing sinister. Just chess and Star Trek so far.'

'What you might call bachelor interests?' Greg suggested.

'Yes, sir.'

The two men exchanged conspiratorial grins: Whittaker's partner while he was in uniform, Chris Clements, was a Star Trek fanatic who regularly went to conventions dressed as Mr Spock, despite being shorter and a lot chunkier than the famous Vulcan. Clements did not have a girlfriend and his regular attempts to chat up new female recruits invariably came to nothing after he tried to impress them with his mastery of the Klingon language which seemed to consist mostly of grunts.

'When I've done his favourites, I'm going to check his most recently accessed websites,' Whittaker added, 'assuming he doesn't automatically delete his temporary files on exit.'

Greg nodded, maintaining the fiction that he had understood a word of this, and said, 'Good work, Andy. What about his office computer?'

'Social Services kicked up about us bringing it in and Babs didn't think it was worth getting into a row with them so Nick's checking it on site.'

'Who?'

'DC Nicolaides, sir.'

'Oh, *George*.'

Whittaker sneezed, making Greg take a step back in alarm. Most people went 'Ah, ah ah' before the explosion. Not Whittaker.

'Sorry, sir.'

'Hope you never have to hide behind an arras, Whittaker.'

'Sir?'

'Never mind.'

Andy had long given up trying to understand the old man's more cryptic remarks. 'Then I'll go through his personal files.'

Greg said, 'If he was planning a disappearance he'd have deleted anything incriminating, wouldn't he?'

'Probably. When I'm done with it it'll go to the lab so they can examine the hard drive properly, retrieve anything he thought he'd disposed of safely. Meanwhile, I've found no sign of a diary at first glance but it might be disguised under an odd name.'

'No sign of a flesh and blood diary, I suppose, bits of paper glued between cardboard sheets: the time in Buenos Aires, sunrise and sunset, new and full moons, best vintage for claret...?'

'Only an appointment diary, no journal. Dentist. Local elections. Boring stuff like that.'

'Do you keep a journal, Andy?'

Whittaker reddened. '...Yeah. Do you, sir?'

'Not since I was a teenager.'

The memory of his adolescent effusions still had the power to make him blush. How deeply you felt things at that age, deeper than you ever would again. He had found the ancient volumes in the attic when clearing out his parents' house after their death and had held a valedictory bonfire.

Who did one write journals for, anyway?

He laid a friendly hand on the constable's shoulder. 'If you can find a diary saying "March 19th: abducted Emilia Troy and took her to such and such an address," we'll make you Chief Constable.'

'Thank you, sir.'

Chapter 7

Barbara was shown straight into Sarah Peach's office when she arrived shortly after three. She saw a woman in her mid fifties who must once have been handsome and still bore her years well. If three decades in psychiatric medicine had left its mark on her, then Barbara saw no sign of it. She seemed relaxed, happy, exuding an air of gentle firmness, like the best sort of mother. Her large, comfortable frame and the floral print dress discernible beneath her white coat only added to the effect.

Barbara half expected to be offered a slice of home-made cake.

'We are not, of course, a psychiatric prison,' she explained to Barbara, once she had made sure she was comfortable, 'like Broadmoor or Rampton. Our patients are not violent or dangerous, except occasionally to themselves. They are ordinary people who suddenly find that they could no longer cope with their everyday lives. Like Roger Troy.'

She leaned across the desk. 'How is Roger? Have you seen him today? I asked Concepta and she just said he was as well as could be expected. Uncommunicative to the last.'

'Bearing up,' Barbara said lamely. 'Is he still your patient?'

'Oh, yes, on an out-patient basis. I see him once a month, review his medication. He's made immense strides since he left us.'

Barbara wondered what he'd been like before. 'I found him a little detached.'

'There can be an element of disconnection with those who've had serious breakdowns. It's a coping mechanism, a form of self-protection. But there's nothing like a happy family to go home to, a warm and loving wife.'

'You expect him to make a full recovery?'

Dr Peach fiddled with a paperweight, a bronze horse. 'At this stage it is largely a matter of will.' Seeing Barbara's puzzled look, she added, 'He will get well when he chooses, when he is ready to put the past behind him and move on to the next stage of his life.'

'Wouldn't we all choose to be sane?'

'Would we? Once you have tried the alternative, it can seem restful – no decisions, no pressures, no expectations.'

'And if some harm has come to Emilia?'

'Then the damage may be irreparable this time. There is only so much pain the human psyche can stand.'

Barbara tried another tack. 'Were you

surprised that Mrs Troy came into work today, in the circumstances?'

'Concepta? No, she's very conscientious. Actually, with Alice Mason ringing in sick again, she's just offered to cover the night shift too. God bless her! I don't know what I'd do without her.'

'She's worked here a long time?'

'Seven, eight years. She came in from general nursing and I've found her an admirable carer. People think that those who care for the mentally ill must be boundlessly compassionate, almost soft. But anyone who is too soft doesn't last in this business; anyone who bursts into tears every time a patient plays up will inevitably be gone by the end of the month.'

She thought about it. 'I have never seen Concepta cry, which is not to say that she doesn't care. Only people are inclined to take Concepta for a fool, you see, just because she's got no small talk, no charm, but she isn't a fool; she's a highly intelligent woman.'

'Is she?'

'Oh, yes! She wanted to be a doctor but her father died when she was sixteen and she had to earn her living so she settled for the next best thing. I have to have complete trust in my nurses, especially when they're here all alone on the night shift, and I have absolute faith in Concepta.'

She added hastily, 'I trust Alice too, of course, and Joan and Moira and Brian, but I'd describe Concepta Troy as my right hand.'

'Isn't it a bit odd that she should marry a patient?' Barbara queried. 'I mean, doctors get struck off for having a relationship with a patient, don't they? And for someone in the position of a therapist almost...'

'But it's not uncommon,' Sarah Peach said, 'in the general wards anyway. The nurse is a fantasy figure for many men, the ministering angel in starched uniform and black nylons. Still, I was surprised to hear the news, I don't mind admitting, but I soon realised that Roger wanted to make his home situation more attractive to Social Services. A nurse who could care for him and the little girl – it must have seemed a heaven sent opportunity.'

'But you weren't surprised that she accepted him?'

Dr Peach slowly shook her head. 'I hope I don't sound bitchy if I say that he was the only chance of marriage she was likely to get. And she does genuinely care for him.'

'She fell in love with him while nursing him?'

'How can I answer that? I know little enough about the human mind, let alone the heart.' She looked a little sad. 'Roger was brilliant once, the nearest thing I've seen to a genius.'

'And not violent?'

'Never. He was a fit man, had once been athletic, but he lived by reason, by intellect, not by his fists. Don't you see? A breakdown doesn't alter someone's basic personality, not in my experience.'

'You treated him – as a therapist, I mean, not just with drugs?'

'Certainly. I'm a qualified psychotherapist as well as a psychiatrist.'

'Was there any indication that he felt resentment towards Emilia for the death of his wife?'

'I think you know, Sergeant, that I cannot possibly answer that question. It's a matter of doctor-patient confidentiality.'

'If you could only say it was out of the question...'

'But if I failed to say that, then you would draw an inference. No, I maintain my right to silence. Either way.' She smiled, softening the words. 'I'm sorry.'

'I understand.'

'Do you really suspect him or Concepta of being behind Emilia's disappearance?'

'We're pursuing several avenues of enquiry.' Barbara felt embarrassed by the dismissive formula and by the sardonic look it elicited from Dr Peach.

'Is that police speak for "Mind your own sodding business"?'

Barbara said in her turn, 'I'm sorry.'

'Granted. I suppose it's only a taste of my own medicine – no pun intended.' Dr Peach got up, putting an end to the interview. 'But if that's what you're thinking then I suggest you pursue some other *avenue*. And why is it always avenues, anyway? Why not streets or roads?'

'Very often it's a cul de sac,' Barbara said and Dr Peach barked out a rather masculine laugh, pacified. The sergeant gave the doctor her card with her mobile number on it and the usual request to get in touch if she thought of anything that might be relevant to the enquiry.

'Genius and madness?' Barbara said, as the psychiatrist showed her out, 'or is that a myth?'

'It's a myth,' Dr Peach said, with that motherly firmness that brooked no contradiction. It was as if she were recommending apple pie and clean knickers.

The psychiatrist sat thinking after her visitor had gone. She wondered if Roger Troy would ever be ready to be sane again since, in order to do that, he would have to let go of his grief for Joanna, and learn to forgive her.

The doctor still hadn't arrived by the time Maybey unlocked the cell for Megan. All the aggression had died from her father and he sat hunched on the hard ledge looking bewildered and rather small.

'I'll leave you to it then, ma'am,' Maybey said, and went out leaving the door open.

Aled said, 'Megan, thank goodness. Where's Matilda?'

'I don't know, Dad.' She sat down on the bench next to him and took his hand. 'At home, I imagine. I'll give her a ring in a minute or two. I expect she's worried about you.'

'Where am I?'

'In a cell at the police station.'

He looked fearful, whispering, 'Did I do something *terrible*?'

'No, Dad, not terrible.'

'Am I going to prison?'

'Not today.'

There was a discreet cough in the doorway and Megan rose to greet the doctor. She saw a woman who looked no more than twenty-five, though she must surely be older than that if she'd gone through medical school, trained as a GP and made it onto the local police panel. 'I'm Tessa MacDonald.' Her voice was musically Scottish. 'Is this the patient?'

'DCI Megan Davies. I'm new here.'

'Thought I hadn't seen you before, though I'm a bit of a new girl myself.'

She was a short woman and very slightly built, hefting a solid metal attaché case in her left hand as she held out the right one in greeting. She had bright red hair, blue eyes and the sort of fair skin that kept women like her out of the sun, a light freckling clearly visible across her cheeks and the bridge of her nose, although it was scarcely spring.

'What's the problem?' Tessa asked.

'This gentleman is my father. He had a stroke about a year ago and now he gets confused occasionally, then he becomes aggressive. Today was one of those days and he picked a fight with a traffic warden who was trying to give him a ticket.'

'Ooh, dearie me! I never pick fights with the wardens even when they ignore my doctor-on-call sticker. It's what my dad would call fighting out of your weight.'

Just about everyone would be out of her weight, Megan thought.

Tessa sat down beside the old man. Megan's initial thought that she was too frail for this job gave way to a realisation that her very smallness would soothe and reassure patients suffering from the stress of arrest and incarceration, not to mention the routine drink and drug problems.

'Is he to be held much longer?' Tessa asked, removing an ocular instrument from her bag.

'We're not holding him at all. I explained the situation to the warden and she was very decent about it. I just wanted him examined before I took him home.'

Tessa smiled at the old man, eliciting a timid response. 'Well let's take a wee look.' She didn't actually say *wee*, but Megan liked to imagine that she had. 'What's your name, sir?' she asked.

'Aled Davies.'

'That's a good Welsh name. I'm Tessa MacDonald and we Celts must stick together. Eh? Can you keep your eyes open for me, Mr Davies, and look up. And down. How are you feeling now?'

'Tired,' he said.

'Do you remember meeting a traffic warden this afternoon, lady in uniform?' He shook his head. 'Do you remember where you were this afternoon at all?'

He thought hard. 'Virgins,' he said finally.

'I beg your pardon!'

'Statues. Incense. Holy Water. Papist filth.'

'He was at the Catholic church behind the station,' Megan translated.

'Oh? Well, I'm a Free Presbyterian myself.' Dr MacDonald took his pulse. 'He's well enough to go home,' she said. 'I don't see anything obviously wrong with him, not physically. Is he on medication?'

'I don't think so.'

'When did he last see his GP?'

'I'll find out.'

'Not that there's a great deal to be done,

126

I'm afraid.' She got up, laying a friendly hand on the old man's shoulder. 'We'll get you home for a rest, Aled, okay?' He nodded gratefully.

Mrs Heston was waiting for them in front of the station, walking slowly up and down, patient. Every so often she darted a look across Mill Lane to where, she was sure, a car was illegally parked.

Megan said, 'Dad, this is Mrs Heston.'

'How do you do.'

'Do you remember her?'

He looked puzzled. 'I'm sorry. Have we met?'

The traffic warden looked crestfallen, deflated, as if her bogeyman in the corner had turned out to be no more than a trick of the light.

Megan said, 'You were rude to her earlier.'

'Rude! Me?' Aled looked as if he might cry and Mrs Heston said hastily, 'Okay. We'll forget about it. This time.'

Megan said a heartfelt, 'Thank you,' and the warden set purposefully off to deal with the miscreant car.

Barbara drove Megan and her father to the church to collect his car, Megan pocketing the parking ticket with a sigh. She then followed father and daughter home and waited outside. That way the two women could go straight back to Peabody Green to see Concepta and she could fill the DCI in on her visit to Dr Peach on the way.

'I may be a while,' Megan said. 'I have to stop Mum being too stoical.'

'Take your time.'

Barbara switched on the radio but she wasn't really listening to the bright chatter of the local station. She examined the house; a 1930s semi, it reminded her of her own parents' place in Hemel Hempstead. Did she have all this to look forward to in twenty years time? She knew in her heart that the burden of caring for her parents would fall on her older sister, Kathryn, who lived locally with her husband and children. She, Barbara, would be the one who visited every couple of months, armed with presents and well-meant advice, glad to escape after a few hours.

Mrs Davies was standing at the open door by the time Megan and her father reached it, navigating the front path between rows of narcissi and early tulips, Aled guided by his daughter's hand in his back. Barbara saw a woman of seventy, her hair totally white but carefully arranged, falling in a neat bob to her shoulder. She was no more than five foot two in height and probably not as slender as she had been in her youth but trim, with clothes that struck a balance between style and comfort. Barbara couldn't make out her face, saw only that the woman embraced her daughter warmly and admitted them both to the house.

The pips sounded for five o'clock and she tuned her brain in for the hourly news bulletin. She learned that some police forces were confiscating shotguns from desperate farmers.

Too late for Mr Halfacre, and his wife.

'This is a fresh blow,' Megan said when she returned to the car twenty-five minutes later. 'The woman I've fixed up to meet Gareth from school and stay with him till I get home can't start till after Easter, and I'd hoped Mum would fill in, but now...'

'What will you do?' Barbara started the car.

Megan didn't answer for a moment. 'Ask Mum as planned and hope for the best. There's nothing else I can do. In a couple of weeks it'll be the Easter holidays and he can go to Newcastle, to his dad.'

'Roll on Easter,' Barbara said.

Megan shook her head. 'Of all the jobs to try to combine with kids! I must be crazy.'

It was almost six by the time they arrived back at Beaumont Tower and it was Concepta who answered the door to them. She led them into the kitchen, motioning them to take seats at the breakfast bar where she was finishing her frugal supper with a hard-looking pear, and went to turn off the blare of the TV in the sitting room.

Megan whispered, 'Do you get a whiff of brimstone?'

Barbara raised her eyebrows, the same way she did to Gregory Summers when he got over-fanciful, and silently indicated the boiled egg in its cup on the draining board, the smell of sulphur lingering.

The shell had been pulverised; no chance of a witch riding in that.

Mrs Troy returned. 'I can't give you long,' she said briskly, 'as I have to be back to the hospital for the night shift by seven.'

'Oh!' Barbara was taken aback. Surely her place was with her husband. Sarah Peach had called her warm and loving. She must have some special vision that Barbara lacked, a mental x-ray.

'A colleague rang in sick,' Concepta said, not defensive, 'and I thought I might as well be there as brooding here where I can be no use. I wasn't here when the abduction took place,' she added. 'Tea?'

'But you've met Mr Salem?' Megan said.

She snorted. 'First time I met him, I thought he was weird.'

'Why?'

She shrugged. 'Well, he's a man for one thing.'

Megan knew what she meant: the caring professions – teachers, social workers,

130

nurses – were predominantly female, especially in the south-east of England where you needed a salary of forty thousand a year to buy a one-bedroomed flat. Women were even in the majority among doctors and lawyers these days.

'You'll have that tea,' Concepta decided and began to busy herself with pots, kettles and cups. Neither police officer objected. It had been a long day, one way or another.

Concepta had little fresh to offer them and they were soon on their way. Barbara caught a glimpse of Roger sitting at his work table, intent on his papers. A shell of a man, she thought.

But had he been pulverised?

Chapter 8

There was something shameful about still being a virgin in your thirties, at least now, in the 21st century; a hundred years ago no one would have thought anything of it, least of all Concepta. Add to that the fact that she had now been married a month and it became a shame that she hardly dared to contemplate.

Her mother had told her that men were ravenous when it came to sex and offered her own seven children by way of demonstration.

'Men are great,' she would say, 'except when they're on their knees,' and Concepta, no more than ten or eleven at the time, had thought she meant at mass and been puzzled.

When she'd left home at seventeen to go to Dublin to train as a nurse, she'd been prepared, armoured against the demands and blandishments of doctors, porters, men encountered in the streets with their devouring, lustful eyes. She had been relieved – with a small leavening of disappointment – to discover that they had no interest in her.

By the age of twenty-four, when she'd set sail for England, relief had become alarm.

She stood looking at herself in the shaving mirror in the bathroom. There was no full-length mirror in the house: her mother had seen no need for such an object of vanity and nor did she. She examined her face in a way she hadn't done since adolescence, then looked dubiously at the Boots plastic bag that lay on the sink. She opened it and took out the make-up she had bought for the wedding, the powder and lipstick, the bright blue eye shadow and black mascara wand.

Wand, she thought: as if it might work magic.

She had had no idea what colours suited her and no girlfriend to ask, but she had been aware of the slightly startled look that Sarah Peach threw her when she walked into the hospital chapel.

Had she been trying not to laugh?

Emilia had been with them that weekend. It had been agreed that she should come for visits for the first month, a day or two at a time, until she grew used to them. Salem had dropped her off on Friday night, remarking, 'Here we are, darling, home to daddy and the wicked stepmother' and she had wanted to slap his stupid face.

The irony was that in fairytales wicked stepmothers were beautiful, like Snow White's, or Rose Red's.

Emilia had wept all Friday evening and most of Saturday, calling for the Fergussons, the people she thought of as her mother and father. Roger had been endlessly patient with her, talking with her, playing the simple games she had brought with her, inventing new ones, and by Sunday she had been cheerful and a little surprised when Salem came to take her away again.

She, Concepta, had busied herself with the child's physical wellbeing, cooking nutritious meals from what she remembered of her mother's limited repertoire. She washed and ironed Emilia's tiny clothes every time they got the smallest mark on them, though she knew that it was like painting the Forth Bridge.

'Relax,' Roger had told her with a smile. He had smiled more that weekend than in the two years she had known him.

'We must get it right,' she had muttered, 'or they'll take her away again.'

She dabbed powder on her face, aware of the cloud floating onto the sink, forming little puddles of mud where it found damp. It was hard to apply eye-shadow when you could see only out of one eye, hard to wave the sticky black wand, harder still to make lipstick with its foul waxy taste curve into the corners of her lips. No sooner had she applied it than it bled into the fine, dry lines and she made a little noise of annoyance.

She smoothed down her clothes: her best blouse, pink silk, a black skirt shorter than she would normally wear. Her legs were bare, her feet in black sandals, her toenails unvarnished. Should she have bought varnish? All the other women she saw wearing sandals had pink or red toes, even blue or green, occasionally silver.

It was too late. If she didn't try now then her courage would be gone beyond retrieval.

She knew that Roger was still in the sitting room, working away at his 'project', the TV on with the sound turned down. 'For company' she'd told him and he'd made no objection.

She stood in the doorway for a moment, trying to calm herself, breathing deeply. 'Roger?' He glanced up. If he saw a difference in her then it didn't register in his eyes. She crossed the room to stand behind him, put her arms round his neck and kissed him softly on the nape.

He sat very still.

She closed her eyes and pulled his face round to meet hers. Her lips reached out for his and she felt them touch, his softer than she had expected, more moist. She let her tongue flicker forward, as she had read in magazines, coming up against the rigid denial of his teeth.

She opened her eyes just in time to see the look of utter horror on his face.

He jumped up, pushing her away. His face was red, then white. She put her hands over her eyes, not because she was crying – she didn't know how – but to blot out the expression on his face, preferably forever.

'I'm sorry!' he said urgently. 'I'm sorry, Concepta.' He put his arms round her, bringing her head to rest on his shoulder and stroking her coarse hair. 'I've been ill. I'm sorry.'

'Yes, of course.' She clutched eagerly at the explanation. She knew what a lengthy depression – let alone the breakdown Roger had been through – did to the male libido, not to mention the medication he took night and morning. 'Only.' She raised her head and looked at him. 'I should quite like a child of my own, before I'm too old.'

Not to leave it too late, the way Mammy had with Tommy.

He said, 'One step at a time. Eh? Walk before we try to run.'

Lying awake in her double bed that night, past midnight, Concepta remembered a saying that had struck her when she was working in a hospital in Liverpool on first arriving in this country.

135

Something pointless had been referred to as 'Like putting lipstick on a pig'.

It didn't surprise Greg that Angie's car wasn't in the drive when he got home. It had gone into the garage that morning to have a new carburettor fitted and get its MOT. Angie had taken the train to college saying that she would a) beg a lift, b) get the train back or c) sleep on someone's floor.

The chances were that he had the house to himself. Well, him and Bellini – the West Highland Terrier bitch he had reluctantly acquired during a recent investigation.

And he had news on that front for Angie.

He noticed a scarlet sports car in the road in front of the house and wondered which of his staid and conventional neighbours was enjoying a second adolescence.

'I'm home,' he called as he removed his key from the front door, just in case. There was an unexpected cooking smell drifting from the kitchen. To his surprise he heard a discreet throat-clearing coming from the sitting room. He poked his head round the door and thought for a moment that his heart was going to stop. For a few seconds he was convinced that the young man on the sofa was Fred, his son, Angie's husband, dead of leukaemia some two years earlier.

He realised his mistake fast enough, of

course, but he felt dizzy with the shock.

The boy rose. He was tall, like Fred, with the broad shoulders of a rugby player; he had Fred's ruddy fairness, so unlike his father. Fred, that is, in the bloom of his health, not emaciated and alabaster-white as he'd been at the end. The shape of his face, the pale blue eyes, all conspired to make Greg's mistake understandable. He could see now that the resemblance was superficial but the boy had been sitting in Fred's favourite place on the sofa and that had clinched the terrifying illusion.

He had a painful flashback to his son sitting in that place with a can of beer in his hand telling him that he was going to get married to some unknown girl – some supermarket check-out assistant – called Angelica Lampton. He had tried to talk him out of it, to tell him he was too young; he had been no more than twenty.

It came to him with a jolt that while he and Angie grew inexorably older, Fred would remain forever twenty-two. He would be spared the long, slow disappointment of middle age.

He realised that the boy was speaking. 'Mr Summers? I'm Del Thomas, sir, a friend of Angie's from college.'

Greg shook hands feebly, not liking the way the boy was talking to him: not as an equal but the way he might have talked to

Angie's father, had she had one. He was wearing a T-shirt over a long-sleeved shirt, a sartorial choice that Greg found incomprehensible. The T-shirt had 'MG drivers do it in top gear' written across the chest.

'I gave Angie a lift home,' Del went on, in the easy, confident manner of the young. He had the faintest of speech impediments: his Rs weren't quite Ws but nor were they entirely Rs. He flicked back his blond hair, worn longer than Fred had worn his. 'She's just gone upstairs to find a textbook she prwomised to lend me.'

'Dr Emeret Warner on *The Modern Mind*, to be exact,' Angie's voice said behind him. She came into the room with Bellini dancing round her heels. 'Hello, Greg.'

'Hello, darling,' he said firmly and kissed her cheek.

'Dr Warner is one of our lecturers,' Del added, 'so *The Modern Mind* is rwequired rweading.'

'Is he the one who keeps calling you Angela?' Greg asked.

It was Del who answered. 'He thinks shortening names is vulgar but he can't be bothered to find out what our names are short for so he calls me Derwek when my name is Delafield, God help me.'

'Bloody hell,' Greg said involuntarily.

'Tell me about it. My sister's called Ankarwet.' Del took the textbook from

138

Angie. 'I must be off. Want a lift in in the morning, Ange – *Angelica?*'

'No, thank you, *Delafield*. My first lecture isn't till one and the garage promised the Renault by noon.'

'Who'd you take it to?' Del asked.

'Smallbills in Hungerford.'

'Could do worse.' People took their cars to Smallbills Garage because they thought it would be cheap when, in fact, it was owned by a man called William who was only five-foot-four.

Angie saw Del out and returned to the sitting room, bestowing on her boyfriend a more lingering kiss on the mouth. Greg heard the firing of an expensive engine outside, the purring as it pulled away.

'Does that sports car belong to him?' he demanded. 'Must be worth a few bob.'

'His mother was the Delafield Detergents heiress.'

'Nice!'

'The rich are different from us.'

'I think they very probably are.'

'I'm glad you're home nice and early,' she said, 'as I put a chicken casserole in the oven on the timer. Should be nearly ready.'

'Smells great.'

He followed her into the kitchen and opened a bottle of red wine, pouring a glass for each of them while Angie donned oven gloves and lifted the lid of the Pyrex dish to

139

smell the stew. Greg stood looking at the entries on the kitchen calendar, sipping his wine, feeling pleasantly domestic.

'By the way,' he remarked, 'I think I've found a permanent home for Bellini at last.'

The sound of Pyrex dish hitting kitchen floor and losing the battle was unmistakable.

'So that's settled then: Bellini stays with us.'

Greg stood in front of the microwave a few minutes later, watching as two lasagnes from the freezer circled round each other on the turntable. He was never sure if it was wise to stand directly in front or if his brains would get gradually boiled but he did it anyway.

Angie was picking up the remains of the casserole from the floor, trying to stop the little terrier from eating it, glass shards and all.

'Who were you going to give her away to?' she asked, in a tone that implied he'd been in the process of sending his first born off to Herod's palace with a goodwill message and an offer of the loan of an axe.

'Sergeant Mistry's boy keeps pestering him for a puppy but he's reluctant to have all the bother of training it and so forth so he thought a well-behaved mature dog like Bellini would be an acceptable compromise.'

'Tough luck,' Angie said.

'Indeed.' Greg opened the door of the microwave and prised up one corner of the lasagne dish, poking the top with his finger. Still cold. He switched it on again. 'Your mate Del ... does he remind you of anyone?'

Angie finished scraping up the ruined chicken and began mopping the floor with a wet J cloth as she thought about it.

'No,' she said finally. 'Who?'

'Oh, I don't know,' he said hastily. 'I just felt like I'd met him before. Do you ever think this house is absurdly big for the two of us?'

'You lived here on your own for almost fifteen years,' she pointed out.

'I did, didn't I?' Why had it never occurred to him how odd that was? 'I wonder why I didn't sell up after the divorce and buy myself a nice little bachelor flat like Barbara's, five minutes walk from the station.'

'I expect you didn't want to *be* five minutes walk from the station,' she said. 'Or you'd probably never have gone home.'

'Fair point.'

'And if you hadn't kept this house then Fred and I wouldn't have come to live with you three years ago,' she added.

And that was an even fairer point.

Angie said, 'I like this house. I have been happy here.'

'It's getting shabby. I noticed coming in just now that the outside painting needs doing.'

'Then we can get it done,' she said patiently.

'I suppose we can.'

And it was no good trying to move away from the memories, he knew; they would only come in the removal van with you.

'Shall we take a last look at Salem's house?' Megan suggested, 'then call it a day?' They walked across the Green to the empty house. There was no sign of life there now, the search team having departed with whatever booty they could find. The two women stood with their backs to it, looking across at Beaumont House.

As they watched, the door opened and Concepta came out, wearing an old tweed coat over her nurse's uniform. She looked neither to right nor left but scuttled away through the car park towards the hospital. It was starting to drizzle again.

'Disconcerting,' Barbara said, 'to have your social worker watching your every move.'

'Yes, but–'

'Can I help you two ladies?'

They spun round to see an elderly man who stood, arms akimbo, eyeing them suspiciously since they were clearly no

142

better than they should be.

'You'll be Mr Mercer,' Megan said. She showed him her warrant card. 'DCI Davies of Newbury CID. My colleague is Sergeant Carey.'

'Oh, right!' The old man visibly relaxed. 'Only I told the young constable I'd keep an eye on the place, like.'

'We're very grateful to you, Mr Mercer,' Barbara said politely.

If Whittaker had not given his age as seventy-eight she would have guessed him at a well-preserved seventy. He obviously took care with his clothes as his slacks and shirt were free of creases and his navy blue blazer looked almost new. He was wearing a tie, like so many men of his generation, unable to give it up once the working life was ended. He was bald on top, a ring of pale brown hair clipped short around the tonsure.

She could not make out his eyes in the twilight and glanced up with annoyance at the non-functioning streetlamp above her.

'Nuisance,' he said, following her gaze. 'I tell the managing company as soon as a bulb goes but they always wait till half a dozen are gone. They say it's not worthwhile sending a man out just to do one.' He snorted. 'I ask you! How am I supposed to run Neighbourhood Watch without decent street lighting?'

'You live at number six,' Megan queried, 'two doors down?'

'Since they built the place,' he said proudly. 'Me and the wife were rehoused when they demolished our cottage down by the canal. It's nice here: bathroom, indoor lavvie, the lot. I own it now. Lived in Newbury all my life, 'cept during the war, of course, when I–'

'Did you know Mr Salem?' Barbara asked quickly before he could get on to the western desert and his part in the downfall of Rommel.

'Since he was a child.'

'Ever been in his house?'

'Not since it's been *his*. I used to call on Mrs Salem from time to time, cup of tea, chat, but she's been gone almost a year now.'

'Did Mr Salem live here when his mother was alive?' Megan asked.

'Oh, yes. Went away to college – what? – ten years ago, more. Grace – Mrs Salem – was that proud. But he came home soon as he'd got his degree and nothing wrong with that.'

'Did he have a girlfriend that you know of?' Barbara said.

'Well, it's funny you should ask really because Grace used to worry that he didn't seem interested in girls, but I thought it was probably more that *they* weren't interested

144

in *him*, what with him not earning a lot of money or having a sports car. I think she was afraid he might be ... you know ... *that way*.' He blushed. 'Begging your pardon.'

'We're women of the world,' Megan assured him solemnly.

'But I said not to worry. I'd come across that sort in the army and he wasn't one. Then, couple of weeks ago, I was just taking the rubbish out and I saw him with a girl, going into the house.'

The two women exchanged glances. 'Did you know her?' Barbara asked.

'Never seen her before. She doesn't live on the Peabody.'

'Can you describe her?'

'It was dark and they were practically in the house. I noticed that she wasn't much shorter than him, which isn't saying much.' He pulled himself up to his full height, a shade over six feet. 'Sorry.'

'When did you see Mr Salem last?' Megan asked.

'Monday morning. Saw him head across the Green towards Beaumont and I thought "Aye, aye, he's off to bother the Troys again".'

'You knew about that?'

'Whole estate knew he was always in and out and not by invitation neither.'

'And did you see him come out later? With the little girl, perhaps?'

The old man was disappointed at having to reply in the negative. 'I'd set off for the shops by then. Do my big shop Mondays when it's quiet.'

The drizzle had turned into steady rain now and the old man said goodnight and went into his house without ceremony.

'There's Nick,' Barbara said suddenly.

Megan turned and saw a man in a black leather jacket and jeans coming out of Kyd House, glancing up with annoyance at the rain. He wasn't overly tall, about five-foot-ten, sturdily built. As they walked to join him she saw that he had dark hair and olive skin, as might be expected with his antecedents.

'Nick!' Barbara said as they moved into earshot.

'Sarge,' he said without enthusiasm.

Barbara did the introductions and Nicolaides shook hands with the DCI and said, 'Us incomers better stick together, ma'am.'

'I'm not sure I'd call myself an incomer,' Megan said. Up close his skin was coarse and pockmarked but he bore himself with an easy confidence. Cockney wide boy, she thought, or more likely Crouch End wide boy.

'I thought you were at Social Services,' Barbara said.

'I was, Sarge, all afternoon. Went through

the files, looking for anything personal he might have slipped in there but there was nothing. They close at six and they wanted me out so I said I'd be back tomorrow. Meanwhile, I thought I'd drop back here, catch some of the people I missed earlier.'

House to house was a thankless task, since half the householders would be out and it often took three or four visits to cover them all.

'Don't suppose anybody saw anything?' Megan said with resignation.

'No, ma'am. They were mostly out at work, mid morning.' He jerked his thumb behind him. 'One woman in Kyd House, single mother, but – would you believe it? – she was out at the Job Centre yesterday morning, having an interview for one of these government schemes to get lone parents back to work, as if they wouldn't be better off at home looking after their kids and stopping them turning into thieves and vandals.'

'I'm a single mother myself,' Megan said.

Nicolaides grinned, unperturbed, and looked down at his black trainers. 'Big mouth and even bigger feet to put in it, ma'am, that's me.'

Megan laughed, liking him.

'What about the OAPs?' Barbara said. 'There must be plenty of those.'

'A round dozen, Sarge. Let me see... Old

bloke lives two doors from the absconder–'

'We've just been talking to Mr Mercer,' Barbara said.

'Yeah? And you still both have your hind legs, I see.'

'Did you just call us donkeys?' Megan queried.

The constable glanced at his feet once more. 'There I go again so I'll quit while I'm behind. Old couple at number three, north side, mister in hospital with his "prostrate", as his missus calls it. She was visiting yesterday morning. Old dear at seven west was watching *Richard and Judy* with the curtains closed because the sun shines on the TV screen. Mr three east and Mrs five east, widower and widow, were in bed all morning.'

'You don't mean together?'

'That's exactly what I do mean, ma'am. She didn't want to let on but I think he wanted to boast, seeing as he took care to tell me he's seventy-seven. Hope I'm still up to it at that age.'

'That's only six,' Barbara said repressively.

'Other six had gone to the day centre for their regular card school.'

'Whist?'

'More like poker. I get the impression their pensions change hands faster than a hot brick.'

'So the upshot of all this is that nobody on

148

Peabody Green saw Joshua Salem leave Beaumont House with Emilia Troy. In broad daylight.'

Nicolaides spread his hands wide. 'Sorry, ma'am. Sod's law.'

As the two women walked back to Barbara's car feeling that they couldn't get any wetter, Megan said, 'I rather like him. Chippy, you said?'

'He is with me. I assumed it was because he didn't like taking orders from a woman, but maybe it's because I'm younger than he is.'

'Yes, well he won't have that problem with me.'

'Hard day at the coal face?' Angie asked when they'd demolished their lasagne and were enjoying the last of the wine.

Greg picked up an orange and began to peel it. It was juicy and his fingers were soon wet and sticky. 'It had its moments. Uniform had to go and rescue a couple of teenage burglars from a house in Winterbourne.' Angie raised her eyebrows. 'The householder kept a pet python,' he explained. 'It had them cornered in the bedroom and they were so terrified they used their mobile phone to call us.'

'I suppose it was called Monty?'

'Clarence, apparently. His owner says he's the ideal pet: not only does he deter burglars but he's a better mouser than any cat and she never has to take him for a walk.'

Bellini said 'Woof!' and went to fetch her lead.

Greg sighed. He passed the rest of the peeled orange to Angie, licked his fingers clean and got up. The night had taken a turn for the worse and he could hear the rain lashing down outside. Or was it sleet? Lucky he knew it was the first day of spring or he might have thought it was bloody miserable weather.

He felt damp already.

Angie said, 'You don't learn from your mistakes, do you? Never use the W word in front of you-know-who.'

He fetched his waterproof jacket with hood. Okay, it was an anorak.

Chapter 9

'Anything I need to know about?' Greg asked on his way into the office the following morning.

'Man exposing himself to schoolgirls in Hamstead Marshall?' Sergeant Maybey offered.

'I'll leave that to Uniform, thanks.' He headed for the stairs, the one piece of exercise he got each day, then paused. 'It's an odd expression, don't you think?'

'Sir?'

'Exposing *himself*. As if the penis is all there is to a man, his essence, his soul. Now, if you went up to schoolgirls and said, "I sometimes cry myself to sleep" – *that* would be exposing yourself.'

'You sometimes cry yourself to sleep?' Maybey sounded bewildered but not unsympathetic.

'That was just an example!'

'Yes, sir.'

'Of course I don't.'

'No, sir. Wouldn't blame you if you did.'

Greg, feeling that the conversation had gone deeply awry somewhere and that his bedtime weeping would be all over the canteen as established fact by lunchtime, made for the stairs again but Maybey called him back.

'Or there's this fire bombing on Peabody Green you might be interested in.'

When Greg reached his office, he told Susan Habib that he wanted to see Sergeant Carey at once.

Barbara presented herself in his office forty minutes later, looking a little flushed. 'Sorry, sir. I was on Peabody Green when I got your message.'

He didn't invite her to sit and something

in his face stopped her from doing so unbidden.

He said, 'At Joshua Salem's house, I imagine.'

'Yes, sir. The house was–'

'Firebombed last night. I know. And how did we let that happen?' Barbara stood in silence, recognising the question as rhetorical. Eventually Greg said, 'You were in charge of searching the house, Sergeant Carey. You were in charge of keeping it safe and now some ... some anti-paedophile vigilante has turned it into a pile of ashes. Why the hell didn't you leave somebody on duty there last night?'

'We're short of manpower, sir, as always. It was a judgment call and I got it wrong.'

'Valuable evidence may have been destroyed.'

'I think we got everything of importance out, sir.'

'And suppose Salem isn't responsible for Emilia's disappearance. Suppose, just for a minute, that he's now happily admiring the architecture of Aberdeen, on holiday, as advertised–'

'Then why didn't he take his car, sir?'

'What?' Greg was irritated by the inter-ruption. 'How should I know? Because he's concerned about global warming and the future of the planet and decided to travel by train.'

'Yes, sir.'

'And when he comes back next week and finds out what's happened, he'll probably sue the pants off us.'

'I know.'

'I'm disappointed, Barbara.'

'Yes, sir.'

'I expect better from you.' He leaned forward in his chair, folded his arms on the desk and sighed. 'Okay, bollocking over. We'll say no more about it.'

'Thank you, sir.'

She turned to leave and he called after her, 'Unless he sues!'

The market was busy that Thursday morning and Concepta moved uncomfortably between the stalls, never happy in a crowd. She had Emilia firmly by one hand and the little girl was taking in the richness of the scene with undisguised glee.

Concepta stopped to finger some blouses hanging on a rail. They were nylon: thin, badly-coloured, cheap. Emilia broke away to explore a nearby toy stall: not the computer games and expensive impedimenta that most children demanded today but a display of garish soft toys: green elephants, yellow cats, red mice.

Concepta, used to caring for those less able than herself, had one eye on her stepdaughter all the time and moved swiftly when she saw a woman stop to speak to her. She dropped the blouse she was holding on the ground, making the stall holder exclaim angrily, and almost pushed over an old lady with a shopping trolley in her haste.

'Millie!'

The woman was crouching in front of the child, holding out a blue toy dog, a hideous creature, in an almost shy offering. In her early thirties, she was not much younger than Concepta but might have been a member of a different species. Tall and slender, she had a mass of untidy blond hair caught back loosely in a scarlet ribbon around a long, almost aristocratic face. Her smooth skin needed no make-up. She wore blue jeans with a fashion label, a thick Guernsey pullover, a blue Barbour jacket and brown suede boots.

Concepta seized her stepdaughter by the hand. 'What do you think you're doing?' she snapped at the woman.

'I ... I meant no harm.' She blinked at Concepta myopically with her huge grey eyes.

Concepta felt more confident now. 'I'm sure you didn't but I don't like her to speak to strangers, you see, let alone accept gifts.'

'Oh, but you don't understand. I'm not a stranger. I'm Annie Fergusson. I fostered Emilia when her father ... when she was a tiny baby.'

'Oh! Oh, I see.' Concepta wanted to feel hostility to this woman who had tried to rob Roger of his child, but she saw only a soul who, for all her grace and beauty, was suffering.

154

'She doesn't seem to recognise me,' Annie went on and tears formed in the corner of her eyes. She brushed them away with her sleeve and sniffed. 'It's not six months since she left us.'

'They don't at that age,' Concepta said kindly. 'Children remember very little of what happens to them before the age of three.'

'You must be Mrs Troy.' She offered her hand and Concepta shook it awkwardly. 'I can see that Emilia is very happy and well cared for,' she ventured.

'And why wouldn't she be?'

'Oh, I didn't mean... I only meant. I'm so glad to see her looking well. I'd better go.' She turned away.

Years of working with the mentally ill had built a protective carapace around Concepta's feelings but she took pity on the woman. 'There's a café in the Kennet Centre. You look as if you could do with a cup of tea.'

Annie Fergusson accepted gratefully.

Emilia was interested in Mrs Fergusson, as she was in any unfamiliar person or experience, but Annie's attempts to make her recall the house in Inkpen, funny incidents and family outings, met with nothing but a shaken head.

'Desmond,' she tried at last. 'Do you still have Desmond?'

'Yes!' the child exclaimed, delighted.

'Oh, she still has Desmond,' Concepta confirmed.

'We bought him in Bristol one afternoon. She

155

saw him in the shop and she wouldn't take no for an answer.'

Concepta sipped her strong brown tea. 'So you have no children of your own, Mrs Fergusson?'

Annie stirred her own much weaker brew although it didn't need it as she'd added neither sugar nor milk. 'In the first eight years we were married I got pregnant five times, no trouble at all. Each time I miscarried in the first trimester.'

'I've heard of such cases,' Concepta said, offering no trite sympathy.

'I've seen any number of specialists and they can't figure out why. The only suggestion they can make is that my husband and I are incompatible in some way, that nature doesn't consider that our DNA will ... fit together, so my body rejects the foetus.'

'It's not an area I know much about.'

'Oh, yes. You're a nurse, aren't you? We've stopped trying now. I couldn't bear it each time I got pregnant. I couldn't stand the hope.'

'That's rough luck.' Concepta regarded Annie Fergusson for a moment with the dispassionate eye of a professional. 'Have you seen a doctor?'

'A doctor? I told you: any number.'

'Not about the pregnancies. I'm a psychiatric nurse and I know depression when I see it... Don't look at me like that, girl. It's not something to be ashamed of. They can do wonders these days with the new generation of drugs.'

They parted outside the café half an hour

later. Annie Fergusson stood watching them go, her oversized bag making her awkward, lopsided, but neither Concepta nor Emilia looked back at her.

Five minutes after Barbara left Greg's office she was back and in much more exuberant spirits.

'I've just had the phone company on the blower,' she said. 'Airways.'

Greg rose to his feet, excited. 'Salem's using his mobile?'

'They got a signal from it a few minutes ago.'

'Yes!'

'He's still here, in Newbury. Well, in Sandleford Park.'

'We've got him. How close can they pinpoint him?'

'To within two square miles though they're trying to narrow that down.'

'That's bigger than the whole park,' Greg pointed out. 'Where's DCI Davies?'

'Still on Peabody Green, supervising the crime scene at Salem's house.' Greg reached for his jacket, glad for an excuse to get out in the field. Barbara said, 'Shall I give her a bell, sir?'

'No, she's needed there. Let's go.'

On the southern borders of Newbury was an area known as Sandleford Park. It was

157

not what most people understood by the word 'park', being acres of arid grassland, unmown and unploughed. It was also ungrazed, which had allowed it to remain open to walkers during the foot-and-mouth crisis. There were no roses except such as grew wild in the hedgerow, no beds of flowers in regimented rows of gaudy colour, only blossoms that would be dismissed as weeds by a suburban gardener: dandelion, buttercup, cow parsley.

The greater part of the park filled the space between two of the main arterial roads that led into town from such distant places as Andover and Winchester, although a few acres had seeped across the A34 to meet the western edge of Greenham Common. It was an unexpected splodge of wild nature among the straggling suburban closes, drives and avenues, the thundering highways, invisible from the roads and unnoticed by casual passers-by. It boasted a series of compact, discrete copses with names such as Dirty Ground, Waterleaze and the more prosaic Corporation Copse.

The river Enborne, more properly a gurgling stream these days, bordered the area to the south, marking the place where West Berkshire met Hampshire and Greg's jurisdiction abruptly ended.

The area had been uninhabited through-out recorded history and a recent proposal to cram the place with 1500 new houses had been rejected by Her Majesty's Inspector, to the joy of most of Newbury and an awful lot of rabbits. So remote was it that the isolation hospital on its western rim had been closed only after the last war when the new wonder drug, Penicillin, had dealt a devastating blow to what had once been man's deadliest enemy.

Greg, as a local boy, could remember when anyone in quarantine was still described as being 'Up at Sandleford.'

He knew the area well as he had often cycled here with his mates on warm summer evenings some thirty-five years ago. They had played games of cowboys and Indians among the trees, cops and robbers, pirates. In the school holidays such skirmishes could last for weeks and result in bruising, gashes, filthy clothes and, in one notable case, a broken arm. Arriving home in this state, they would be scolded, punished, even clipped round the ear, but no one forbade them to play there or dreamed that they could come to significant harm.

These days children stayed at home with their computer games under the eyes of their anxious parents and the copses were the domain of enthusiastic joggers, dog walkers and the occasional illicit couple.

Theoretically a single footpath led across

the park from east to west and 'keep out' notices, crudely lettered in red paint, had sprung up for those inclined to stray. They'd not been there in Greg's youth and he wouldn't have paid them any mind if they had been.

He drove them there as Barbara had her mobile clamped to her ear, hoping for more detailed information from the Airways phone company. He veered off the main road at the roundabout, doubled round the new Hilton hotel and left the car at the bottom of the sinister sounding Deadman's Lane, a few feet from the highway. They sat there for a moment, as traffic tore past, waiting for the squad car that Greg had summoned to his help.

Barbara had a large-scale Ordnance Survey map on her knee and was tracing her finger along the marked footpath. Greg knew just how many unmarked ones there were. He grew impatient, fed up with sitting in the car, and got out, striding the few paces up the bank to the grass verge. His sergeant hastened to join him.

'There are hardly any buildings here,' he mused as he stood looking into the wilderness opposite, waiting for a Norbert Dentressangle lorry to pass and stop blocking his view. It took some time. They had to be that big to get the man's name on the side.

'Could he have rented a house on one of those lanes that peter out at the far side of the park?' Barbara asked. 'What?' She was speaking into her phone again and Greg waited as she struggled with the map with her spare hand in a stiff breeze.

'Okay.' Barbara examined the co-ordinates on her map and pointed due west. 'I think that's our best bet.'

'High Wood?'

'If you say so.'

She folded the map and stuck it in the pocket of her overcoat. By unspoken agreement they stopped waiting for backup. Greg scribbled a note and put it under his windscreen wiper. After an impatient wait, they crossed the road.

'When I was a boy there was a footpath leading directly to the wood from here,' he said crossly. 'It's gone.' He could just about identify the gap in the hedge where the stile had been, overgrown and blocked with barbed wire. In the distance he could make out some kind of works site or excavation: a tractor, piles of earth.

'Would he come here with a load of workmen about?' Barbara asked.

'They've not been working all winter. It's been too wet. The site's been virtually abandoned for months.'

'What are they doing here anyway?'

'God knows.'

161

He moved the barbed wire carefully aside. Much of it was rusted. He took his coat off, glad that it wasn't his new one, and laid it along the barbs, allowing them both to climb into the field. He removed it with difficulty and a few rips in the fabric and shrugged it back on.

'This way,' he said, striking out in the direction of the wooded hillock a hundred yards ahead.

'Could he be camping?' Barbara suggested.

'In this weather?' Their boots were squelching in the mud as they bent their faces into the wind and trudged towards the wood. Much of the ground was still waterlogged from the wet weather of the preceding autumn and winter and they had to take frequent detours round quagmire and swamp. 'Good luck to him... Well, obviously not. I mean, I don't wish him luck.'

Barbara didn't bother to reply. She knew what he meant.

'Was there any camping gear at his house?' Greg asked.

'No, but then there wouldn't be if he'd taken it with him!'

They could hear voices as they entered the wood and exchanged looks. Greg was getting cold feet. Not literally – that ship had long sailed – but metaphorically.

'Should we go back for that squad car?' he whispered.

'There are two of us,' Barbara pointed out, reluctant to be deprived of action, 'and only one of him.'

'As far as we know. What about this alleged girlfriend?'

'We only have the word of one old man for that. I think she's pie in the sky, personally.'

'But he could be dangerous if he's cornered. He could be armed. We don't want to escalate it into a hostage situation.'

'I think we should go in, do a recce at the very least. If we keep undercover then we can always back off if it looks like turning nasty.'

'Then let's do it.' They separated slightly, heading into the thickest part of the copse, coming at the sounds from two directions.

Greg was troubled by what he could hear. It was distinctly two voices, neither child nor adult, both probably male. He had lost visual contact with Barbara and had to rely on their years of working together and their mutual understanding to do this right.

He was making more noise than he'd hoped and he stopped as he heard the voices fall silent.

One said, 'What was that?'

'I can't hear anything.'

'I heard something.'

163

'Just a fox.'

Two adolescent boys, he thought, disappointed.

The second voice said, 'Which one shall we try next?' and they both giggled guiltily.

It was all suddenly obvious to him and his heart felt heavy with frustration. He stepped out from the shelter of the trees and into a clearing, startling the two boys so that the taller one dropped the mobile phone he was examining with such delight. They moved instinctively closer together: a short, ginger lad with puppy fat and troubled blue eyes; a tall dark one, slender from his adolescent growth spurt; the classic odd couple.

'We'll scream if you come any closer, you old perv,' the shorter one said, with more confidence than he obviously felt, since he was trembling.

Greg took out his warrant card and held it up. 'Police,' he said, not thrilled at being taken for a child molester.

'Police!' The boys edged nearer, still glued together like contestants in a three-legged race, the better to see his credentials. They were half frightened, half excited. About thirteen, he thought, their voices breaking but not yet reliable, growing hairier, not men, not children. They wore the uniform of nearby St Elfreda's – a school where the children needed high IQs and the parents deep pockets – but with their black and green ties knotted round their brows as headbands and their shirts undone, their hair defiantly dishevelled.

He saw Barbara come out of the woodland opposite, softer on her feet than he was, unheard by the boys whose eyes were intently fixed on himself. She bent to pick up the mobile phone using a clean handkerchief, a reflex action despite the odds against taking any useful prints from it.

'We only bunked off for an hour,' the taller boy said, his eyes moist. 'Or two,' he added with a rush of honesty. 'It's only double Geog. We didn't mean any harm.'

'I'm not a truant officer,' Greg said hastily, determined that the lad should not humiliate himself or his friend with tears. He'd never been able to see the point of geography lessons himself, which probably explained why Barbara was a much better map reader than he was.

'What we need to know,' Barbara said, making them whirl round in alarm, 'is when and where you got this mobile phone.'

It was a nuisance that they were so young as it meant that he was forbidden from questioning them without a responsible adult present.

He apologised. 'I'm sorry, lads. If there was any way I could do this without involving the

165

school and your parents, then I would.'

Subdued, they followed him and Barbara back to their car. They were Timothy Mitchell and Jack Bacon, they offered, and they were twelve and three-quarters, Jack two weeks older. Tim was the ginger one, his hair so bright it glowed, Jack the handsome ascetic.

The squad car was now parked next to Greg's. One constable was reading the note and saying, 'Which one's High Wood then?' to his partner.

'Too late, constable,' Greg said, making him spin round, red-faced.

'Sorry, sir. We got here quick as we could. Had to attend some ruckus in the retail park.'

Another 'park' that was no such thing, Greg thought. 'Never mind.' He plucked the note from the young man's hand. 'You might as well be on your way.'

The constable looked with curiosity at the two boys. 'See you picked up a couple of hardened criminals,' he ventured with a grin.

'Don't we get to ride in the squad car?' Tim piped up, disappointed.

'Not today, son.'

'Aww!'

Greg drove round the park to the school and asked to see the head teacher, a woman called Harriet Steele whose grey eyes suited her name although a small smile played on her lips as she looked at the boys.

'Well, Tim, Jack, I trust this is the last time you bunk off school.'

'Yes, Mrs Steele,' they chorused.

'Hmm! We'll discuss it later. Wait here.' She led Greg into her office and looked up the emergency phone numbers of their parents.

'I wouldn't like to be in young Tim's shoes when Mr Mitchell hears about this,' she remarked as she reached for the phone.

'They haven't done anything wrong,' Greg pointed out.

'I take a dim view of truanting, oddly enough.'

'Nothing criminal, I mean. They're literally helping me with my enquiries.'

'I always thought that was a euphemism for "we know he done it and we just gotta prove it",' she said.

Greg smiled politely. 'Their evidence could be invaluable and–'

She held up a hand to stop him as the phone was answered.

'Mrs Mitchell? Harriet Steele. Yes. I'm afraid we have a small problem...'

Mrs Mitchell, who never divulged her first name, if she had one, was a tall and overly thin woman of about thirty-five, wearing an expensive suit. She had come straight from

167

her office in Hungerford where she worked, it seemed, as an independent financial advisor. She was keen, for some reason, to emphasise the independence.

She was visibly angry but Greg got the impression that free-floating anger was her normal state. It was a phenomenon he had observed among many working mothers of her age and class. She shook hands with him on arrival, tight-lipped, her eyes boring into her son who flinched. Greg, following the boy's gaze, saw her flexing the fingers of her left hand as if she longed to lash out at him. He sensed that Timothy's copper head and puppy fat pained her, like a personal failing.

'My husband won't be coming,' was her first remark. '*He* can't be spared from his office. Apparently.'

'I need only one responsible adult,' Greg replied. 'It's the law, I'm afraid.'

'I should think so!' She turned her attention to her son, raising her voice as she did so. 'How many times have I told you to keep off Sandleford Common? There's no knowing what sort of weirdos you might meet there, it's so cut off.'

Part of its charm, no doubt, Greg thought.

'It's not as if he hasn't got everything he could possibly want to play with at home,' she complained. She sat down on the chair opposite Greg's and crossed shapely legs in sheer tan nylon. One hand reached nervously for her blonde bob, smoothing and adjusting that which was already perfect. At close quarters he could see how skilfully her makeup was applied, giving the illusion of no make-up at all. She would be attractive, he thought, without the endemic fury.

With it, she was faintly repellent.

He had decided to talk to the boys in his office rather than subject them to the full panoply of bare, windowless interview room and tape recorder. Jack had looked a little disappointed when he'd said this. It was obvious that both boys, now that the first shock was over, viewed this as a terrific adventure and a great improvement on a morning of double Geog.

Mrs Mitchell leaned forward and spoke confidentially as if she thought the boys couldn't hear. 'I blame the Bacon boy for leading Tim astray. Single parent family, if you know what I mean.' Her son blushed for shame at his mother's words. Jack's face froze. Greg pretended that he had not heard but it didn't shut her up. 'We're thinking seriously of sending him to boarding school,' she sniffed, 'where he'll make a better class of friend.'

Barbara had swiftly fetched extra chairs from the conference room and she sat against the wall, a boy on either side, a notepad on her knee.

Mrs Bacon – Emma, as she swiftly introduced herself – arrived to complete the group. She was quite unlike Mrs Mitchell and Greg detected no sign that the family friendship extended to the older generation, although they nodded acknowledgement to each other cordially enough. Emma was much the same age as the other woman but looked older through lack of grooming. Her brown hair was streaked with grey at the front and her cheeks were rosy by nature and not blusher.

She wore a denim skirt that fell to her calves and a baggy jumper which might have belonged to her husband. Bare legs ended in red espadrilles. Greg would have taken her for a cheery housewife if he hadn't known that she was senior partner in Bacon, Travis, Maxton, one of Newbury's most ruthless estate agencies. It was said that Emma Bacon herself could sell air-conditioned houses to Eskimos and her voice was out of keeping with her appearance, husky, persuasive, sexy.

She smiled reassuringly at Jack as she took her seat and he returned the look with gratitude. Greg opened his mouth to begin the interview but was interrupted by Mrs Mitchell.

'I must say,' she commented, 'that I don't pay the exorbitant fees of that bloody school so that Timothy can be wandering round

Sandleford Park at all hours of the day and night. Anything might happen.'

'Boys will be boys,' Emma Bacon said.

'Oh, department of bloody cliché,' the other woman muttered.

'Ladies...' Greg said, since there seemed no other way he could address them. 'I'm grateful to you for giving up your time and, while I know that truanting is to be discouraged, your sons may hold the key to an important case, so, if I may...?'

Mrs Bacon said, 'Of course, Superintendent,' while Mrs Mitchell said irritable, 'Yes, can we get on?' as if she wasn't the one holding up the proceedings. Greg caught Barbara's eye and she raised hers briefly to his artexed ceiling.

Greg fingered the evidence bag containing Salem's phone. 'The boys were using this mobile when we came across them in High Wood this morning.'

'Just phoning some numbers we saw in the local paper,' Jack piped up, his voice, which had sounded fully broken an hour earlier, now firmly back in the realm of pre-pubescence.

'What sort of numbers?' his mother asked. He mumbled a reply but she persevered. 'I can't hear you, Jack, dear.'

'Ring 0898-whatever to talk to a busty lady?' Barbara suggested.

Both boys flushed scarlet.

Emma Bacon said, 'Oh, Jack!'

Mrs Mitchell said wearily, 'Like father, like son.'

Greg remembered how desperate he had been at that age to get more inside information on the female anatomy. He had envied boys with sisters who could often be persuaded to permit a brief look on payment of half a crown, double if you wanted a feel. But surely the television screens throbbed with naked women these days.

Half a crown was a lot of money back then.

There had been rumours of a housewife in Avington who answered the door to the paper boy wearing nothing but a see-through nightie, but Greg's parents weren't keen on him doing a paper round and there was a waiting list for that route.

'Since you obviously couldn't make such calls from home,' Barbara said, 'finding the mobile must have seemed heaven-sent.'

'Is that right, boys?' Greg said. They nodded.

Tim spoke in a big rush, not looking at his mother. 'It was switched off when we got it and we thought it'd have a pin code so we couldn't use it but there wasn't one which was pretty silly of whoever it belongs to 'cause we could've been phoning Australia or anything so we sneaked out of school this morning to use it.'

'What's this all about, anyway?' Mrs Mitchell demanded. 'Who does this phone belong to?'

'I can't discuss the case at the moment, madam.'

'Oh, no! I can be dragged away from my desk to "help you with your enquiries" but you can't answer a civil question.'

'Is it a murder?' Tim asked.

'...No.'

'Aww!'

'Drug dealing, I suppose,' his mother said. 'Has it been checked for disease? There's no knowing what the children might catch.'

'Okay, can we back up a bit?' Greg said, ignoring her. 'How long have you boys had the phone?'

'Last night,' Jack said. 'We'd been to the school chess club and we were cycling home together only Tim's light went out and we didn't have a spare battery so we walked our bikes home in the end, along the pavements, and we didn't get back till it was dark.' He looked at his mother. 'Remember?'

'I certainly do. I was just about to set out to look for you.'

'And we were walking along Monk's Lane when a car stopped just beyond us. It was dark and I don't think he saw us.'

'I don't like them cycling along Monk's Lane at the best of times,' Mrs Mitchell interrupted. 'Cars fly by at sixty miles at

173

hour. It's a death trap.' She looked accusingly at Greg, deeming all policemen responsible for traffic control.

Greg continued to ignore her since this seemed the only way to deal with her given that he wasn't allowed to thump her. He concentrated on the boys. 'You don't think *who* saw you?'

'The driver.'

'You're sure it was a man?'

They looked at each other in surprise. Tim said, 'No. We assumed...'

'He didn't get out,' Jack explained. 'Just opened the window and threw something out into the bushes, something quite heavy I mean, it flew through the air and landed in the undergrowth with a bit of crash and he just accelerated away.'

'You couldn't make him out?'

They shook their heads solemnly and repeated, 'It was dark.'

'We went to look,' Tim went on, 'and found the phone lying on the ground. Course, we thought it didn't work and that was why he'd chucked it away but it did. We couldn't believe our luck.'

He paused and looked a little doubtful about this assertion in the cold light of Greg's office.

'And it didn't occur to you to hand it in to the police, Timothy?' Mrs Mitchell said icily, 'or at least to your father or I?'

Greg forcibly restrained himself from correcting her grammar.

'N ... no,' Tim said.

As if.

'I hid it in my rucksack,' he offered, 'and Jack and I agreed we'd sneak out and try it this morning.' He looked puzzled. 'Is it a crime to keep something you find then?'

'Of course it bloody is!' Mrs Mitchell snapped. 'It's stealing by finding.'

'It *had* been deliberately thrown away,' Greg pointed out. 'Okay, now if I know anything about boys you're quite interested in cars, right?'

Tim shrugged but Jack said, 'Yes!' with some enthusiasm. 'It was only a small hatchback, though,' he added, 'so it wasn't very interesting. Not like Mr Mitchell's Porsche. That's brilliant.'

Mrs Mitchell sighed and raised her eyes to the heavens: the Porsche was clearly a sore point.

'What colour was it?' Greg asked gently.

'Dark. Blue or green.' He glanced at his friend for confirmation. 'I think.'

'And did you notice any of the registration?' The boys shook their heads. 'It didn't have – you know – any of your initials, or a number like your birthday?' Memories could be jogged that way but the boys were adamant that they hadn't noticed any of the number plate.

'I think it was a woman,' Tim said suddenly.

'No, it was bloke,' Jack said.

'Wasn't very tall.'

'So?'

'It was sort of ... well, *shaped* like a woman.'

'You're talking rubbish,' Jack said. 'It was just a dark shape. S'all.' He turned to Greg. 'We couldn't see. Honest.'

'I'd like you to come with me to Monk's Lane,' Greg said, 'and show me exactly where the car stopped and if you can be precise about the time...'

'It was five past seven,' Tim said. 'I was looking at my watch because we were late and I was thinking my mum would go mad.'

Watching Mrs Mitchell's thin lips compress themselves into an even narrower line, Greg didn't blame him.

Monk's Lane: it was strange how inappropriate road names often were, Greg thought. This was no country lane but a busy highway with, as Mrs Mitchell had complained, cars and lorries whizzing past incessantly at high speed. The medieval monk who had lived here or who had walked this way would be bewildered by its modern incarnation.

The boys pinpointed the place easily

enough and Greg left Barbara to organise a scenes of crime team. He thanked both mothers profusely, receiving a warm smile from Emma Bacon and a haughty toss of the blonde bob from Mrs Mitchell.

Mrs Bacon gave him her business card before leaving saying, 'If you're thinking of moving...'

'Not just now.'

'Where do you live?'

'Kintbury.'

'Ah! Always demand for a nice little village like that.'

The nameless Mrs Mitchell looked mildly annoyed, as if she wished she'd thought of claiming him as a client first. But then it was a well-known fact that police officers were not rich, unless they were on the take, and so had no need of financial advisors.

Greg drove the boys back to school himself, despite their protests that it was maths and physics this afternoon and that there must be lots of other questions they could answer for him, or maybe they could help at the crime scene.

Having dropped them off and watched them inside, Greg headed back to the station.

Chapter 10

In number two cell, Tessa MacDonald was tending to a man named Geoffrey Napier who'd been brought in a few hours earlier much the worse for drink. He had been reported for verbally abusing shoppers in the Kennet Centre, then fallen unconscious in the police car after his arrest. Sergeant Maybey was concerned about his health and had asked the doctor to check if he needed hospitalisation.

'He's clearly used to it,' Maybey said, 'but I'd guess he's had enough to kill many a man and most women. At least a bottle and a half of whisky would be my estimate.'

Tessa had winced, recalling the time she'd sneaked one too many of her father's best malt one Hogmanay when she was fifteen. It had been an eighth of a bottle, at most, and it had been a sharp lesson.

Napier seemed barely conscious and Tessa regarded him anxiously, wondering if she should transfer him to hospital to be on the safe side. She checked his pulse and found it strong and regular. Laying a hand on his forehead, she thought he was feverish but not alarmingly so. She lifted one eyelid and looked into a brown iris surrounded by whites streaked with pink. Nothing unusual in a man of his age – she gauged him to be in his early thirties, in what ought to be the prime of life – who drank his breakfast, lunch and dinner out of a bottle.

He was lying on his back on the wide, hard shelf which served as a bed, one leg slightly bent, both arms hanging limp. His clothes were worn and torn, the bottoms of his flannel trousers caked in mud. It looked as if he was living rough and that could mean any amount of disease including TB and even Aids.

She decided to check his blood pressure and then take a blood test. She turned away to get some equipment from her bag.

She didn't hear him move before he was upon her, his strong fingers closing round her neck. Tessa had done elementary self defence and swung her elbow back into his solar plexus, stamping one foot hard on his instep as she did so. But what had worked so beautifully in class turned out worse than useless in the real world: she angered him and he merely tightened his grip.

She could hear his breath in her ear but he didn't speak, as if he didn't consider her worthy even of abuse. She could feel consciousness slipping away and a pain in her throat like the worst kind of infection, burning, raw.

Tessa had looked death in the face since the day she started medical school at the age of eighteen, only it had always been someone else's death. Now her panicking brain told her that if she didn't act in the next few seconds, the death she faced would be her own. She twisted her head and bit him hard on the right wrist, her sharp teeth drawing blood. The thought of what contamination this blood might contain terrified her, but not as much as the lack of oxygen to her lungs. He made his first sound, a yell of pain and fury, and relaxed his grip for a second.

It was enough: Tessa now had hold of the personal alarm which she carried with her at all times in her jacket pocket. She pressed the catch, releasing a screeching sound that almost deafened her.

Napier hauled her round to face him and she saw the insane rage in his eyes. His fingers closed on her throat again, but now he was banging her head against the cell wall as he throttled her. Her hands flailed helplessly at him while, all the time, the alarm pulsed on the floor at their feet where she had dropped it.

The madman stamped on the alarm, abruptly silencing it but she could hear another – a more insistent – alarm bell, somewhere beyond the tiny world of the cell. She was dimly aware of yelling in the corridor, commotion. Help was on its way and she offered up a small prayer to the God of the Free Presbyterians that it would not come too late, that this dismal hole would not be the last thing she saw on earth, the man's stinking breath her final smell.

She felt bone splinter in her skull, blood pouring from her nose and mouth, even her ears, pain such as she had never experienced. She took refuge in blessed insensibility as four uniformed men crashed into the cell and seized Napier from behind.

Greg was just slipping down the back stairs on his way to a late lunch when the station alarm went off, a continuous ringing that startled him in its loudness. It was a long time since he had heard it. He took the last few steps at a run and jump and almost collided with four large constables who were heading for the cells at high speed.

He debated whether to follow them, decided in the end that a middle-aged superintendent might be one cook too many, and headed off to get the full story from Dick Maybey. He found the custody sergeant looking worried. He was on the phone saying, 'I want an ambulance *here*. Yes, at the police station. And I want it now!'

He hung up and Greg said, 'What's going on?'

'Dr MacDonald's personal alarm sounded a minute ago,' he explained. 'She was dealing with a bloke the night shift brought in early this morning, big bruiser of a man high on something, though I'm not sure if it was booze or drugs.' He gazed down the corridor towards the cells, the look of a concerned father on his face. 'She's such a little thing too. I always said she was too frail for this job, with the scum we get in here some nights, but you can't tell women that these days or they tick you off and report you to the Political Correctness Police.'

'Do they need any help?' Greg asked.

The sergeant shook his head. 'Plenty of big, fit blokes in there.' He looked at Greg in his well-pressed grey suit and maroon silk tie. '*Young* blokes,' he added.

'I think you've made your point, Dick, thank you.'

Greg stood with him, uncertain what to do, waiting for the outcome, the bell continuing to shrill.

'Can't you switch that off?' he asked at last.

'Now, there's a good idea. That must be why they made you superintendent and not me.' Maybey hit a button under his desk and the ear-splitting noise ceased as abruptly as it had begun.

'Blimey,' he said. 'That's better.'

'I can still hear it echoing in my head,'

Greg said adding, as Maybey opened his mouth to speak, 'and if you say it's because it's empty in there I shall put you on report.'

'Thought never crossed my mind, sir.'

After two minutes of what now seemed like unnatural silence, PC Tom Reilly joined them from the cells.

'We need an ambulance, Sarge.'

'It's on its way, son.'

'How bad is it? Greg asked.

Reilly wiped some sweat off his forehead. 'Bad enough. It took the four of us to drag the bastard off her and we were only just in time. He'd half choked the life out of her and she's bleeding like a stuck pig.'

They heard sirens at that moment and two paramedics ran into the building, pushing a gurney. They followed Reilly to the cells, returning at high speed. Greg caught only a glimpse of the young doctor, of the alarming amount of blood that was still pouring from her skull.

'Skulls bleed a lot,' he offered as the ambulance got under way again, screeching out of the station, heading for Accident and Emergency.

'Means she's still alive n'all,' Maybey added. He picked up the phone. 'I'd better get on to the doctor's panel, get coverage.'

'Is there anything I can do?' Greg asked idly, expecting the answer no.

Maybey grinned as he waited for the connection. 'You can give blood.'

'I had to ask, didn't I?'

'Apparently.'

It was a tradition in the force that when an officer was wounded in the line of duty, colleagues would give blood. He had never met Tessa MacDonald and she wasn't even a colleague, not exactly, but he would afford her the same courtesy. Thoughts of lunch banished, he got into his car and drove to the Kennet Hospital.

The trouble was that Greg could remember only too clearly the days when needles were like darts and the phrase 'this won't hurt a bit' was an outright lie. His brain told him that modern hypodermics were so tiny that they slipped into your arm before you knew it, but his body wouldn't listen and still flinched from the needle.

He drove, perhaps, more slowly than he might have done.

Megan Davies was seething with resentment that afternoon, barely able to respond civilly to anyone who spoke to her, from the hair-netted woman in the canteen who asked if she wanted gravy with her pie and chips, to that over-hearty custody sergeant who had enquired after her father and been visibly affronted by her brusque reply.

She was making a bad start in her new

posting, she knew that, and the fact that none of it was her fault didn't make it any easier to bear.

She was supposed to be the officer in charge of this case, yet Gregory Summers had summoned Barbara back to the station this morning to deal with the mobile phone business, leaving her to the tedious donkey work of the firebombing.

She had been surprised when Barbara's mobile had rung and the sergeant had excused herself, saying that the boss wanted to see her urgently, but had assumed that it was some minor matter, some piece of paperwork that needed sorting out. It was only on her return to the station three hours later that she was brought up to speed on the trip to Sandleford Park.

It might have been a crucial break in the case. They might have picked up Salem and the child. He should have called her, Megan, explained the situation and left her to handle it, not gone rushing off himself, without proper back-up. So, okay, in the event he had found nothing but a couple of schoolboys but he hadn't known that, couldn't be sure that he wouldn't be confronting some maniac with a knife or a gun.

He was the superintendent. He had a proper office, a desk, a secretary. He should bloody well stay there, sit at it, dictate policy documents.

Was it possible that he was deliberately trying to undermine her position, anxious to get rid of her, embarrassed by the memory of that weekend at Bramshill? It had been a very long time ago and he had seemed friendly enough yesterday morning.

Could he really be that petty?

She gritted her teeth, making a nervous tea lady glance at her in alarm: she'd be damned if he was going to drive her out. She needed to be here, in Newbury, it was her home town and her parents could no longer manage on their own.

She had a feeling that there was going to be a confrontation – and sooner rather than later.

Greg came out of the hospital feeling a little light-headed. As ever, the reality had not matched his fears and the sticking plaster on his arm masked only the faintest throbbing. Bruising took longer to heal as you grew older, he knew; it was a reliable gauge of how decrepit you were.

He touched the sore spot gingerly.

He'd been to check up on Dr MacDonald after giving blood and been told that her injuries were less severe than they looked, the dramatic bleeding normal for head wounds. She had some bruising to the throat and would be kept in for a day or two for observation. She was now conscious and could be seen for a few minutes.

Like a suspiciously large number of NHS doctors, Tessa MacDonald had health insurance and had been moved into a private room with a TV and fresh flowers. She was still groggy, propped up against a pristine pair of pillows, but responded when he introduced himself by saying, 'I feel so stupid.'

'Not your fault.'

'But it was. I turned my back on him. That was pretty much the first thing they told me when I took this job: don't, under any circumstances, turn your back on the prisoner.' She yawned hugely, then winced as it hurt her throat. She reached for a glass of mineral water, sipped it and flinched again as the cold liquid hit the inside of her gullet. 'I thought he was catatonic.'

'There's many a police officer has made that same mistake.'

'It's not one I shall make again, I can promise you.'

'So, you'll be coming back?'

'You don't think I'm going to let a little thing like a near-death experience put me off?'

Her pale lips were set in a determined line and he admired her spirit. He gave her a big grin of encouragement. 'I'll let you get some rest now.'

'Be seeing you – at the station.'

The door was flung open at that moment and a man of about thirty erupted into the room, followed by an irritated nurse who was trying to tell him that Dr MacDonald was allowed only one visitor at a time but was being roundly ignored. He was wearing a conservative grey suit, blue shirt and tie, but contrived to look dishevelled.

'Tessa! My God! What have they done to you?' He flung himself on his knees by the bed and seized her hand, pressing it fervently to his lips.

'I'm all right, Donald.'

Donald MacDonald, Greg thought with amusement. Or had Tessa, like so many young professional women these days, kept her own name?

The nurse said, 'Really, Mr MacDonald, what your wife needs now is peace and quiet, not melodrama.'

The agitated husband ignored her. 'I could never understand why you wanted to take such a dangerous job. I knew it was a mistake.' He seemed to become aware of Greg's presence and scrambled to his feet. 'And who might you be?'

'Superintendent Gregory Summers.' He held out his hand but the man deliberately didn't take it.

'My wife may well be bringing an action for negligence against the Thames Valley Police,' he announced.

188

Tessa laughed. 'My husband, the lawyer. I've already told Mr Summers that it was my own fault, Donald.'

He threw his wife an exasperated look and Greg silently slipped away. He could imagine the scenes in the MacDonald household over the next couple of weeks. His money was on Tessa.

Chapter 11

It had stopped raining for once, and Greg decided to leave his car at the hospital for half an hour and take a walk over to Peabody Green. He had no desire to encroach on Megan's conduct of the case – let the new DCI win her spurs and the respect of her men – but he wanted to get the atmosphere of the place.

He skirted a group of shabby portakabins at the front of the hospital, by the main road. One was the VD clinic – although they didn't call it that any more – nicely sited so that any patient going in could be seen by a neighbour passing by on the bus. Next door was the substance abuse centre, but people wore their addictions with pride these days.

He passed through the gate that led from the hospital grounds into the Peabody car park and strode along past the garages, the Green in his view. He didn't know this district of Newbury well – during his uniform days it had never been part of his beat – but had often driven past it and thought what a change it made from some of the municipal housing he policed.

On the tarmac beyond the garages someone had chalked out a hopscotch course. Greg had been a champion at the game in his youth. He stopped and looked furtively round to see if anyone was watching. There was no one in sight. He picked up a flattish stone, took up his position in front of number one and threw the stone to land plumb in the middle of the furthest square. Hurrah. The old magic was there. He hopped up the course, retrieved his stone, did a 180-degree turn on one leg and hopped back down again. He dropped the stone, took one last look round to make sure he was not observed, and went whistling on his way.

He walked slowly round the Green, stopping for a moment outside each of the towers: Beaumont, Fletcher, Middleton and Kyd. Somebody at the council in the late 1970s had had a taste for Jacobean revenge tragedy: incest, murder, torture and rape; brothers having their sisters whacked; daughters taking out contracts on the old man. Happy families.

To each his own.

The rows of cottages were more prosaically named North, South, East and West, each numbering from one to nine which might be confusing to a postman unfamiliar with the route. He could see where each council tenant, on becoming an owner-occupier, had stamped his individuality on his home, usually with a new door, often a porch; in one case an elaborate stucco portico which looked embarrassed by its own inappropriateness.

Salem's house, boarded up and with a line of police tape forbidding entrance, also looked out of place amid the neatness.

Satisfied, he retraced his steps. He noticed that the rows of garages were carefully numbered: N1-9, S1-9, W1-9, E1-9 for the cottages. Then B1-8, F1-8. K1-8, M1-8. Salem's garage, S4, like his house, was sealed with police incident tape, blue and white.

So the Troys had a garage allocated to them, even if they had no car. He pressed his ear to the door but could make out no sound. He tried the lock but it didn't yield to his thumb. He could see that the hinges of the up-and-over door were well-oiled as if the place was in frequent use. He took out his mobile phone. He told himself that he was not looking for a child's body and yet this garage was just the place where such might be concealed.

191

'Barbara, it's me. Is DCI Davies with you? Can you both meet me in the car park at Peabody Green right away?'

Roger Troy looked enquiringly at Greg as he produced his warrant card. The superintendent was surprised by him: from his tragic story he had expected a shambolic wreck. He saw only nobility in this man who had lost his sanity when his wife died: a memorial, in its way, as poignant as the Taj Mahal.

'Dr Troy? I'm Superintendent Summers. I was wondering if you'd be good enough to unlock your garage for me and let me take a look round.'

He didn't want to have to get a search warrant and surely if Troy had nothing to hide then he had no reason to refuse. He scanned the man's face for fear or nervousness but Troy merely looked puzzled.

'I haven't got a garage. I haven't got a car.'

He had had a car once, he thought: a Golf GTi convertible, white. He had had a widescreen TV and a video recorder and a DVD player and a state-of-the-art stereo system. He'd had a supple leather sofa and a Georgian tallboy. He'd had holidays in the Caribbean and New Zealand and Brazil. He had had a wonderful wife, a terrific job and a glowing future.

Or had that been some other man?

Greg looked at him in mild exasperation. 'But you do have a garage! B8. It's allocated with the flat and the door and locks show signs of regular use.'

'Oh!' A light came on in Troy's eyes. 'You mean my workroom, my laboratory. Yes, you're welcome to look round. Let me get the key and put some shoes on.'

Greg waited in the doorway for two minutes until Troy rejoined him. 'You'll be wanting a coat, sir,' he suggested, 'it's cold out.'

'Good idea.' Troy disappeared again and returned with a ratty old anorak, its collar torn, its pockets bulging. 'Shall we go?'

Although he gave the impression of a shambling man, Troy walked with speed and vigour and Greg had to bustle to keep up with him. Half way to the car park he said, 'It would have been more helpful if you'd told my officers about your "workroom" earlier, Dr Troy.'

'I'm not sure I'm entitled to the honorific of *doctor* any more.'

'They haven't taken your PhD away, have they?'

'True.'

Greg felt he was being side-tracked. 'The garage. Dr Troy?'

'I used to be a scientist,' Roger said, 'as I say. It makes one literal minded and my illness seems to have aggravated that.' He wasn't apologising, merely explaining. 'I don't think of this building as a garage. It's where I work on my project. Cold Fusion. No?'

'I'm not familiar...'

'Well I won't try to explain. I only bore people.'

'No, I'd like to understand if you can do it in words of one syllable.'

'All right.' Roger looked at him with respect. As when he'd been talking to Barbara and Megan, all hesitancy dropped from his speech as he began on his subject. 'You're familiar with the concept of energy produced by nuclear fusion, I take it?'

'I'm aware that it happens,' Greg said carefully. And that it could blow people into the middle of next week. Or was that nuclear *fission*? He should have paid more attention in Physics class.

'Two nuclei are fused to make one bigger nucleus,' Roger went on, 'but that new nucleus is unstable and breaks down, releasing energy With me so far?'

'That sounds simple enough,' Greg said gratefully.

'The problem is that the two initial nuclei are both positively charged and so naturally repel each other. Conventional wisdom is that the only way to make them fuse is by subjecting them to inordinately high temperatures – something of the order of 50 million degrees Celsius.'

Greg whistled. 'That's hot! But you clearly believe it can be done cold.'

'Well, at room temperature and it's not just me. Most conventional scientists would tell you that it violates the laws of thermo-dynamics but then they said that it was impossible to split the atom.'

'Until they did.'

And look at all the trouble that had caused.

'Precisely. People have been trying to do it since the 1920s but without success. Then in 1989 two researchers in Utah used electrochemistry to fuse deuterium nuclei, but I'm working on a completely new methodology which I will keep to myself for the time being, if you don't mind.'

'It'd be perfectly safe with me,' Greg said truthfully. 'What are the chances?'

'At a conservative estimate?' Troy asked. 'About one in a trillion.'

There was something attractive about a forlorn hope on that scale, Greg thought, the grandmother of all lost causes.

'I can see now that it looks suspicious,' Troy added, 'but my workshop is quite blameless, as you will see.'

'Can you drive, sir?'

'I suppose so.'

'You *suppose* so?'

'I haven't been behind the wheel of a car

for three years but I expect it's like riding a bike: once learned never forgotten.'

Barbara and Megan were waiting when they got there and Roger Troy nodded a greeting before unlocking the door and pushing it up and over.

'You are giving us permission to enter these premises, Dr Troy?' Greg checked.

'I'll show you round.' He clicked a switch and a single unshaded bulb lit up in the middle of the ceiling. 'There's an electricity supply,' he explained, 'so I can work here at night when Emilia is asleep.'

The three police officers followed him into the cold oblong space. Greg's garage at home was so full of junk that he hadn't put his car in there for six years, but this was no lumber room. An expanse of concrete floor stretched out before him, bare brick walls, cobwebs in the corners.

At the far end a length of wood stood on two trestles to make a table or workbench. On it was the sort of scientific equipment he remembered dimly from his chemistry lessons at school. Science had not been his forte and the classes had been endured rather than enjoyed but he recognised test tubes and retorts and a Bunsen burner. A glass bottle with a skull and crossbones sticker was labelled sulphuric acid, half full.

'There's no room for experiments in the

196

flat,' Roger explained, 'and my wife complains about the mess and smell. My work is mostly theory, of course, but I have to run the occasional test.'

Greg walked slowly round the garage, examining the floor. There was no break in the concrete: nobody had been digging here. There was no sign of blood spilt and hastily mopped up. He looked at the ceiling where brackets hung, but they were empty. There was one small cupboard, containing a few bottles of chemicals and a shelf decked with the more usual garage paraphernalia of half empty tins of paint, clogged-up brushes and a bottle of turps.

That he could identify with.

A computer stood at one end of the trestle and he noted the proliferation of plugs crammed into a single socket via a three-way adapter inserted into a second three-way adapter: the sort of fire hazard that was unavoidable to anyone whose premises had been rewired before about 1990. He'd been guilty of many such a transgression himself.

'Money is tight,' Roger said, eyeing the computer, 'but you can pick up an obsolete model for fifty quid; everyone wants the latest technology, the most up-to-date chip to play the latest games on, so the second-hand market is a buyer's market. It earns its keep.'

There were no tarpaulins, torn sheets,

sacks: nowhere to hide even the smallest body. It was, to use Roger's word, blameless. Greg glanced at Barbara and Megan. 'Thank you, Dr Troy. You've been most helpful. We needn't disturb you further.'

'I might as well stay,' Roger said softly, 'do some work. I forgot for a moment that I don't have to be indoors to keep an eye on Millie.' He looked stricken and Greg felt uncomfortable. He said goodbye again, and left.

'He said he didn't have a garage,' Barbara said when they were out of earshot. 'I should have checked!'

'He doesn't think of it as a garage,' Greg said, 'since he hasn't got a car.' He looked at Megan. 'You're very quiet, Megan. Anything wrong.'

'No, sir. I'm fine.'

This was not the time to complain that he was encroaching on her case, not when he'd just demonstrated her inadequacies.

Pull yourself together, woman, she thought. You're a highly competent officer, highly decorated, and you're conducting this investigation like a rookie fresh out of police college.

Father, husband, son; superintendent; Roger Troy and Joshua Salem: that was a lot of men to be carrying about in your mind all the time, fighting for position. She closed her eyes briefly and ran her hand across them but neither of her colleagues was watching her.

Barbara was glancing round the car park. 'Do you need a lift, sir? I don't see your car.'

'No, it's at the hospital. Meet me in my office in half an hour and we'll have a confab – see where we've got to and where we're going.'

He set off back to the Kennet, scuffing over the hop-scotch course without seeing it.

Salem's mobile phone had already returned from the lab and was sitting on Greg's desk when he reached it, still in its evidence bag, flanked by official forms. The gist of the report was that there were enough finger-prints on it for him to put on a small display at the town museum.

He took it out of the bag and held it lightly in his hand for a moment before activating it and pressing the redial button. A woman boasting the unlikely name of Chesty answered and provided some details of her anatomy that made his eyes water.

He smiled and disconnected.

He wondered what Social Services would make of it when they got the itemised bill.

'Call the police!'

Matilda Davies jumped up, startled, as her husband burst into the kitchen where she'd been enjoying a quiet cup of coffee and a Bourbon cream. 'What's the matter?'

'There's a boy – a youth – in the garden, trespassing.'

'Aled–'

'Probably planning a break-in.'

'Aled...'

'Good God, woman, what are you waiting for? Call the police before we get murdered in our beds.'

'Aled!' He fell silent, shocked by her unaccustomed display of ill temper. 'That boy in the garden – that *youth*, as you call him – is our grandson, Gareth.'

'Grandson. What are you talking about?' He seized her by the arm and almost dragged her along the hall to the sitting room at the back, digging finger-shaped bruises into her flesh as she struggled. He gestured through the patio doors. 'There.' His voice dropped to a shrill whisper. 'You call the police while I make sure the doors are bolted.'

Matilda gazed in despair as he rattled the bolts on the glass doors. Beyond him she could see Gareth, happily amusing himself in the garden, bouncing his ball against the shed till she called him in for supper. Such a good boy, she thought, pretending that he didn't mind being dumped on a couple of old fogeys.

As she watched he glanced round and

waved at her. She waved back. 'That's Gareth, our grandson, Megan's son.'

'How can it be. Look at him, woman.'

'He's Megan and Philip's son, Aled. You remember Philip?'

The old man looked at her for a moment. 'Philip?'

'Yes. Our son-in-law. Megan's husband. Gareth's father. Remember last Christmas how the two of you had that long argument over dinner about what you would do if you were in charge of the England cricket team?'

'Well, it'd be a start if they put them back in white flannels instead of those bloody stupid fluorescent tracksuit thingies...' He stared out of the window, then something seemed to click in his head as if his brain had slipped back into gear.

'Gareth,' he exclaimed. 'My grandson.'

'That's right.'

He fumbled to unbolt the french windows and ran out, startling the lad, throwing his arms round him. Gareth would be as tall as his grandfather, Matilda thought dispassionately. She liked a man to be tall. She saw Gareth embracing his grandfather, soothing him, his eyes, a little troubled, darting back to the house.

He offered the old man the ball and soon they were bouncing it back and forth between them. Matilda went to phone

Megan, to ask her to collect Gareth as soon as possible.

'So how far have we got in two days?' Greg asked.

'Nowhere would be the frank answer,' Barbara said. 'Or, given the damage to Salem's house, we could be said to be going backwards. By the way, I just stopped in the office and picked up the lab report on his computer.' She flourished the papers. 'His hard disc's been wiped recently, cleared of all deleted data files.'

'That's interesting. Could he have done it himself?'

'I spoke to his boss who said he's no boffin when it comes to modern technology – knows how to operate a PC but not how to programme it. In fact, he's bit of a joke in Social Services for having to ask people for help whenever his screen freezes or his computer crashes.'

'Which brings us back to this possible mystery girlfriend,' Megan said, 'except that no one knows who she is, assuming she exists.'

'Should we be making a media appeal?' Greg asked. 'Get the Troys to talk to the press?'

Megan and Barbara looked at each other, neither anxious to voice the thought that Roger and Concepta Troy would hardly make a good impression on television.

It was Megan, as the senior, who finally spoke. 'I don't think we'd be doing the Troys any favours.' Greg raised his eyebrows. 'I mean, they're both so very odd.'

He said, 'I didn't find Dr Troy especially odd.'

'He can be, and Mrs Troy is...'

'What?'

'Different.'

'And that's a hanging offence now?'

'You know what the public is like: they'll take one look at the Troys and decide that they've murdered their own daughter.'

'Their lack of obvious concern bothers me too,' Barbara added. 'I've seen parents hysterical because they've lost sight of a child for two minutes. Mr Troy is very ... laid back about his missing daughter.'

'But if they're responsible for her disappearance then they wouldn't appear unconcerned,' Greg pointed out. 'They'd be weeping and wailing and demanding justice and vengeance. We've all seen it.'

After all these years, it still had the power to sicken him.

'I'd still like to keep a TV appeal for an emergency,' Megan said. 'I have a nasty feeling we'd be loosing a lynch mob on the Troys. For the time being I'd like to release Salem's name and picture to the press, see if we can find out where he's gone to ground or if there's some long-lost friend who can give us more details about his private life.'

'It's your case,' Greg said. 'Your decision.'

'Yes, sir.' Both women rose to leave but Megan, suddenly determined to clear the air, said, 'Can I have a word, sir, in private.'

'Of course.'

Barbara said, 'I'll be in the CID room, ma'am,' and left.

Greg leaned back in his chair. 'What can I do for you, Megan?'

'The thing is–' Her mobile phone rang. She gave a tut of exasperation, checked the incoming number, said, 'I'd better take this,' and answered it. 'Yes, Mum?' He saw her face grow paler as she listened. She said, 'I'll be right there. Sorry, sir. It wasn't important. Some other time.'

'Would you like me to release Salem's details to the press?' he asked gently, 'in time for tomorrow's papers.'

She flushed. In those few minutes she had forgotten. 'Thank you, sir.'

By the time Megan arrived at her parents' house, Aled was sitting quietly in the living room watching TV while Gareth ate his supper in the kitchen.

Megan said, 'Hello, darling,' and dropped a kiss on his forehead.

'I thought I was staying over with Gran

and Grandad tonight, Mum.'

'Change of plan.'

He nodded philosophically and said, 'Grandad's having one of his bad days, isn't he?'

Matilda said, 'Run and get your overnight bag, Gary.'

'Okay.' He went obediently upstairs.

'You'd be surprised how resilient kids are at that age,' she added.

'I hope so.'

'We've been invited to a golden wedding do on Saturday,' Matilda said, while they were waiting. 'In Marlborough. You remember Tim and Pat Machin?'

'Uncle Tim and Auntie Pat? Course I do.'

'They're pushing the boat out: hired a hall, champagne, sit-down dinner, dance band, formal wear.'

'Sounds like fun.'

'I'm dreading it. There'll be a crowd of people there who hardly know Aled, who don't remember him the way he was, who won't understand that this isn't him, this isn't Aled Davies. It's some imposter, some bodysnatcher.'

Megan looked at her mother in surprise. Matilda had never been an imaginative woman and it was disconcerting to hear her talk this way.

'Not long till *your* golden wedding,' she said in an attempt at cheerfulness. 'Only three years. We shall push the boat out too. Don't want Tim and Pat outdoing you.'

Matilda looked at her with sad eyes, unable even to appreciate the effort. They both knew it would never happen.

'Look.' Megan laid an affectionate hand on her mother's arm. 'If I can grab a couple of hours on Saturday morning, we'll go shopping together, get you a lovely new dress for the party. Red; you look good in red.'

'He always liked me in red.'

She was speaking of him as already dead, Megan noticed, talking like a widow.

Chapter 12

Megan wearily unlocked the door of the house that wasn't home, allowing Gareth to scamper ahead of her. He made for the stairs.

'Where do you think you're going?' she asked, more sharply than she had intended.

He paused on the third stair. 'I thought I'd play with my computer for a bit before bed.'

'Come and talk to me instead. You haven't told me anything about your new school yet.'

He shrugged. 'Okay.'

They settled in the bland sitting room, at either end of the sofa. He took his trainers off and turned sideways, drawing his knees up to his chin, resting his socked feet on the cushions a few inches from her thigh. Neither of them could think of anything to say and after a moment she got up to fix herself a drink, pouring a generous measure of whisky into a tumbler and filling it with water from the kitchen tap.

At home Philip would have fetched drinks for them both and they'd have sat laughing in the elegant drawing room that they had put together over the years, bitching about their colleagues and the events of the day. She'd liked being single the first time round, playing the field the way Barbara did, but it was another story when you were past forty and had a child to raise.

Look at Gregory Summers, an attractive, personable man of her own generation: if canteen gossip were to be believed he was shacked up with a girl half his age; whereas if she made a grab for Bubble Nicolaides, as his flirtatious dark eyes half suggested, then she'd be the laughing stock of the station. She had aged, she thought, these last months. She sat heavily back on the sofa and smiled at her son. He had aged too, though in his case it was more a matter of maturing. There was nothing like your parents separating to make you grow up fast.

'New school,' she prompted.

'It's okay. Not much different.'

'Making friends?'

'A few. People made fun of my name for a couple of days.'

'You know how people are about the Welsh.'

'That must be it!'

He spoke for a few minutes: the teacher who could easily be induced to lose his temper, the one who could be pushed to tears, the occasional eccentricities of the Head with his tendency suddenly to mispronounce an everyday word, sending them into fits of giggles at the morning meeting, which she took to be what had been called Assembly in her day.

She sat half listening, unaware for some time that Gareth had stopped talking. When she roused herself, she saw that he was watching her with compassion in his eyes. Oh, God, she thought, I'm already at the stage where my child pities me; my parents had to wait till they were nearly seventy to achieve that distinction.

'So, what about you?' he asked gently. 'How's your new school?'

She laughed at the image of Gregory Summers as the benign headmaster, Andy Whittaker the eager first-former, Nick the kid who could be relied on for an illicit packet of fags, and Barbara Carey the school swot and know-all, always the first to put her hand up squealing, 'Sir, me sir'. Not that she didn't like Babs, but she resented the fact that the sergeant had been right about leaving someone on overnight guard at Salem's house. It had been a serious error of judgment on her part and she was only surprised that there had been no comeback, not a word of criticism from the kindly headmaster.

'I've been pitched into the middle of a difficult case,' she said.

'But you like difficult cases.'

'Up to a point.'

''Cause you're the best.'

'Thank you, darling.'

'Should you be working now?' She didn't answer. 'I mean, I was supposed to stay at Gran's tonight.'

'There are plenty of people to do the donkey work,' she lied.

'Only I don't mind being left on my own. I won't set the house on fire or anything.'

'I know, but you're just too young to be left. I could get into trouble.' She leaned forward and ruffled his black curls. She'd forgotten how like his father he was with his thin, intense face, his intelligent dark eyes. She thought of Gregory Summers' son, dead at twenty-two, and had an overwhelming desire to take her child in her arms and inhale the scent of his hair.

'C'mere.' She lunged at him.

'Mum!'

'Gi'ss a kiss.'

'Geroff,' he protested, laughing. She was stronger than he was and he submitted to her kisses and hugs for two minutes before breaking away.

'Now you can go and play with your computer,' she said.

'Okay.'

He went bounding off up the stairs with the energy of a puppy and she remembered that she hadn't eaten. She went into the kitchen and made a sandwich, then another. She dutifully ate a wizened apple, rendered sweeter by its near-decay.

The telephone on the kitchen wall made a small noise. She went to the foot of the stairs. She could hear the game on his PC: whistles, bangs, the sound of gunfire, a prolonged scream. She hoped that these games weren't bad for his character.

'Gareth?'

No answer.

She went back to the kitchen and picked the phone up carefully. She wasn't surprised to hear her husband's expensive voice, the tones he used to such good effect in court, impressing the judge, lulling the jury, hypnotising them.

'But you're okay?' he was saying.

'I'm fine, Dad.'

'You seen Aled?'

'He's not so good.'

'I'm sorry.'

'It's tough on Mum and Grandma.'

'How's your mum coping?'

Gareth hesitated. Megan didn't wait to find out how she was coping but put the receiver back on its rest, hoping that no sound would betray her eavesdropping.

It was gone nine by the time Barbara left the station that evening. Slipping out the back way, she ran into Andy Whittaker.

'Fancy a quick drink?' he asked.

'Well, just a quick one.'

As they fell into step, making their way through the underpasses to one of the scruffy pubs on the far side of the round-about, he said, 'Only I don't feel much like going home evenings since Tina left.'

'It must be tough.'

'I sit there with a takeaway, TV on but I'm not watching it, just put it on for company, to get rid of that awful silence. Place is a tip and I can't be bothered to do anything about it. I sit there waiting for the sound of her key in the lock, to see her standing there with her suitcase telling me it's all been a terrible mistake.'

'And how does this fantasy end,' Barbara

211

asked, not unkindly, 'with you taking her in your arms or telling her to bugger off?'

'Hugging her so tight she can't breathe,' Whittaker said ambiguously. They reached the pub, ducking into the welcome warmth of the saloon bar. 'What're you having?'

Barbara thought about it. 'Tonight, whisky.'

'Good choice! Grab a table.'

He brought over two large whiskies and a jug of water. 'I wanted to ask how you thought I was doing, Sarge,' he said.

'Oh, don't call me that when we're off duty. You're doing good, Andy. How are you liking it?'

'I like the work fine.' He drew up his chair and sipped his whisky, added a few drops of water and tasted it again. 'Only thing is that the others are a bit funny. I mean, Chris Clements and I were partners for years and now he hardly talks to me. He's not deliberately rude or anything, just "Hello, Andy, how you doing?" and doesn't wait for an answer.'

'Jealousy,' she said. 'It'll take them a little while to get used to you not being in uniform any more.'

'It's what I've wanted for years.'

'I know. I was the same.'

'But I don't want to end up like Nick.'

'How's that?'

'Cynical. Claimed this evening he'd got

the DCI eating out of his hand.'

'Did he now? If only he'd employ a bit of that Mediterranean charm on me.'

'You're not important enough.'

'Cheers.'

'His words, not mine. I think you're ever so important, Sarge.'

'Oh, shut up.'

Andy drained his glass and Barbara rose automatically to get the next round in. When she returned, he said, 'You seem a bit subdued yourself, Babs.'

'Got carpeted by the old man this morning.'

'What! Why?'

'Because of the damage to Joshua Salem's house, of course.'

Andy was shocked. 'But that wasn't your fault! It was the DCI. Didn't you tell him?' She shook her head. 'That's not fair.'

'Who said life was fair? I wasn't going to stand there like some school kid going "Please, sir, it wasn't me, it was Megan Davies".'

'Well, somebody should tell him.'

She eyed him over the top of her glass. 'But not you, Andy. Promise me you won't say anything to him.'

'I'm mostly too scared of him to speak to him. Didn't think Mr Summers went in for bawling people out, though.'

'He doesn't, not usually. On this occasion

he was justified, it's just that he happened to choose the wrong person. I don't hear that promise, Andy.'

'I promise. And you mustn't say anything to Chris about what I said.'

'It's a deal.'

It was not much after ten when Barbara got home. They could have stayed in the pub till closing time. They could have put away another half dozen large whiskies, but that would have been a bad plan.

There was a message on her answering machine and she pressed the button to play it back.

'Babs, it's me.'

Typical man, she thought, sure that there was only one *me*. But she had no trouble recognising the voice of Trevor Faber, inspector in the National Crime Squad and occasional date.

'I can't make Saturday night. Sorry. I've got to fly to Amsterdam. Can't even tell you why.' There was a pause. 'Call you soon.'

She snapped off the machine and switched the TV on. As Andy said, it chased out that awful silence, like turning a spotlamp into a dark corner.

Five miles away, in Kintbury, Gregory Summers also had the TV on, although he was watching it. At least, he was sitting in front of it facing the general direction of the screen.

Angie had gone out. Studying, which he had found to be a solitary business in his far-off schooldays, was now apparently done *en masse* and to a background of tuneless pop music. Well not *en masse*, exactly, more *à deux*: she'd gone round to Del Thomas's place, wherever that was, to 'work on an essay'. Trouble was there were so many things other than studying that could be done *à deux*. He sucked in a mouthful of tepid coffee and tried to concentrate on the news.

French police were rounding up sheep for slaughter as the foot-and-mouth outbreak crept across continental Europe, no doubt as part of some evil plot by perfidious Albion to undermine the European Union and the single currency. How could anyone take them seriously, he wondered, with their silly little képis and their blousons?

Perhaps the pistols at their hips helped.

At least here in Berkshire they had none of the burning pyres that were blighting so much of the British countryside, the smoke spiralling into the air, a column, and the stink of rotting flesh.

The news ended; the weather girl told him that the rain would be more organised tomorrow, but failed to divulge by whom. He picked up the remote and clicked it off.

He heard Angie's key in the door and rose

to welcome her home.

He met her in the hall where she'd just dumped a carrier bag full of books onto the floor, only to have it spill its contents over the parquet. She muttered a curse and started gathering the volumes back together. He had assumed that the computer revolution would mean less carting about of books but it seemed to mean more, rather in the way that the paperless office had resulted in piles of printout clogging up his desk.

He waited impatiently as she dumped the books in a more or less neat pile on the hall stand and turned to receive his kiss. His lips nuzzled her cheek and neck before settling on her mouth.

Then he recoiled.

'You've been smoking dope!' he exclaimed, in what he was sure must be capital letters.

She shrugged. 'I had one or two puffs, that's all.'

'And you drove home?'

'Yeah! Same as you drive home from the pub after a couple of beers or the restaurant after half a bottle of wine. What is your problem?' She broke away from him like a stroppy teenager and walked towards the kitchen.

He ran after her. 'I haven't finished talking to you.' He had to restrain himself from adding 'Young lady'.

'Are you really going to make a big deal out of this?' She was running water into the kettle. Bellini, curled up warm by the radiator, raised her head and turned mournful brown eyes on them both, more in sorrow than in anger.

Greg, on the other hand, was full of anger. He wanted to lash out at her, almost physically. He bellowed, 'Do I have to tell you the damage it could do to me if you were to bring marijuana into my house? It could be the end of my career.'

Angie exploded, slamming the kettle down on the draining board. 'Thank you for reminding me that this is *your* house, that I'm nothing but a lodger who doesn't even pay rent.'

'I didn't mean–'

'I haven't brought marijuana into *your* house, I would never bring marijuana into *your* house. I'm insulted that you should think I might, that you think I don't know or don't care what it could do to your career.'

Bellini began to whimper. Angie, abandoning thoughts of a late cup of tea, ran upstairs. He saw that she was gulping back tears and thought cynically that women always turned on the waterworks when they wanted to win an argument. He heard her go into the bathroom and lock the door. Soon water was cascading from the taps.

He sat down at the breakfast bar and Bellini came to butt his foot. He leaned down and scratched behind her ear. 'Sorry you had to see that,' he whispered. He wondered why he felt in the wrong. Was he in the wrong? How could he be in the wrong?

He went up and tapped on the door.

'I'm in the bath!'

She drenched her face in hot soapy water, obliterating the tears. She hated the way she sometimes cried when they rowed; it gave him such an advantage when she couldn't speak coherently to put her point of view.

'Oh, Angie. Darling. Let me in.'

He heard a sigh, a whoosh of water as she stood up and the turning of the key. She stood on the bath mat before him, dripping and naked, with her hands on her hips.

'I'm sorry,' he said. 'I overreacted.'

'All right,' she sniffed. 'Can I get back in the bath now?'

He went in and sat on the closed lavatory seat while she finished washing. 'This house will be yours one day,' he ventured, trying to introduce a lighter note, 'when I'm gone.'

'Good, because right now I could cheerfully murder you.'

'Ah, but you wouldn't inherit then. They'd confiscate my estate from you.'

'But how would they solve the crime,' she

218

asked, 'without you to head up the investigation?'

They both began to laugh. She stood up and he held the warm towel out for her, wrapping her in it and rubbing her down. Then he stood with his arms tight around her, still aware of the faint sweet odour on her breath which had set him twitching like one of Pavlov's bloody dogs.

'Are you involved with a missing toddler at the moment?' she asked suddenly. 'Emily something?'

'Emilia Troy. Yes, though Megan Davies is running the case. Why?'

'Del's worried about her. He knows her.'

'He does? How?'

'Seems his sister and brother-in-law used to foster her, when she was a baby.'

Greg mulled this over. 'Annie Fergusson is Del Thomas's sister?'

'They certainly call her Annie. I don't think I've ever heard their surname. You know what people are like about introductions these days.'

'Oh, I know.'

'She's fifteen years older than he is and more or less brought him up after their mum died.'

'What about the father?'

'Long gone... Del's worried about his sister,' she added. 'Seems she's been depressed since she lost the little girl. She struck me as a wishy-washy type.'

'Depressed enough to do something desperate?' he asked.

'Suicide, you mean?'

'I was thinking more along the lines of kidnapping.'

Angie thought about it. 'It's a big house but I can't believe they could hide a young child's presence from Del.'

'Maybe he's in on it.'

'Then he wouldn't be so worried about her.'

'Hmm. Good point. But I forgive you. How big is this house exactly?'

'Rambling old place, Victorian Gothic.'

'Attics? Outbuildings?'

'Loads of them but, to answer your question, no, I don't think she's desperate in that way. It's the sort of depression where you don't want to do anything, where it takes all your energy to get out of bed in the morning.'

Greg went into the bedroom while Angie finished drying herself. The lights were off and the curtains still open and he stood looking over his garden, his territory, thinking. The idea that the Fergussons had persuaded – or bribed – Salem to abduct Emilia for them made no sense. They couldn't just acquire a new child, not in one of the most populous areas of Europe. They'd have to move to another part of the country where they weren't known, or even abroad.

And Salem? He'd thrown away his career. He would surely need a big incentive to do something so reckless. Like something from the Delafield Detergent millions?

He sighed and pulled the curtains shut. He heard Angie come into the room behind him. He turned as she let the towel fall to the floor.

'Kiss and make up?' she suggested.

Chapter 13

She liked the night shift. It was a time of privacy and peace.

During the day there were constant calls on her time. Now that it was public policy to keep the mentally ill in the community if at all possible, wards like Edith Austin dealt with the worst cases, the people who could not conceivably manage on their own. During the day she had to dress them, feed them, even bathe them and take them to the toilet, gritting her teeth into a smile to pretend that she didn't mind.

As if she hadn't seen enough degradation in her life.

But by nine o'clock they were all in bed, lost in their drugged sleep, the ward in darkness. She could settle at the nurses' station with its small, intense reading light, a good romance and endless cups of tea. Each patient had an alarm but they had quickly learned to use it only in a real emergency while she was on duty, and that did not include wetting the bed, as Mr Aimory had discovered after the first time.

Let them lie in the filth of their own making.

It was rare for the phone to ring. Only once in the past three months had Dr Peach called to warn her of an emergency admission. She had put down her book and made up a bed, greeting the doctor when she arrived with gentle concern, brisk efficiency.

The romances made her laugh, which was why she read them. She didn't have to buy them: there was always a stack left by the other nurses, even Brian. She wondered how many women's lives had been ruined by this sort of trash. True, the heroines were not as passive as they had been; true, they now had sex, some of it quite racy, if not wholly convincing; but still they waited, still they yearned, for the male, the Yang, the decisive one who would relieve the burden of their existence.

More likely to end up with someone like Roger, she thought, kept by his wife, leaving the choices to her.

Sometimes she thought about Joanna and how much she hated her, how much she had ruined things. That passed the dark hours nicely. She was glad she was dead, hoped there was a *hell and that she was in it.*

But her ghost lingered.

And the child, Joanna's child, her flesh, her blood, her genes: Emilia, of all the stupid pretentious names.

Let her join her mother in hell, the real hell or a living hell; it hardly mattered.

Greg usually woke up a few minutes before the alarm went off but this morning it shrilled into his unconscious, interrupting a disturbing dream. In the dream there was no Angie: it wasn't that she had left him or had not come into his life, but that she didn't exist, that Rita Lampton had never met the shadowy and nameless man who had left her nothing but his sperm and a fiver for the taxi at the end of a drunken night's clubbing.

His hand groped to her side of the bed, meeting emptiness and cold sheets, and he sat up in a panic.

This was it: he'd woken in a parallel universe. He felt sick and dizzy, his stomach churning. He hadn't felt this physically ill since the day in 1961 when he'd discovered what he thought was a cache of chocolate in his mother's bedside drawer and eaten the lot.

It was Ex Lax.

He shook his head to knock some sense into it and became aware of breakfast noises rising from the kitchen through the open bedroom door.

He made his way groggily to the bathroom, peed and splashed cold water on his face. He looked at his naked body in the full-length mirror beside the bath and turned sideways. His belly sagged. Why did his belly sag? He was a naturally thin man who hadn't gained weight in the last ten years and yet his belly was moving steadily south.

There should be a law against it: then he could arrest someone.

He dressed hurriedly and went down. Angie was sitting at the breakfast bar sipping from a garish Pokémon mug, while Bellini ate a bowl of smelly dog food with such concentration that she didn't bother to look up when he entered the room.

'Tea's mashed,' Angie remarked.

'You're up early.'

'I was awake so I thought I'd put in an hour on that essay before I went in to college.'

He poured himself tea and sank down on a chair. Angie said, 'You all right? You don't look like a man who's just had eight hours refreshing kip.'

'Bit groggy. You know how it is when the alarm wakes you up.'

'Yeah. You were dead to the world when I got up.'

'Stomach's a bit dicky too. Need something to settle it.'

She drained her mug and descended gracefully from her stool. 'I bought some hot and cross buns yesterday. Want me to toast you one?'

'Thanks.' He smiled gratefully. Hot and cross buns: it was a family joke, a misunderstanding by the infant Frederick which had stuck. Suddenly the universe was all right again. This was his kitchen; this was his girlfriend and that was his dog wagging her tail hopefully at his feet. He bent to scratch behind her ears.

Only proper couples had dogs.

A minute later the phone rang. Angie said, 'Keep an eye on the grill,' reaching for the receiver. 'Hello? Yeah. Hi... All right! Brilliant. See you then.' She hung up. 'Del Thomas,' she explained.

'Oh.'

'There's a fancy dress party in Marlborough Saturday night.'

'You know I hate fancy dress parties,' he grumbled.

'Ooh! Well, perhaps that's why he didn't invite you.'

Hurt, he said, 'Then I shall invite Piers round for the evening. His love life's been in the doldrums lately.'

'What happened to ... what was his name – the black-haired Adonis with the biceps?'

'Karl, with a K. He went off with a professional badminton player from Portsmouth and Piers' most expensive video camera.'

'That's Karl with a K,' he'd said when Piers had introduced them. He'd given Greg a firm handshake and looked him straight in the eye like they told you in the conman's handbook.

'Did he report it to the police?' Angie asked.

'Not unless you count moaning endlessly to me about it. He says he's not going to tell some desk sergeant that his homosexual lover robbed him and see the look on his face that says "Well, what did you expect, you little poof?"'

'Surely you can do something.'

'I offered, as it happens, but I was told to keep my nose out of it. Threats were uttered. Dire threats. Anyway, the upshot of this is that he's feeling a bit sorry for himself.'

'A bachelor evening's a good idea then. You can cheer him up.'

They could cheer each other up.

Greg sat brooding for a few minutes until Angie pointed out that smoke was billowing from the grill. He jumped up and managed to burn his hand trying to salvage the scorched bun. He swore.

Now he really was hot and cross.

Barbara went to the canteen for a bacon sandwich, something you couldn't get at the town's coffee shops on those mornings when a Danish pastry or a biscotti would not hit the spot. She spotted Chris Clements sitting by himself behind the remains of his own bacon sandwich, gazing at page three of the *Sun* with a longing that was almost poignant.

They should rename the canteen the bacon sandwich shop.

'Oy!' she said.

'Sarge!' Clements slammed the paper shut as she loomed over him.

'Why aren't you talking to Andy any more?' she demanded.

His face took on a look that closed her out. 'I dunno what you mean. Who says I'm not?'

'He does.'

Clements looked uncomfortable. 'Thing is, I dunno what to say – about Tina buggering off like that.'

'How about "Sorry to hear about Tina buggering off like that, mate"?'

'What if he doesn't want to talk about it?'

'Only one way to find out... Honestly, Chris, you and Andy were partners for years. He saved your life.'

'Eh?' The man stared up at her, open-mouthed. She could see brown sauce on his gums. Yeuk. 'When?'

'No, well, okay. He didn't. But he might have done. Close your mouth while you're eating. You're disgusting.'

'You want this sandwich or not?' the woman in the silly hairnet called to Barbara.

She collected it and left. She'd broken her promise to Andy in speaking to Chris. Would he break his to her in the same way? Part of her hoped that he would: she respected Gregory Summers and she needed his respect in return.

And if Megan Davies had an ounce of decency then she would have put the record straight by now.

The photograph that Greg had released to the newspapers had been taken from a snapshot, an office outing to Bath. Salem was the only one in the group not smiling, Greg thought, though it wasn't easy to tell with a beard. Was that why he mistrusted men with beards? He was also the only male in the group, his face a little fuzzy, standing between two women colleagues, staring with defiance into the camera.

A man who didn't like having his picture taken, thought Greg, who sympathised. Trouble was the photo made him look mad, even dangerous, but perhaps he was. They were all assuming that he would do Emilia no harm but what if this was a delusion? He might be a closet paedophile, spending

228

years in Social Services, biding his time, waiting for just such an opportunity.

The papers had cleaned the photo up a little, made it larger. It was on the front page of the tabloids opposite the picture of a haggard Prince Charles, himself a gentleman farmer, who had been told to keep his mouth shut about the foot-and-mouth outbreak.

The headline was 'Have you see this man?'

In the broadsheets, a smaller picture lurked in the bottom right hand corner under the same photo of the Prince of Wales. The story was brief, the headlines less stark. Salem was a man the police wished to interview urgently, travelling alone or with a woman, accompanied by a girl of three, almost certainly by car.

After much internal debate, Greg had added the usual rider about how the public shouldn't approach him directly but should contact Newbury police station on the above number. He had a short fantasy of reported sightings in Windsor, at Buckingham Palace and at Highgrove in Gloucestershire.

'Glum looking bloke in the paper, mate? Sticky-out ears. I seen him and he looks a right villain.'

'What do you think?' he asked Barbara and Megan.

'Should do the trick,' Megan said.

'I think we should warn the Troys to expect press on their doorstep,' Barbara added.

'We haven't released the child's name,' Greg pointed out, 'or even said what we want to talk to Salem about.'

'But half Newbury's talking about the abduction. I heard somebody in Starbucks on about it when I stopped for my morning triple espresso with extra caffeine.'

'I'd hate to see the lining of your stomach,' Greg commented.

'I trust you never will, boss.'

It was shortly before lunch when Barbara got an emergency call to a remote corner of Halfacre Farm. A woman, believed to be Mrs Halfacre, was holding a rambler at gunpoint and was refusing to surrender to police.

'You've met the woman, Babs,' the inspector in charge of the day relief concluded. 'My boys could really use your input.'

Barbara glanced at Megan who nodded. 'I'm on my way.

'A rambler?' Megan said as they sped through the streets of suburban Newbury. 'Surely footpaths that cross farmland are still closed off.'

'That may be the problem,' Barbara said. 'If some twerp of a walker has ignored the keep-out signs, that may have pushed Mrs

H over the edge.'

They saw the red and white police car from a distance, pulled up by the hedgerow so as not to block the narrow lane. Barbara parked immediately behind it and the two women got out with circumspection, grimly aware of the effects of a shotgun at close range.

A five-bar gate led into a field in which sheep grazed at the far end. Beside the gate was a well-maintained stile with a footpath sign, but tacked to the signpost was the now familiar red notice announcing that use of the path was suspended until further notice.

'Oh my God!' Megan said. 'Oh, sweet Jesus, no.'

Startled, Barbara followed her eye and gave a yelp of her own.

'It's your dad!'

Megan swung her leg over the stile without further ado and Barbara hastened to follow her. Mrs Halfacre stood at a distance of about ten yards from them, holding a double-barrelled shotgun pointed steadily at Aled Davies's head. The old man was standing very still since, confused as he was, he knew himself to be in mortal danger.

If Mrs Halfacre had noticed the new arrivals she gave no sign of it. Her eyes were fixed on her prey with a messianic glare.

Inside the gate two uniformed PCs, Sharon Moore and Tom Reilly, an old-established partnership, stood helplessly watching.

'Thank God you're here, Sarge,' Sharon muttered.

'Let me handle this.' Barbara walked a few paces forward towards the woman and said in a clear but low voice, 'Mrs Halfacre? Charlotte? Do you remember me?'

Charlotte Halfacre spun round so that it was now Barbara who was in her sights. She pointed the gun first at the sergeant's head, then at her abdomen, as if unsure where she could cause the most devastation. Barbara had a sudden image of Gregory Summers standing gazing at her stomach lining at the post-mortem, saying, 'Look at those caffeine stains. I warned her.'

She didn't flinch, however, keeping her cool, maintaining eye contact with the distraught woman. Megan took the opportunity to join her father, pulling him away towards the safety of the hedge. He looked at her without recognition.

'It's me, Dad. Megan.'

He shook her hand from his arm, looking her up and down with contempt. 'Don't be stupid, woman. My Meggie's just a little girl.'

She stared at him in despair.

'Do you remember me, Charlotte?' Barbara said. 'Barbara Carey. I came to your house on

232

Tuesday morning when David died.'

'He didn't die,' the woman bellowed, her finger tightening on the trigger. 'He didn't just sodding *die*. He killed himself, and he didn't even have the decency to kill me first, left me to carry it all by myself, and do you know what pisses me off the most? Do you?' Barbara shook her head. 'That I haven't got the guts to follow him.'

'Charlotte...'

'And you know the other thing that pisses me off? People like *him*–' She jerked the gun back towards Aled, making Tom and Sharon move smartly away from him, '–Who think that the law doesn't apply to them, who think they can come for a quiet stroll in my fields whenever they feel like it, spreading infection, spreading disease.'

'Charlotte,' Barbara said calmly, 'this old gentlemen is ill. He's not responsible for his actions.'

'Heh?' Mr Davies bridled. 'What's she on about?' he demanded of no one in particular. 'Who you calling irresponsible, young lady.'

Barbara took another step forward and the gun swung back towards her. She held out her hand. 'We can work this out, Charlotte.'

'Can we? We can work it out, can we? You can give me back my husband, I suppose, and my livelihood.'

'No,' Barbara said. 'I can't do that, but if you would lower the gun, then we can at least put an end to this.' The woman seemed rational enough, coherent, and Barbara appealed to reason. 'I mean, where are you going with this, Charlotte? You've made your point. You've given Mr Davies here a lesson he won't forget in a hurry. You can't stand here holding us all at gunpoint indefinitely, so if you're going to shoot me you might as well get on with it.'

'Oh, bollocks!' Mrs Halfacre hurled the gun to the ground. 'It's not even loaded. I don't know how to use it. David was the marksman of the family.' She sat down rather abruptly on the grass and buried her face in her hands.

Barbara stepped forward without haste, picked the shotgun up and broke it open. It was not loaded. She threw it to Sharon Moore.

'Hang on to that, Shaz.'

'Nice work, Sarge.'

'Yes,' Megan agreed. 'Well done, Barbara.'

'Megan?' Mr Davies said. The police officers all looked at him. 'I've got a daughter called Megan,' he added doubtfully.

'Yes, Dad. It's me. Let's get you home.'

'Yes, let's get out of here before we all get fined five thousand pounds,' Barbara said. 'Tom, Sharon, take Mrs Halfacre home, call her family doctor, stay with her till he gets

234

there. Make sure she hasn't got any more shotguns in the house. If she has, confiscate them.' She lowered her voice. 'The licence-holder is dead.'

'Are we charging her with anything, Sarge?'

'God, no! Give the poor woman a break.'

'I was only asking.'

'I'll join you at the farmhouse after I've run Mr Davies home.'

'No one is going anywhere,' Charlotte Halfacre said with a sudden return of spirit, 'until they've been disinfected.'

Barbara sighed. Megan murmured, 'She's right. We're just as likely to spread infection as anyone else. We can't exempt ourselves.'

'There isn't even any bloody disease in Berkshire,' Barbara muttered.

'Let's keep it that way.'

Barbara said, 'Tom,' and Reilly began to talk into his radio. After a short exchange he reported back.

'Best part of an hour to get a van here, Sarge.'

'Then we wait.'

They waited. Mrs Halfacre stayed sitting on the ground, her arms wound round her knees, her face pressed into the green and white tartan of her skirt. Tom and Sharon wandered round the field, not straying far from the gate, trying not to manifest impatience. A curious sheep came towards

235

them at one point and was shooed away by Sharon.

Barbara and Megan waited by the gate while Mr Davies sat on the stile, breathing heavily as he tried to make sense of recent events. The fields around Newbury were still waterlogged from the autumn and winter of heavy rain and Barbara looked without enthusiasm at the mud on her suede ankle boots, boots which were soon to be hosed down with a pungent disinfectant. She had congratulated herself too soon on the fact that she hadn't been wearing them during the excursion to High Wood.

'They're practically new,' she complained to Megan. 'I ruined the last pair when I stepped in a bucket during a dawn raid at Christmas.'

'Dare I ask what was in the bucket?'

'It was being used as a chamber pot.'

'Lovely.'

'I was in Marks,' Mr Davies announced.

'Dad?'

'I was in Marks and Sparks looking at shirts.' He glanced round at the boggy field, at the sky with its layers of cold white cloud. 'Then next minute I was here and that woman was shouting and swearing at me. Not at all ladylike. If your mother had ever used that sort of language, she'd have felt the flat of my hand, let me tell you.'

'Dad!'

'Not literally, Meggie.'

'How did you get here, Dad?'

'Don't know.'

'Where's the car?'

He thought about it. 'Car park near Marks,' he suggested doubtfully.

They were all grateful when the van arrived, two men in white overalls and masks solemnly hosing them down, then doing the wheels and underneaths of their cars for good measure. They started with Barbara and the two Davies.

It was like a medieval plague, Barbara thought. They should walk about with a handbell chanting 'Unclean.'

When they were done, she put Mr Davies in the back of the car and went to get into the driving seat but Tom Reilly was gesticulating wildly at her from the far side of the gate.

'Sarge, I think you ought to see this.'

'I've just been disinfected, Tom,' she said with more patience than she felt. 'I'm not coming back in there.'

'I think I've found something.'

'What sort of something?' Barbara slammed the driver's door shut and stood in the lane, her hands on her hips.

'Looks like someone's been digging, here by the hedge. Recently...'

He hesitated. 'Sarge, it looks very much like a grave.'

Chapter 14

Gregory Summers reached the field in ten minutes flat.

Barbara and Megan had gone back through the gate, asking the men from the disinfectant van to wait for them. The narrow lane was growing crowded with vehicles by the time Greg parked his Rover behind Barbara's car. He glanced over the gate, fetched a pair of wellingtons from his boot, changed out of his good shoes and climbed over the stile.

He stood looking down at the disturbed earth with Megan, Barbara and Sharon while Tom Reilly politely kept Mrs Halfacre away.

'Recent,' he said.

'It's a big grave for a child,' Megan pointed out. 'If a grave is what it is.'

Greg measured it with his eye: a good six feet. There was loose earth on top, raising the level of the ground by a few inches, patted flat by the mark of a spade. A few shovelsfull of soil lay in the ditch under the hedge.

'That's the farmer's wife?' Greg glanced at Charlotte Halfacre. 'Let's see if she knows anything. It could be a dead sheep, for all we know.'

'A dead sheep?' Barbara echoed.

'Suppose, for a moment, that one of her sheep showed signs of disease, the first outbreak in the county. Instead of calling the vet, she shoots it herself and buries it secretly here.'

'You think she'd try to conceal a case of FMD?' Megan asked.

'In a misguided attempt to salvage the rest of the flock, maybe.'

'She can't have been thinking very straight these last couple of days,' Barbara added. 'It's not such a daft idea as it sounds.'

Pausing only to shoot her an indignant look, Greg walked across to Mrs Halfacre and introduced himself. 'It seems that something's been buried in your field in the last few days,' he said. 'I was wondering if you could shed any light on that.'

'Any chance of me getting a closer look?' she asked caustically.

Greg hesitated; he didn't want a possible crime scene contaminated. 'All right but don't touch anything and don't go too close.'

She stood with him a few feet from the mound and slowly shook her head. 'I know nothing about this.'

'Are you sure? If you're trying to cover up that you've failed to report a notifiable disease, or that your husband–'

'I know nothing about this,' she said at a considerably increased volume.

'When were you last in this field?' he asked.

'I come every day to check on the sheep, make sure they have enough water.' She glanced round at the animals, grazing in the distance, indifferent to human machinations. 'They're running short of grass here but I'm not allowed to move them. We ... *I* may have to shell out for feed, on top of everything.'

'And have you noticed this mound before?'

'No, but I don't come over this end much. The water trough's up the top of the field. I only came over today because of the old man trespassing.' She looked at Mr Davies with a tired eye, all passion gone.

'Thank you, Mrs Halfacre.' Greg nodded his head at Tom Reilly. 'Get her home, Reilly.'

'Sir.'

'Barbara, get a forensic team here ASAP.'

'Sir.' Barbara pulled out her mobile phone.

'Who's the elderly gentleman?' Greg asked.

'My father, sir,' Megan said. 'I don't know if you heard about the incident at the Catholic church on Tuesday...'

As if a juicy morsel like that wouldn't have reached his ears. He said kindly, 'I heard.'

'My father had another of his blackouts today, I'm afraid.'

'Then you'd better take him home,' Greg said.

'But, sir, if we're looking at a murder investigation–'

'Which we don't know yet.'

'I mean, I know you'll want to head it up nominally–'

'I shall head it,' Greg broke in. 'Full stop.'

Megan was trying very hard not to lose her temper with her father; she kept telling herself that it was not his fault that he was ill and that he was ruining her life and her career.

'How do you suppose you got out to Woodhay?' she asked as she drove him back to town in Barbara's car. 'It's a good two or three miles.'

Aled snorted. 'I walked three miles to school every day when I was growing up in Pembrokeshire, girl, and three miles back. We thought nothing of it.'

'That was a long time ago, Dad.'

'Yes,' he sighed. 'And a long way away.'

They eventually found his car in a pay-and-display car park in the town centre. He'd got a ticket for overstaying his two hours. Megan pocketed it. She would pay the fine herself.

Again.

'Are you okay to drive home?' she asked, since he seemed completely normal now that the episode had passed.

'Never felt better,' the old man said stoutly.

'Only I need to get back to Halfacre Farm.'

'I'll be all right,' he insisted. 'Meggie, love. There's no need to tell your mother about this morning. Eh?'

'I have to, Dad.'

'She'll only worry.'

'She needs to worry. We're all worried.'

'Got an appointment to see Dr Simmons on Monday,' he said, his face pathetically eager. 'Matilda fixed it up yesterday. He'll sort me out in no time. You'll see.'

'I hope so, Dad,' she said but there was little hope in her heart.

The forensic team had moved as small an amount of soil as was concomitant with finding out what the hole contained. They'd chosen an end at random and had uncovered a pair of human feet within minutes. Medium size feet in brown leather loafers, presumably male.

At that point Greg rang for Dr Chubb, the pathologist, who promised to be there within the hour. He also summoned an

242

ambulance and sent the disinfectors away.

'There's no chance of keeping this field quarantined now,' he explained to Barbara. 'I'd better get on to MAFF, put them in the picture.'

As he set about the long task of getting through to the Ministry of Agriculture and making them understand the situation, Barbara looked gloomily at the wet patches on her boots, at the suede drying hard and scaly under the chemicals. Gumboots, she thought, like the boss. Mental note: buy a pair first thing tomorrow.

By the time Dr Chubb arrived, a full-sized corpse had been unearthed, lying on its face where it had been dropped, higgledy-piggledy, into the makeshift grave. It was male, by its clothing, and certainly no child. There was no appreciable decay as yet and, as they carefully turned the body over, neither Barbara nor Greg had any difficulty in recognising Joshua Salem from the photograph in the papers.

Dr Aidan Chubb, in overalls and boots, kneeled by the body, oblivious to the mud. After a moment he looked at his watch. 'I'm certifying death at 13:35 hours.'

'How long?' Greg asked.

Chubb raised his head as if sniffing the air. 'It's been colder than usual for the time of year, but no frost. Wild guess is two to three days.'

Greg mulled this over. 'So he could have been killed on Monday evening or even afternoon.'

Within hours of the abduction.

'Or any time up to Tuesday afternoon,' Chubb pointed out.

'Cause of death?'

Chubb pulled back the collar of Salem's checked shirt. 'There are signs of manual strangulation, if you look. I'll let you know if that was the cause of death when I've done the PM.'

'Manual?' Greg examined the marks on the dead man's neck. 'That takes some strength.'

'Strong hands, certainly, but he may have been drugged or drunk when it was done.' Chubb picked up the right hand which hung limply in his. 'His fingernails aren't exactly clean. Curious.' He picked up the left hand. 'Yes, look. He bit the thumb nails but not the fingers. Trying to give it up, I suppose. Now, there's a habit I can't understand – not like drink or fags where you get an obvious high. We'll see if there's any tissue, any sign of struggle, defence injuries.'

'Some skin tissue would be very helpful,' Greg said.

'I'll do my best.'

'Can we move him?'

'Yes.' As Greg gestured to the waiting

244

ambulancemen, Chubb said, 'Know who he is?'

'Unofficially? One Joshua Salem, social worker of this parish.'

'In *The Times* this morning? I thought he looked familiar. I didn't do more than glance at it but from the headlines I assumed he was villain not victim.'

'Yes,' Greg said, 'so did I.'

Megan returned as the body was being driven away.

'No doubt that it's a murder investigation,' Greg told her. 'I'm sending Barbara to arrest the Troys, with Tom and Sharon for muscle. They have some explaining to do. Can you get off to the mortuary and attend the PM. I need the results as soon as possible.'

'Yes, sir.' Megan was a little sullen. It was an important job, but one which she would have delegated had she been in charge. She was being marginalised in this investigation again, but what could she expect if she was always running off to deal with a domestic crisis?

She was sure that the other officers were avoiding her eye. She knew that they were embarrassed for her.

When he got back to the station, having left a full team going over the scene of crime,

Greg looked in on Chief Superintendent Barkiss to tell him the bad news.

Barkiss's office was palatial in comparison with his own: nicer carpet, better desk, less miserable view. Greg's eye was caught, as always, by a framed photo on the wall by the window. It showed a thirteen-year-old Jim Barkiss, the cox, seated cross-legged on the ground surrounded by four enormous rowers in baggy, knee-length shorts. They were all a head taller but he was the one holding the silver cup.

The Chief Super was sitting at his desk staring gloomily at a sandwich in one of the plastic boxes favoured by supermarkets.

'Corned beef sandwich?' he asked.

'No thanks.'

He sighed and pushed it away. 'I hate corned beef. She knows that. Disgusting concoction.'

Greg was surprised. Jim Barkiss claimed that after six years at a minor English public school he could eat anything. He had endeared himself irrevocably to his men at Whittaker's stag party three years ago by eating an earwax sandwich on a five-pound bet.

'It's all in the mind,' he had said at the time: 'just don't think about what you're eating.'

Still, he was right: corned beef was peculiarly disgusting.

She was Mrs Asquith, the Chief's secretary, the power behind the throne. She was efficient but Greg had yet to meet anybody at the station who admitted to liking her.

'So what can I do for you?' Barkiss asked, pitching the sandwich neatly into his rubbish bin.

'We have a dead body,' Greg said bluntly.

'Not another depressed farmer?'

'I'm afraid not, unless he strangled himself with his own hands. It hasn't been formally identified but there's little doubt that it's Joshua Salem.'

Barkiss whistled. 'The missing social worker? Then where is the child?'

'That's the sixty-four-thousand-dollar question,' Greg said. 'Thing is, Jim, I need to keep this discovery as quiet as possible since the murderer clearly didn't anticipate the body being found for a long time.'

'No one will hear it from me. You didn't get any spectators at the site?'

'It's down a dead end and with the footpaths being closed to ramblers I'm optimistic that we'll be able to go about our business free of gawpers.'

'Is the little girl's body there too?'

'We're looking, in that field and the neighbouring ones.' He glanced out of the window. 'And it's bloody raining again.'

'I suppose you're here to tell me that you

want a lot of help from Uniform on overtime.'

Greg said hastily, 'Thanks for the offer, Jim. Much appreciated.'

And left.

He went down to the CID office and found that Barbara had returned. She was filling Andy Whittaker in on the latest developments as he entered the room.

'They came quietly, sir,' she reported, 'and are being processed and put in the cells as we speak.'

'We have to get the body formally identified,' Greg said. 'We may be certain that we've got Joshua Salem but somebody has to look him in the face and say "This is he". Any offers?'

'It's between his boss, Caitlin Kramer, and the neighbour, Digby Mercer,' Barbara said. 'Mercer's known him since he was a child.'

'I haven't met either of them,' Greg said, 'so tell me which one.'

Whittaker chipped in. 'Mr Mercer's almost eighty, sir. We don't want to give the old chap a heart attack.'

'But he went through the Western Desert,' Barbara reminded him. 'He's seen dead bodies whereas Caitlin probably never has.'

It was a phenomenon of the last fifty years, Greg thought, a social upheaval. Before the last war most people had a friend or relative who died young and the body would be laid out in the front parlour so that everyone could pay their respects. But the post-war generation, the baby boomers, had been spared this ordeal – or deprived of the experience, depending on your point of view – and death had become an unknown horror for them. Barbara was almost certainly right: Caitlin Kramer had not been blooded.

'And if there's one thing old people can't stand,' Barbara concluded, 'it's being mollycoddled.'

'Mercer it is,' Greg said. 'If he's willing.'

'I suspect he will be,' Barbara said, 'partly because he'll see it as his duty and partly because it'll get him out of the house. Shall I deal with it?'

'Please. I'll go and see about my prisoners.'

'Do you want the bad news or the bad news?' Sergeant Maybey asked Greg.

'Just get on with it.'

'The bad news is that Mrs Troy is asking for her solicitor and the bad news is that it's Deirdre Washowski.'

'What about Mr Troy?'

'He seems ... hardly with us, but Mrs Troy says Deirdre's to represent them both so I guess we'll have to go with that.'

'Okay, let me know the minute she gets here.'

'Don't hold your breath. She was lunching with a client in Reading when I rang her and can't get here before three.'

'In that case,' Greg said, 'I have a visit to pay.'

Sunita Lawson was a busy woman. She imported Asian art – quality stuff, not the tourist tat that people brought home from 'finding themselves' in India – and had a retail outlet in Notting Hill Gate. She had three children. Jayesh, who was fourteen, and Geoffrey junior, at twelve, were largely self sufficient; but then there was baby Astrid, who was two and a half and had been an accident, albeit a much-loved one.

She would sometimes remember with nostalgia her childhood in New Delhi, in a household with a cook, two maids, a man-servant, a nanny, two gardeners and a chauffeur: normal middle-class life in a country where labour was cheap. Here she managed with a cleaning service one morning a week and a mother's help for Astrid.

Shortly after the wedding she had swallowed her pride and enrolled in an evening class on Indian cookery.

She found time to sit as a magistrate on the Newbury bench four half days a month because she believed that ethnic communities needed representation and role models, and because her mother could still make her feel guilty about marrying out, about falling for Geoffrey Lawson sixteen years ago during a post-graduate year at Oxford.

'It'll never last, *beti*.'

She'd shown her, although her mother still regularly exclaimed in horror over the lengthy pauses and mysterious echoes of the long-distance telephone at the idea of her daughter doing her own cooking, shopping and washing like some untouchable woman from the slums of Bombay.

She took a special interest in domestic and family cases.

Greg knew he'd been lucky to catch her in when he'd phoned and he arrived at record speed outside the Lawsons' house in a smart square on the northern outskirts of Newbury. It was semi-detached like his own house but there the resemblance ended: the Lawson place was twice the size, early nineteenth century, four storeys high and faced with a pleasing cream stucco. He admired it while thinking that he wouldn't like the trouble and expense of the upkeep.

Sunita answered the door and he held up his warrant card. She looked instead at his face. 'Yes, I recognise you from court, Superintendent Summers. Please come in.'

They had never met except across the

polished wood of the bench, yet he felt that he knew her. She was about forty, of medium height and rounded in all the right places. He thought her easily the best-looking JP on the Newbury circuit but the competition was not fierce.

In court she wore her hair severely up, now it hung in one fat plait down her back. Her smooth pale skin was free of make-up, those almond eyes and full brown lips needing no cosmetic enhancement. She was dressed simply but, even to Greg's amateur eye, expensively, in a beige silk jersey two-piece which swirled around her body as she walked.

She had no accent – courtesy of the best girl's school in New Delhi – and people assumed that she'd been born in England.

He followed her down a white hall which displayed some of her best pieces. He would have liked to pause to admire them but she led him down the stairs to the semi-basement: a kitchen-cum-family room that ran the full depth of the house. She clicked off a radio which was tuned to *The Archers*, pulled a plain wooden chair up to a long pine table and gestured him to do likewise.

Food was being prepared – an aromatic scent issuing from a cast-iron pot on the Aga brought saliva to his mouth – and he could see smudges of coriander on her hands.

'Thank you for seeing me at such short notice,' he said.

'Something about a missing child, you said?'

'I wondered if you recalled a visit you had late one night from a social worker called Joshua Salem. It would have been a month or two back.'

'I'll say! It was gone ten and I'd just persuaded my elder son to switch off Lara Croft and go to sleep. My husband was pouring us both a large brandy by way of nightcap when there he was banging on the door demanding a POSO.'

'But you do get urgent applications for Place of Safety Orders?'

'Sure, from time to time, but Social Services always ring me first and I insist on concrete evidence that the child is at risk. I happen to think that rushing in mob-handed and snatching a child from its bed in the middle of the night is pretty traumatic. Caitlin Kramer knows that. I gave Salem short shrift, I'm afraid.'

'He offered no such evidence?'

'Nothing but a lot of waffle about a feeling – a *hunch* – that the girl was in danger. Some nonsense about her sleeping in the same room as her parents...' She raised her eyes, not in supplication to the gods but in the direction of the master bedroom suite on the second floor. 'My little girl won't sleep anywhere else!'

'And that was all?'

'Not quite. He insisted he had it on very good authority that the stepmother hated the child and wanted rid of her.'

'And did he specify what this authority was?'

'I'm afraid I wasn't prepared to listen to any more. I sent him away with a flea in his ear.' She leaned back in her chair. 'I heard a rumour that Salem has abducted this same child. Is it true?'

'It seems so, but things are not as simple as that. I don't think I can say any more at the moment, not even to a representative of the bench.'

'I understand.'

She got up and he rose with her. 'Thank you for your help, Mrs Lawson.'

'Am I likely to find him up before me for committal?' she asked.

'Very unlikely indeed,' Greg said.

Digby Mercer insisted on changing his jacket before he would accompany Barbara. The new one was clearly his best, kept for funerals and memorial services, so dark grey as to be black in most lights.

On the doorstep he stood looking round the Green for a moment and waved to a stooped elderly woman who was letting herself in at a house on the east side. She stared openly at them but did not return the salute.

'Thinks I'm being arrested,' he said jovially. 'It'll be all over the Green in an hour. Mrs Dace. No better than she should be.'

The merry widow, Barbara concluded, who had spent Monday morning in bed with the merry widower two doors down.

She'd heard that love was blind but had taken it for granted that lust was not.

Digby Mercer held himself very upright in the mortuary as the assistant drew back the sheet. He looked carefully at the face and drew in a long breath before speaking.

'That is the body of Joshua Salem,' he said, 'of number four south side, Peabody Green.' His formality cracked as he added, 'I'm glad that Grace isn't here to see this,' and wiped his hand across his eyes although there was no tear visible. 'Poor little bugger.'

So there was somebody who cared that Salem was dead. 'I'm very grateful, Mr Mercer,' Barbara said. 'And sorry that we had to put you through this.'

'No, I'm glad to do it. You should have seen the way Grace looked after me when my Edna died.'

'I'd be grateful if you'd keep this strictly to yourself for the time being, for Emilia's sake.'

255

'I'm no gossip and I wouldn't do anything to risk her safety. She's such a nice little girl. I had a little girl like that once, you know – pretty, bright as a button.'

'What happened to her?' Barbara asked nervously.

'She grew up! Lives in Norwich. Doesn't visit.' He fixed a steely eye on her. 'How often do you visit your parents, Sergeant?'

'Oh, I get over once a month.' Barbara crossed her fingers behind her back. 'At least.'

'Hmm. Good.'

'Come on, I'll run you home.'

'Think I'll walk.' He gulped in oxygen. 'Spot of fresh air.'

He drew himself up to his full height, saluted Barbara and marched from the room in regular time, his stiff arms swinging.

Chapter 15

Greg hadn't been back in his office ten minutes before Maybey rang up to say that the Troys' brief was there. He hastened down the back stairs to greet her. She wasted no time on formalities.

'I'd like a quick word, Superintendent

Summers, if you please.'

'This way, Ms Washowski.'

She was a tall woman who had grown stout since turning fifty. She wore the sort of floaty garments that cover a multitude of chins. Greg felt that she used her size as a weapon since she made a formidable obstacle. He shepherded her into a vacant interview room. She slammed the door shut, leaned against it with her arms folded across her shelf of a bosom, and said, 'I hope you've got some very good reason for detaining my clients.'

He laughed. 'Come off the high horse, Dee! This is a murder enquiry.'

'One to which the Troys have no connection.'

'I can't agree. Their story was that Joshua Salem abducted Emilia and now what do we find? Salem dead in a ditch. Literally. Strangled.'

'Has there been a post mortem?'

'It's going on now. DCI Davies is attending.'

'Davies?' Deirdre searched her excellent memory with the speed of a computer. 'I don't know him.'

'Her,' Greg said, feeling he had scored a minor feminist point. 'Megan Davies is my new second in command.'

'Taking over from Harry Stratton and – what was his name? – Monroe. Better luck this time.'

'DCI Davies is a first rate officer,' he said stiffly, 'and the fact remains that the Troys lied to us about the disappearance of Emilia.'

'Not proven!' she snapped. 'He could have taken Emilia, then been murdered by a third party.'

'Oh, very plausible! You knew Salem, I believe.'

'I've met him, in court.' She grinned, showing healthy but yellowing teeth, a hint of malice. 'He was not a worthy opponent.'

'There are few in your league, Dee.'

'What about the Fergussons? They fostered Emilia—'

'I know who the Fergussons are.'

'I saw them in court too, when they tried to get a compulsory adoption order. They were determined to get their hands on Emilia at any cost. Who's to say they didn't get Salem to kidnap her for them? Have you brought *them* in for questioning? No? Now, why would that be, I wonder? Not because they're such a nice, rich, middle-class couple with Barrington Chitty as their lawyer by any chance?'

'He's not in your league either,' Greg said.

If ever he got arrested he would send for Deirdre Washowski.

'He looks the part but do you know he left Cambridge with a *third?* Not something he

258

tells his clients, you can be sure.'

Greg was used to Deirdre's antics and unbowed by her. 'I'm not playing games with you, Dee. I have good reason to question the Troys, to go over their story of the abduction again, and you know it.'

'All right!' Deirdre held up her hands in surrender. 'I'm prepared to let you interview both my clients—'

'That's very good of you.'

'—but I'd ask you to remember that Roger Troy is not a well man.'

Greg had had enough. 'You can't have it both ways. Either Roger Troy was fit to have care and control of his infant daughter, in which case he's fit enough to answer a few simple questions; or he wasn't well enough to look after her, in which case you did the world no favours by standing up in court and maintaining that he was.'

Deirdre bared her teeth again but there was no malice this time, merely amusement. 'Always good to spar with you, Gregory. You *are* a worthy opponent.'

'The pleasure is mine.'

Greg pondered how best to set about the Troys. The clock was ticking – twenty-four hours in which to charge them or release them – and normally he might have asked Barbara to handle the wife while he talked to the husband, or vice versa. But Deirdre

Washowski insisted on sitting in on any interview with both of them, so he decided to start with Roger since he was the one alleging the abduction.

He saw what Maybey meant: Troy seemed detached, sitting motionless on the hard chair in the interview room, his hands neatly folded in his lap. Greg wanted to be brusque with him, to shock him into admissions, but something in the stillness of the man invoked compassion and he couldn't do it.

Gently, he said, 'Dr Troy, I'd like to take you again over the events of Monday morning when you allege that Joshua Salem kidnapped your daughter Emilia.'

'I told the whole story to Sergeant Carey,' nodding at Barbara, 'on Monday night and to Chief Inspector Davies the following morning.'

For a confused man he was pretty on the ball, Greg thought. 'Bear with me, Dr Troy.'

Roger collected his thoughts, as usual, then told his story again. It did not differ from the account he had given Barbara on Monday evening or Megan on Tuesday morning.

He concluded, 'And when I woke up they were gone.'

'So you can't actually be certain that Salem took Emilia,' Greg said.

'It's too much of a coincidence otherwise,'

Troy pointed out.

'But you did not witness the alleged abduction.'

'If you put it that way.'

'Are you worried about your daughter?'

'I miss her,' Roger said simply. 'I wish she would come home.'

'And your wife?'

'Concepta loves Emilia.'

That fairytale ogre, the wicked step-mother, drifted into Greg's mind, the beautiful queen with her poisoned apple. These days she had been largely replaced by the wicked stepfather, a huge shift in the social fabric since the days when women routinely died in childbirth and a widow with children seldom remarried.

Roger had roused himself a little. 'It was not an *alleged* abduction before.'

Greg had to remember that a brilliant mind was hidden beneath this unpromising exterior, this regular sedation. He glanced at Barbara, but it was Deirdre Washowski who spoke.

'The police have found the murdered body of Joshua Salem, Dr Troy.'

'But that's ... it makes no sense.' He looked at the three representatives of the law one by one and there was hostility in his eyes. His voice rose, a wail of despair. 'Then where is my daughter?'

Greg was finally ready to go in hard. 'If

you are responsible for her disappearance, then best say so now.'

'Don't answer that,' Deirdre snapped.

'I don't believe you hurt her on purpose, Dr Troy. It was an accident, wasn't it? She was in your workshop and drank from your bottle of sulphuric acid – something like that. And then you panicked.'

'Don't answer that, Dr Troy.'

Roger said, 'I don't know what you're talking about. I would never harm a hair of her head.'

'Accidents happen.'

'Dr Troy has told you that there was no such accident, Superintendent, that it is a figment of your overheated imagination.'

The door opened and Andy Whittaker poked his head round. 'Sir?'

Greg didn't take his eyes off Troy's face. 'Is it important?'

'I think so.'

Greg nodded to Barbara who slipped out of the room. She returned almost at once. 'I think you should hear this, sir.'

'Right.' Greg clicked off the tape recorder. 'We shall take a break. Perhaps Dr Troy would like a cup of tea.'

He left a uniformed policeman with Troy and Deirdre and followed Barbara into an unused interview room where Whittaker was holding a sheaf of papers. 'This had better be good, Andy.'

'Got the phone logs from BT,' he explained, waving them at Greg. 'DCI Davies told me to go back six weeks.'

'And?'

'Three calls, roughly one a fortnight, latish, between eleven and midnight. It's the direct line for the psychiatric ward at the Kennet Hospital, sir, for the nurses' station.'

When Greg returned to the interview room, Deirdre and Troy were silently sipping brown liquid from plastic cups.

Greg said, 'That's all for now, Dr Troy. Ms Washowski, I'm going to interview Mrs Troy.'

'If you're finished with Dr Troy then I'd like him released,' Deirdre said promptly.

'Not yet. I shall almost certainly need to ask him some more questions later.' He turned to the uniformed PC, 'Take him back to the cells and see about getting him something to eat.'

'I'm not hungry,' Roger said, 'but I'd like something to read.'

'We'll see what we can do.'

Concepta's first words when they brought her into the interview room were, 'I want to see my husband.'

'Not at the moment, I'm afraid, Mrs Troy.' He would not have them conferring.

She sat down. 'Then I won't answer any

questions until I know that he's all right.'

'He's fine,' Deirdre said.

'Where is he?'

'Back in his cell.'

'It's not good for him to be shut up for a long time.'

Greg felt like saying that he'd been shut up in a psychiatric ward for almost two years, but perhaps that was the point. He sat down, put new tapes in the machine and activated them. He, Barbara and Deirdre Washowski identified themselves for the recording.

Greg felt none of the compassion for her that he felt for her husband. Seeing her for the first time, he saw her plain face as secretive and sly. He felt a purely masculine revulsion from her lack of charm or beauty, a distaste that grew in his loins. He looked at her strong, red hands, peasant hands, well up to strangling an un-suspecting man. Salem had told Sunita Lawson that he had it on good authority that she hated Emilia.

Something, or nothing?

'What I'd like to know, Mrs Troy,' he said, leaning forward aggressively, 'is the precise relationship between you and Joshua Salem.'

She stared back incredulously. 'We had no *relationship*. He was an interfering know-all who wouldn't leave us in peace.'

'Then why did he make three separate phone calls to you at your place of work over the last six weeks?'

'I haven't the faintest idea what you're talking about.'

'Perhaps you could elucidate,' Deirdre said.

'We have obtained Salem's telephone records from British Telecom.' Greg glanced down at the papers in his fist. 'They show calls from Salem's house to the nurses' station in Edith Austin Ward on the 18th of February, the 3rd of March and the 17th of March. Each lasting from three to seven minutes, late at night, just short of midnight.'

'May I see?' Deirdre said. Greg pushed the sheaf of papers toward her. She read out the highlighted telephone number.

'Do you recognise that number, Mrs Troy?' Greg asked.

'Yes.'

'Is it the number of the nurses' station?'

'Yes, but...' She paused. 'What days are those dates?'

Deirdre produced a pocket diary. 'Sunday then two Saturdays.'

'I don't work the night shift at weekends.'

'Never?'

'In an emergency maybe.'

'But you were working those nights.'

'I was not.'

Greg looked coldly at her. 'I put it to you that you found your stepdaughter a nuisance. That you hated her.'

'No.'

'That you thought she came between you and your husband.'

'I was right fond of the child.'

'Was?'

'Am. Besides...'

'What?'

'Nothing.'

She wasn't going to tell this hateful man that the reason Roger had married her was to help get custody of Millie, that without the little girl he would have no more use for her, and that to lose him would be more than she could bear.

Greg went on. 'I think that you conspired with Joshua Salem to abduct Emilia and take her away somewhere, maybe sell her to a childless couple.'

'This is ridiculous,' Deirdre said, 'and my client will not respond to these wild allegations.'

'That you drugged your husband's food on Monday morning so that he would fall asleep. That, fearing Salem would give you away, you murdered him and buried his body in a field.'

'Murdered!' Concepta half rose to her feet. 'Are you telling me that Joshua Salem is dead?'

'I don't think you need me to tell you that, Mrs Troy. I suppose you thought his body wouldn't be found for a very long time, but you were unlucky... Please sit down, Mrs Troy, or I'll have to call my constable.'

She sank back into her seat. After a moment, she said, 'I know nothing about Joshua Salem's death, however hard I might have prayed for it at times. May God forgive me.'

'I want you to go down to the Kennet,' Greg told Andy Whittaker, 'see the doctor in charge of Edith Austin Ward and check that Concepta Troy was on duty on the dates those calls were made.'

'Right away sir.'

'Here's DCI Davies,' Barbara said, as he left.

'Megan!' Greg turned to her eagerly. 'What have you got for me?'

'The immediate cause of death was manual strangulation,' she reported, 'but he was drugged beforehand.'

'That makes sense,' Barbara said, 'with no real sign of a struggle.'

'Drugged how, with what?' Greg demanded.

'Hypodermic mark in the left thigh, straight into the bloodstream. Dr Chubb says he was probably unconscious before he knew what was happening.'

Barbara and Greg exchanged meaningful glances. 'A hypo,' Barbara said. 'That says doctor or nurse. After which, it was an easy matter to throttle him.'

'As for *what*,' Megan went on, 'we've sent samples to the lab but Dr Chubb's guess is a strong sedative of the sort used in hospitals to subdue a dangerous patient in an emergency.'

'A hospital like the Kennet,' Greg said.

'Dr Peach was very quick to tell me that the patients on Edith Austin Ward aren't dangerous or violent,' Barbara said.

'But they might keep a stock of such a drug, just in case.'

'I'll catch Andy on his mobile and he can check that out too.' She retired a few feet away and made the call.

'Is he any closer to a time of death?' Greg asked Megan in the meantime.

'He's sticking to two to three days. He says if you need a more precise time then you'd better get a forensic entomologist to look at the larvae in the body'

'Time of death is probably not crucial,' Greg said.

'Have we enough for a charge?' Barbara asked, returning.

'Are we talking about Mrs Troy?' Megan asked, still feeling that she was being sidelined.

'Sorry Megan. Yes.' He explained about

the phone calls and invited her to join him in further questioning Concepta Troy.

'Do you ever have occasion to use a fast-acting sedative on a patient in Edith Austin Ward, one you would administer with a hypodermic?'

'I've been there seven years and it's never been necessary. Our patients are mostly depressed. Violence is too much effort for them.'

'But there are such drugs available?'

'Naturally in places like Broadmoor they need them regularly.'

'But do you have them available at the Kennet?'

'There's a small supply of Sodium Pentothal,' Concepta admitted, 'for emergency use. As I say, I cannot conceive of having to use it.'

'And what does the drug do exactly?'

'As you say, it acts quickly, usually within twenty seconds, to disable someone who is violent or dangerous. It's also used on animals in zoos or big game parks in the same way. The effect soon passes off – fifteen, twenty minutes – but during that time the patient is helpless.'

'Unconscious?'

'Not always. It would depend on the dose.'

'And you have access to it?'

Concepta paused a long time before

answering. Deirdre said, 'Where is this leading. Mr Summers? Am I to understand that Joshua Salem was killed with an overdose of some sedative drug? You told me he had been strangled.'

'That was the direct cause of death,' Greg agreed, 'but whoever strangled him drugged him first, so that he would not be able to struggle.'

There was a silence. Greg imagined Joshua Salem, comatose on a bed, a sofa, the floor, while the murderer throttled him at her leisure. As he visualised the scene, the killer's face came clearly into vision and he saw the unaesthetic features of Concepta Troy.

'Perhaps you would answer my question now, Mrs Troy. Do you have access to this drug?'

'The senior nurse on each shift has a key to the drug cabinet in Dr Peach's office. We have to be able to get our hands on it without delay in an emergency, not wait for the doctor to be paged.'

'And you are such a senior nurse?'

'Yes.'

'Was your husband involved with you in the murder of Joshua Salem?'

'Don't answer that,' Deirdre snapped.

Concepta gave Greg a sardonic look. 'I thought I'd done it because I'd used Salem to get rid of Emilia, according to you.'

'That was just one theory. I'm not clear on

your motive yet. In fact, there's another scenario running through my mind, perhaps a more plausible one.'

Concepta sighed. 'I'm listening but since you're telling fairy tales, why don't you begin "Once upon a time"?'

'Roger killed Emilia—'

'No!'

'Oh, not on purpose, an accident, but you knew that no one would believe such a story. Joshua Salem would be vindicated for his vendetta against you.'

'And,' Megan added, 'with Mr Troy's history of mental illness, he could easily find himself in Broadmoor, maybe for the rest of his life. Juries are very vindictive these days. They'd sooner bring in a verdict of murder than manslaughter any day.'

'This is speculation,' Deirdre said.

'This isn't a court of law, Ms Washowski,' Greg said. 'I'm allowed to speculate. You came home on Monday, Mrs Troy, earlier than you later claimed to police, I think. Perhaps you popped home at lunchtime – it's only a few minutes walk – and found Emilia dead. Maybe Roger had fallen asleep, as he said, and she'd injured herself somehow, left to all intents and purposes alone like that.'

Concepta didn't answer but sat listening to him intently. He could not read the expression on her face.

271

He went on.

'You're used to caring for Roger, to looking after him and you wanted to clear up this mess he'd made, to protect him. You knew that Joshua Salem would never rest till he'd crucified you and Roger, so he had to be got out of the way. It dawned on you that he would also make the perfect scapegoat. His obsession with Emilia was well known to his colleagues and a story of his having abducted her would be believed.'

'It was believed,' Megan said.

'You lured him to the flat somehow, no doubt telling him that Emilia was asking for him – the one thing that could be guaranteed to fetch him running – and you drugged him with the medicine you'd stolen from your work. Then you strangled him with your bare hands.'

They all looked once more at Concepta's hands as they lay flat on the table before her, large with prominent knuckles, the sliver of gold wedding band almost lost in the flesh of the left hand.

There had been no money for an engagement ring, no diamonds and sapphires for Concepta Tobin.

Greg leaned back in his chair and folded his arms. 'Well, Mrs Troy?'

'Roger knew nothing about it,' she said. 'It was I who killed Millie and then I killed Joshua Salem.'

272

Chapter 16

'I didn't mean to kill her, but she was a demanding child: always chattering, asking questions. She got on my nerves. That day I just snapped and lashed out. I'm strong and she was such a little thing. She flew back and hit her head against a sharp corner of the kitchen cabinet. There was nothing I could do. She died instantly.'

'And when was this?'

'Early Monday. Roger was still in bed. I went in and gave him a double dose of his medication so he'd sleep through it all. I stole the drug and the hypodermic from the hospital that morning and in the afternoon I enticed Salem round, just like you said, and killed him.'

'And what did you do with the body?'

She said, 'I would like to take a break now and confer with my solicitor.'

Greg was too surprised not to agree. He left the two women alone. When they called him back in, Deirdre Washowski said, 'Mrs Troy takes full and sole responsibility for the deaths and will tell you all about them, but not until her husband has been released from custody and allowed home.'

Greg stood internally debating it, then said, 'Very well.'

He despatched Barbara to drive Troy home and install a SOCO team to check out the kitchen. Even with careful cleaning, they should find evidence of the accident that had ended Emilia's short life.

He and Megan resumed their seats in the interview room.

'So you called Salem,' Megan said.

'I rang him from the hospital that morning and asked him to come round straight after lunch. I said I had something I wanted to discuss with him, about Millie.'

'And what time did he arrive?'

'Just after two.'

'Weren't you supposed to be at work?'

'Dr Peach was away that afternoon and I left my deputy in charge. I told her I had a migraine.'

'What happened?'

'I stood holding the door open for him and he passed into the hall.' Her expression darkened. 'Strutting in, all cocky, the way he always was, like he was putting something over on me. I wasted no time. I grabbed him from behind; I've been trained to restrain a patient physically, if necessary, like a policewoman. He wasn't a big man, not fit, and I had surprise on my side. I injected the drug into his arm and held him for a few seconds till he collapsed on the floor.'

'Into his arm?'

'...I think so. It happened so quickly.'

'Did he cry out?'

'I had my other hand over his mouth.'

'So he's on the hall floor?'

She nodded. 'Unconscious. I strangled him. I knew where to press. When I was sure he was dead, I carried the body down-stairs–'

'Somebody must have seen you, surely. It's a very open area.'

'I suppose I was lucky. I took his car keys from his jacket pocket.'

'You drive?'

'I have a licence, but no car. I used Salem's car to transport the body to where I buried it.'

'And Emilia's body?'

'Hers too, of course.'

'Did you bury them both in the same place?'

'...No.'

Greg looked at her in silence for a moment. He felt Megan move to speak and laid a hand on her forearm to stop her. It was perfectly clear to him now that there wasn't a word of truth in what Concepta was saying, that she was making it up as she went along.

Finally he said, 'Where?'

'What?'

'I asked you where you buried it?'

'...You know where. You found it.'

'I want you to tell me where I found it. Let's say I'm amnesiac.'

Concepta looked at him helplessly. 'In the woods beyond Welford.'

'That's not even close,' Greg said.

Concepta was taken back to the cells and Deirdre Washowski prepared to depart saying, 'Remember that you can reach me on my mobile at any time. You're not to question either Troy in my absence. Don't even ask them the time. Understood?'

'Understood,' Greg said, 'and you, Deirdre, are on no account to mention the fact that we've found Salem's body to anybody. The murderer believes that it's safely hidden and I want to keep it that way.'

'Trust me.'

'I am.'

'It could be a clever double bluff,' Megan suggested, when the solicitor had gone. 'Mrs Troy admits to the killing, then is hazy or plain wrong about the details, leading us to think that she's lying and so must be innocent.'

'Is she clever enough for that?' Greg asked.

'I think she is.'

'So she could still be our murderer?'

'Either that or we're back to our original idea: that she's covering for her husband.'

'Maybe I made a mistake in letting him go.'

A slight tap at the door preceded the return of Andy Whittaker. Greg called to him to come in.

'Mrs Troy definitely wasn't on duty on any of the nights Salem phoned the hospital, sir,' he reported.

'Definitely? No last minute substitutions which didn't get recorded on the shift rota?'

'Definite. The nurses sign in and out of the ward at the start and end of their shifts, just in case.'

'In case of what?' Greg wondered.

'Trouble – patient running amok, hostage situation, anything like that.'

'I see. And did Dr Peach check her medicine cabinet?'

'Yes, sir. She's missing several doses of a drug called Thiopental.'

'Thiopental?' Greg queried. 'Not Sodium Pentothal?'

'It's the same thing.'

'Who was on duty those nights?'

'There was a male nurse called Brian Andrews but a woman called Alice Mason was in charge. She's fairly new to the hospital, came to work there just before Christmas.'

'Is she there now?'

'Odd thing: she's been away since Sunday. She was due to do four shifts this week but she rang in sick on Monday and hasn't been in since.'

Greg sat up, taking notice. 'Are you saying that she's not been seen since Emilia disappeared?'

'No, I thought that was a bit of a coincidence.'

'Perhaps it is. Did you get an address for her?'

'Flat nine, 114 Doncaster Road.'

'I think we need to take a look,' Greg said. 'Ring Barbara and tell her to get SOCO to look for any trace of that drug at the Troys' flat. What was it?'

'Thiopental.'

'Megan, can you go and pick up this Alice Mason for questioning.'

'And Mrs Troy, sir?'

'Let her go. On police bail.'

Megan had no trouble in finding Doncaster Road, a long, featureless thoroughfare just outside the town centre, perpetually busy with traffic. The houses were tall and had once been prosperous but now this was bedsit land. A plausible address for a nurse who was new to the area, not well off and finding her feet.

Number 114 was a three-storey Victorian house with hard standing on what had once been the front garden, space for four or five cars. There were already five there but

Megan squeezed in anyway

There was an array of bells in the porch, two columns of four, but she didn't need to ring as the front door stood an inch or two open and she went in unannounced. In the hall was a table laden with post, much of it junk mail but some bearing the letters OHMS: welfare cheques, probably, or some bloodhound of a tax man. Somebody had scrawled 'gone away' or 'not known' on some of the letters but had not bothered to repost them. She picked one up and found the postmark to be three months old.

She knew houses like these, their itinerant residents, here today and gone tomorrow.

She leafed quickly through the envelopes and found only one addressed to Alice Mason, a greetings card of some sort by the look of it, with a Newbury postmark. She went back to examine the bells. They were numbered one to eight and Alice had given her address as number nine. To make sure she did a quick tour of the building: three bedsits on each of the ground and first floors, two, numbers seven and eight, on the top and smallest storey.

She knocked at each door, spoke to the three men and one woman she found at home, wary, tired people with a smell of takeout food in their bedrooms. None of them had heard of an Alice Mason, but then none of them had heard of each other.

It was so easy, she thought. Alice had given this address and could come at her leisure and collect any mail that arrived.

So where was she?

By six o'clock they were all reassembled at the police station. Megan explained her findings at Doncaster Road and handed over the envelope addressed to Alice which she had pocketed as she was leaving. Greg tore it open without ceremony and took out a cheap card with a pattern of pink roses on the front and the words Get Well Soon embossed in gilt above them.

'Hope you are feeling better,' he read out, 'with much love from Concepta.' He examined the large, childish handwriting as if it might offer inspiration but none came. 'This was all there was?'

Megan nodded. 'It's possible Alice Mason was there when she first arrived in Newbury,' she said. 'It's not somewhere you would stay longer than you had to. There may be nothing sinister in it at all. Chances are she found a flat share and forgot to tell the hospital she'd moved ... except that there is no flat nine.'

'And Concepta Troy got her address from the same source we did?'

'It would seem so.'

'And the fact that she sent a get-well card suggests that believes in the woman's

280

illness,' Barbara pointed out. '...Unless she's very cunning indeed.'

'And there's this mysterious girlfriend the neighbour claims to have seen Salem with,' Greg said. 'If she's not in it up to her neck then why hasn't she come forward to report him missing at the very least?'

He considered saying *Cherchez la femme* but thought better of it.

'You think Alice Mason is that girlfriend?' Megan said. 'But what's her motive for abducting Emilia and killing Salem?'

'That, I don't know. Yet. Let's see if we can track her down. Andy, social clubs, gyms, even the local library. Anywhere you can think of that she might have joined since her arrival in Newbury and who might have an up-to-date address for her.'

'Right away.'

'George.'

No reply.

Greg said more loudly, 'George?'

Still no reply.

'GEORGE!'

Barbara poked Nicolaides sharply in the ribs and he jumped an inch off the ground. 'Sorry, Sir! Were you talking to me?'

'Well of course I was,' Greg said, baffled. 'Has there been any progress in finding a cottage or holiday flat that Salem might have rented?'

'I haven't checked since we found the

281

body sir. I'll chase it up now.'

'Do.' Nicolaides left the room, rubbing his ribs. Barbara smothered a smile. She'd just realised that the boss was being neither bloody nor absent-minded, that he'd simply not been told that Nick the Bubble didn't answer to his given name. She would have to enlighten him.

Eventually.

Greg went on, 'Meanwhile, we'll keep our options open. I want a search warrant for the Fergussons' place.'

Barbara puffed out her cheeks. 'Tall order, Guy. They might co-operate if we ask them nicely.'

'I doubt it,' Megan said. 'Fergusson sounds like the type who knows his rights and will reach for his solicitor.'

'And then we'll have tipped our hand,' Greg agreed, 'given them time to get the girl away before we get there with the warrant.'

'If she's there,' Barbara said, 'and that's a big if.'

'Who else would Salem and Mason have kidnapped her for?'

'Any childless couple who're not too fussy and are prepared to pay,' Barbara suggested. 'Or simply for themselves.'

'I'll do my best with the warrant,' Megan said.

'Just do it! Call me at home when you've got it.'

He found Angie slumped in front of the TV watching *Who Wants to be a Millionaire?* She was in the armchair but was sitting sideways it in with her legs over the arm, cradling a glass of red wine. As he came in she was yelling, 'How could anybody not know the answer to that?'

'First sign of madness,' he said and bestowed a kiss on her forehead.

'You home for the night or is that a silly question?'

'How could anybody not know the answer to that?' he echoed.

'I'll take that as a no.'

'I'll probably have to go out in a bit. I'm expecting a call. Is there any food?'

'I picked up an Indian on the way home. Your half is in the fridge.'

'Oh, good. I was just in the mood for curry.'

It didn't smell half as appetising as Sunita Lawson's kitchen but he scooped the contents of the foil containers into a heap on a plate, microwaved them for five minutes, grabbed a fork and rejoined Angie in the sitting room. She'd turned the sound down for one of the seemingly end-less commercial breaks that the TV com-pany had chosen to inflict on its viewers recently.

'Good day?' he asked between mouthfuls

283

of basmati rice.

'I seem to spend half my life listening to the collected woes of Del Thomas. This party Saturday night's going to be like a wake if he doesn't buck up.'

'Still worried about Emilia?'

'That and being homeless.'

'Huh!' His food had spent too long in the microwave and a piece of chicken biryani had just exploded in his mouth, burning his tongue. He grabbed Angie's glass of wine and drained it.

'Hey!'

'Sorry. Tongue incineration emergency. I thought he lived with his sister.'

'He does, except the husband's been posted to his bank's New York office. They leave at the end of the month... Greg!'

'Gotta go, honey-bunny.' He thrust the rest of the curry into her hands. 'Final answer.'

He pulled out his mobile as he headed for the car, trying Barbara's car phone first. He got the sergeant. 'What about this search warrant?' he snapped without preliminaries.

'I'm on my way there now, sir. DCI Davies had to rush home.'

'Her son?'

'The mother can't care for him any more because of Mr Davies's ... problems, and the temporary babysitter Mrs Davies found rang to say her own teenager's been whisked into hospital with suspected meningitis. But she said to tell you she's putting him on a train to Newcastle first thing tomorrow morning, to spend a few days with his dad.'

'Okay it can't be helped. I'll meet you there. Wait for me.'

He'd pull rank, if necessary. Whatever happened, he was going to search the Fergusson house tonight.

Ten minutes later he was speeding towards Inkpen in his own car with Barbara at his side.

'Intuition, sir?' she asked.

'It's only intuition if I'm right. Otherwise it's a wild stab in the dark.' He explained about the Fergussons' imminent departure for the United States.

'Hmm,' Barbara said. 'The States are very good about upholding the Hague Convention on child abduction, though.'

'But that assumes we even knew Emilia was with them,' Greg pointed out. 'They might have quietly left the country and arrived in – I don't know – Poughkeepsie–'

'Is there such a place?'

'–complete with infant daughter and no one thinking twice about it.'

He was chilly. There was something wrong with the heating but he hadn't had time to take it to the garage and get it fixed. He took his hands off the wheel alternately and blew on them.

'Pass me my gloves,' he said, 'they're in the–' he gestured.

'Glove compartment?'

'That's the one.'

Barbara pulled down the flap and drew out a pair of brown leather gauntlets lined with fake fur, passing them to him. She turned her own collar up against the cold night. 'I never met anyone who kept gloves in their glove compartment before,' she remarked.

'What do you keep in yours?'

'Oh, you know: maps, service manual, boiled sweets, cassettes, condoms. The usual.'

'I've been meaning to ask someone: what are those dents in the flap?'

'These? They're cup holders.'

'Eh?'

'You buy a Styrofoam cup of coffee and it fits there so it doesn't fall over while you're driving.'

'God help us!... Is Styrofoam what I call polystyrene?'

'Yes, sir.' Barbara indulged her boss's periodic outbreaks of fogeyness. 'This is it!'

Greg swerved off the road and took the turning into the drive a shade too fast. The two squad cars behind him followed at a more sensible pace. He had told them not to use their sirens but one of them had its blue light flashing. As they all drew to a halt, Whittaker, Nicolaides and four men in uniform emerged.

'Take a man and go round the back,' Greg told Nicolaides, 'in case they try to sneak her out that way. The rest of you wait here. And switch that light off!'

He strode up to the front door with Barbara and pressed the bell.

It was a big house, almost sinister in the darkness with its gothic turrets and gables, its arched windows. It stood well back from the road in a generous garden and even the lights of passing cars didn't penetrate the mature hedges. There were a number of lamps on in the house, however, and three cars stood by the front door. There was a Range Rover, a vintage Bentley, and Greg recognised the sports car which had been standing outside his house on Tuesday night: Del's car.

'Come on!' Greg pressed the bell again and held it down this time. 'There's clearly someone home,' he grumbled, his tongue still raw from the biryani disaster. 'I don't like this.' He'd be within his rights to break the door down but it was a tough-looking door and he didn't have a 'master key' – police slang for a sledgehammer

Besides, he preferred the civilised approach where possible.

'I expect they all think someone else is going to answer it,' Barbara suggested. 'That's how it was at home. The phone, now, that was different: we all dived to answer ... here's someone.'

They heard a male voice call, 'Isn't anyone going to get that?' and the door opened to reveal Del.

He said, 'Oh!'

'Hello, Mr Thomas,' Greg said, holding up his ID to the light that spilled out from the hall. 'My name is Gregory Summers, as you know, and I have a warrant to search this address. Are Mr and Mrs Fergusson at home?'

Del fell back in surprise. 'I never knew you were a policeman,' he muttered. 'Angie never said.'

'No, well.' Social death, living with a copper. 'Don't look so worried,' he added more kindly. 'I'm not here in search of a bit of illegal substance that you keep for your private use. I'm far too important for that. I'd like to see Mr and Mrs Fergusson.'

The boy, relieved, turned away calling 'Annie! Rwupe!'

He'd left the door open so Greg, choosing to take this as invitation, nodded to his men and they followed him into the hall. The entrance space was the size of his sitting room in Kintbury, rising high into a vaulted stairwell with an elaborately carved

288

balustrade. He found himself standing on an exquisite wooden floor, eyeball to eyeball with a piece of modern sculpture – all elegant curves and cavities – which stood on a marble plinth and the meaning of which he could not hope to guess.

Everything spoke comfort, luxury and taste. The Delafield Detergent millions were being well spent. Greg thought, a little sententiously, that all their money couldn't buy them the child they longed for. But maybe they thought that it could, if there had been enough spare cash to buy the treachery of a man like Joshua Salem.

A door opened to their left and a man came out, late thirties, average build. Greg caught a glimpse of a study behind him: walls of filing cabinets, a computer glowing incongruously on a Georgian desk.

'What's going on?' he said. 'Is this some nonsense of yours, Del?'

'Mr Fergusson?'

'I'm Rupert Fergusson.'

Greg explained his errand and handed him the search warrant. Out of the corner of his eye he could see a woman half way down the stairs, frozen into immobility. If she tried to retreat upstairs he would stop her, bodily if he had to. He felt Barbara tense beside him, also aware of the woman, also ready to move.

Rupert Fergusson scanned the paper and

said, 'I'm calling my solicitor.'

'Very well, sir. In the meantime...' Greg gestured to his men but Fergusson stopped him.

'And I'd like you to wait till he gets here please.'

Greg hesitated, assessing him. He had some prejudices about city bankers, especially if they were called Rupert, but they didn't fit the mild-mannered man before him in his unremarkable clothes – jeans and a scarlet sweater, canvas trainers – his wire-rimmed spectacles. He had a tousle of black hair which made him appear younger than his years and his dark eyes looked directly into Greg's without disguise. He displayed concern but not blustering arrogance. He was asserting his rights without aggression. He was polite.

'All right,' he said at last. 'I'll give him twenty minutes but I must insist that the whole family stays where I can see them till he gets here.' He glanced up the stairs, acknowledging the woman for the first time. 'And that includes you, Mrs Fergusson. I take it that's who you are.'

'My wife, Ankaret,' Mr Fergusson said. 'Come down, darling.'

She descended the last few steps and Greg could see her clearly and what he saw in her face was puzzlement. She didn't look younger than her years, he thought: worry had impressed its lines upon her face.

Intuition? Only if he was right.

He said, 'Mrs Fergusson, if you have Emilia here then it will save a lot of time and trouble for all of us if you admit it now.'

'I don't know what you're talking about.'

Fergusson went to make his phone call and Barrington Chitty arrived in the drive with an audible screech within the time allotted. Greg had to stifle a smile, remembering what Deirdre Washowski had said about him. Chitty did look the part in his designer suit and club tie but Dee's caustic voice echoed in his head: 'Left Cambridge with a *third*.'

He must live in that suit since he surely wouldn't have had time to change. Greg had a mental image of him retiring to bed in it, his tie still tightly knotted round his chubby pink neck.

Chitty read the search warrant quickly, accustomed to such documents. 'Are my clients under arrest, Summers?'

'There's no question of that, *Mr* Chitty.' Greg had often found it a useful ploy to repay rudeness with courtesy. 'At this stage.'

'And may I ask the purpose of this search?'

'I think you know that Emilia Troy has been missing since Monday–'

'And that she was taken by the socia

worker,' Chitty broke in, 'Salem. His picture was all over the paper this morning: wanted to help police with their enquiries. I think we all know what that means. What has that to do with Mr and Mrs Fergusson?'

'We're not satisfied that Mr Salem was working alone,' Greg explained, 'and there have been developments today. We've found a body–'

Chitty drew in a sharp breath.

'No!'

Annie Fergusson began to scream and Greg cursed himself for a fool. Which was apt, since this was starting to look more and more like a fool's errand. Rupert Fergusson darted to comfort his wife, throwing Greg a look of unmitigated hatred.

'The body of a male of about thirty,' Greg added hastily. Annie groaned and slumped onto a handsome oak settle at the foot of the stairs. Her husband kneeled at her feet and began to rub her hands.

'Del, get her a glass of water,' he said.

The boy set off for the kitchen, Barbara close on his heels. Greg wouldn't have minded a glass himself as his tongue was still throbbing but the householder didn't look in the most hospitable of moods.

Chitty said, 'You've found Salem's body? Is that what you're saying, Mr Summers? Murdered?'

Oh, so it was *Mr* Summers now. He said,

'It looks that way.'

'So there's some doubt?' Fergusson queried.

'Not really sir.'

'But it makes no sense,' Chitty muttered.

'We believe that Mr Salem may have abducted Emilia at someone else's behest,' Greg said, trying to remember when he'd last used the word *behest*, 'and that that somebody has now sought to cover their tracks by killing him.'

'But not us, Superintendent.' Fergusson, calmer now, was on his feet again. He had gone a little paler at the news of Salem's death.

'If you will let me quickly ascertain that the little girl is not on your premises, sir, then we will leave you in peace.'

Fergusson made a dismissive gesture and the men began to fan out. Del and Barbara returned with the water and Annie sipped it gratefully. Barbara laid a hand on Whittaker's arm as he passed her.

'Start in the bedrooms, Andy,' she whispered. 'You may find her curled up fast asleep.'

'Right, Sarge.'

But Emilia was not sleeping in any of the bedrooms. She was not playing with her toys in any of the living rooms. She was not splashing happily in either of the bathrooms. Nor was she hiding in the attics. A

search of the garages, sheds and outbuildings was no more productive.

'Satisfied?' Fergusson asked when they
were done.

'Yes, thank you, sir,' Greg said with
dignity. 'May I have a word?'

'In here.' Fergusson went back into his
study

Greg said, 'Wait for me outside,' to
Barbara and followed Fergusson.

'I suppose I can understand your reason-
ing,' he began before Greg could speak, his
anger gone. 'Just about, but my wife has
been very depressed lately...'

'I'm truly sorry to add to your woes,' Greg
said, 'but I learned tonight that it was your
intention to leave the country in the near
future.'

'I see!' Fergusson sat down at his desk
while Greg leaned against the back of the
door. 'You thought we planned to take
Emilia with us?' Greg nodded and the other
man was thoughtful for a moment.

'Part of the reason we're leaving is to put
all that behind us,' he said finally. 'In
Newbury there's a danger that Annie will
run into her, you see. It's already happened,
in fact, about six months ago, in the
market. She was in a terrible state when she
got home, hardly slept for days. We're
hoping that doctors in the States will be
able to help us have a child of our own or,

if all else fails, adoption is so much easier over there: none of those endless visits from Social Services and arbitrary age limits and rules against inter-race adoption that we have here.'

'I hope it works out for you,' Greg said, liking the man. 'But no more fostering, eh?'

'No.' Fergusson let out a sad little laugh. 'It seemed like a good idea at the time, a stop-gap measure that would satisfy Annie's maternal longings. Now, what was it you wanted?'

'I wanted to ask you to say nothing to anyone about the discovery of Salem's body. The murderer doesn't know that we've found it and if he or she finds out then it could endanger Emilia's life.'

'Then naturally you have my word.'

'And Mrs Fergusson too, of course, and your brother-in-law.'

'We shall be as the sphinx, Superintendent. Emilia was – is – very precious to us all.'

'I'll say goodnight, sir.' Greg held out his hand and Rupert Fergusson rose and shook it, not warmly, but with a sprinkling of respect.

'Come on,' he said to Barbara once they were outside. 'Let's get ourselves home, maybe an early night.'

A big grin spread across her face. 'Cry ourselves to sleep?'

'Just ... shut up.'

Concepta let herself into the flat. She'd been walking the streets of Newbury for hours since they'd released her, wondering what kind of fool she was. Had she really thought, if only for a moment, that Roger could have hurt Millie, might have killed Joshua Salem?

Her dear, gentle, beloved Roger.

To her surprise, he came to meet her in the hall, almost running from the sitting room. He put his arms loosely round her.

'You've been a long time,' he said. 'I was getting worried. They let me come home but nobody would tell me what was going on or when you would be released. The police have only just left. They spent ages searching the place. God knows what for. Are you all right?'

She thought she had never heard such a long speech from him and gave him a brave smile. 'You know me, tough as old boots.'

'No, you're not.'

She was not comfortable discussing her own feelings and needs. 'How are *you*?'

'I'm all right.' His tone was surprised. 'My daughter is missing and the man who abducted her has been found dead and I'm worried sick but somehow I feel better than I have for years, better than since Joanna died.'

It was the first time he had mentioned her predecessor by name.

'It's having something external to focus on,' Concepta said, 'something that's concentrating your mind and bringing you out of yourself.'

'I must have been incredibly self-centred these last three years.'

'Understandable.'

'It's as if I've found the key to a gate,' he added, 'and passed into a different garden.'

'With greener grass?'

'I hope so. You know, when you're in your twenties you think you're immortal. Even when they tell you you've got cancer you don't expect to die of it. You think I shall fight this and I shall win but sometimes you don't; sometimes cancer wins.' He drew in a deep breath. 'It's taken me all this time to forgive her.'

She kissed his cheek without comment since there seemed nothing further to be said. 'Roger, I was thinking. Have you fed Desmond since...?'

'Oh, bloody hell!' He darted away towards to the second bedroom. 'That's all we need – for Millie to come home and find her beloved hamster starved to death. She'll kill me.'

'He's probably just eaten the rest of the bedding.' Concepta followed and watched as Roger shook a selection of seeds into the feeding bowl.

'He needs cleaning out too,' he said. 'I'll do that before he wakes up.' He started to pull out the metal tray that held the hamster's flooring. The nocturnal creature, disturbed by all this activity, stuck his nose out of his box and gave a suspicious sniff.

Concepta said, 'Have the hospital phoned?'

'Oh, damn the hospital. They can manage without you. I know you're the best nurse they've got but you're not indispensable.'

'I wouldn't worry but with Alice Mason being off sick all week–'

He stared at her, letting the hamster's tray clatter from nerveless hands. 'Who did you say?'

'Alice Mason.' She looked at him in exasperation. 'My friend Alice, Roger. I've only mentioned her every day for the last three months.'

'But not her surname.'

'So?'

'So, I must ring Superintendent Summers.' He waved vaguely at the cage. 'Deal with this, will you?'

She followed him into the sitting room instead. 'Why?'

'Because Joanna's maiden name was Mason and she had a sister called Alice.'

Chapter 17

'Tell me about your wife's sister,' Greg said. He looked apologetically at Concepta. 'Your first wife, I mean.'

'I never met her,' Troy said. 'I didn't even know she existed till my first visit to the Masons' house just after Jo and I got engaged. Mr and Mrs Mason behaved as if Alice were dead and Jo never mentioned her in their presence for fear of upsetting them.'

A conspiracy of silence, Greg thought.

'But Jo dug out an old photo album from her room and there were the two of them, outside a tent on a camping holiday in the Lakes. Jo was about fourteen and Alice eleven. Obviously I asked who she was and Jo told me the whole story: how Alice had run wild in her teens, got into drugs and shoplifting and underage sex, anything she could think of to hurt their parents, until she finally decamped at the age of fifteen and was never seen or heard from again.'

And good riddance was the unspoken finale to this tale.

'How did your wife feel when her sister ran away?' Greg asked.

'I got the impression that she was relieved,

to be honest, that Alice had been giving her a pretty hard time.' Poor unloved Alice, Greg thought, the number two daughter, the second best. 'What I'm trying to say, Mr Summers, is that there was no love lost between Joanna and Alice and if Alice has taken Emilia, then it's not out of affection for her little niece.'

Barbara's mobile rang and she went into the hall to take the call.

'What is it, Babs?' he asked as she returned.

'Dr Peach, sir.'

'The psychiatrist?'

'She sounds very agitated. She wants to see us at once but won't tell me why over the phone.'

'Then let's go,' Greg said.

Sarah Peach had none of the maternal calm Barbara had seen during her previous visit, sitting in her office in semi darkness in the quiet of the night, the lights of Newbury distant through the window.

So much for an early bed, Greg thought.

She jumped up as they came in. 'I don't know how this can have happened, and on my watch.'

Greg said, 'What is it, Dr Peach?' He reached over and clicked on a spotlight, illuminating half the desk and the doctor's agitated face.

'It's ... it simply never occurred to me. I mean, it doesn't.'

'Dr Peach,' Barbara said kindly, 'please calm down and explain yourself.'

'Yes!' Sarah Peach flung herself back into her chair. 'Sorry. Maybe I should prescribe myself some valium.' She gave a little laugh. 'After your constable came here, Miss Carey, asking about Alice being on duty those nights and I found the phials of Thiopental missing, naturally I was very disturbed and I started looking back through her records and I made a few phone calls.' She paused as if for dramatic effect. 'It's all fake. Her application, the previous experience she claimed, the glowing references. I can find no sign that she's even a qualified nurse at all.'

Greg let out a deep breath. There had been such cases, often involving fake doctors: men – it was usually men – who worked in hospitals for years, even performing surgery, before being rumbled. Often people said what good doctors they were, admired and respected by patients and colleagues alike. If you had enough cheek; if you looked the part; if you strode through the wards with confidence – even arrogance – and all the jargon, then no one would question your credentials.

'Didn't you check her references?' Barbara asked.

'She came via a reputable nursing agency and you assume that they've done the checking up front. It's pretty much routine, though, since no one expects fraud on this scale. It's not like it's a glamorous job that people are aching to get into. She's been very clever.'

'I don't think we need look any farther for Salem's girlfriend,' Greg murmured to his sergeant, 'or for his killer.'

'Except that we don't know where to look for her at all,' Barbara said.

Alice couldn't remember a time when she hadn't hated her sister Joanna. On sleepless nights, she liked to visualise herself lying in her cradle in her lacy frock and bonnet, hating Joanna. Comparisons, endless comparisons. In infancy, it had been her parents: 'Joanna is a good girl; she doesn't break things or shout or throw tantrums. She doesn't tease Fluffy till she scratches. Why can't you be more like her?'

She had come to a speedy realisation that the family had already been complete without her, the three of them, that she was surplus to requirements. Perhaps if she'd been a boy...

When she started school she'd heard the same tune from the teachers, with the same lyrics: 'Your sister was a pleasure to deal with. She was obedient and clean and polite.

She didn't start fights in the playground. Why can't you be more like her?'

As a teenager she chose the usual unimaginative rebellions, striving to be less like Joanna: shoplifting, drugs, truanting, the wrong sort of boys. She demanded to be called Al, saying that Alice was a stupid, girly name and that she wouldn't answer to it so they needn't bother trying.

When Al was fifteen, Joanna went up to Cambridge with a full scholarship and a great fanfare. Al thought that things would get better with her gone, that maybe some of that parental love and pride would come her way at last, but she was soon disillusioned. After two months she couldn't bear to hear another word about how proud her parents were of the absent scholar.

With the Christmas holidays looming and the return of the conquering hero imminent, Al ran away. Stealing the few banknotes her father kept about the house for emergencies, she headed for London like every foolish, hopeless misfit before her.

At the darkest and coldest time of year she hitched a lift, shivering in her short skirt, along road and monotonous motorway. Within a week she was living in a crummy flat in Kennington with four other teenage girls, wearing her hair in pigtails with a gymslip that barely covered her bum, telling strange men that she was twelve years old.

She thought about Joanna occasionally as the years went by, but she had more immediate problems. Sometimes, when she felt hopelessness and despair, she deliberately thought about her to invoke the rush of anger – the bitter taste in her mouth – that told her she was still alive, that she could feel.

She met Jonny ('without a haitch,' he would say to each new acquaintance, 'I can't afford a haitch') Baird when she was twenty-one and for a while she could see a future that might be bearable. But he had fled his home in Glasgow, running from his stepfather's fists, and was no more a rock for her to cling to than she was one for him.

At best, they propped each other up.

She had left the flat in Kennington by this time, thrown out as too old to pass for twelve. She and Jonny found a squat nearby, a boarded-up house not far from the Oval cricket ground, prime property in its way. Logic suggested that it would be a wide and easy path downhill from now on.

Jonny was into heroin. Plenty of other stuff too – crack, ecstasy, angel dust, Special K, grass if it was all he could get – but always heroin the drug of choice. When he needed it he didn't care what he did to get it: stealing, mugging, selling his own body or hers to anyone who could pay.

He wanted her to try it, the greatest high

of all, to join him in that world of rapture and of death. It would make them truly one, he told her, again and again, more than any marriage contract, any priest.

But her urge for self-destruction was not so strong as his. She had something that kept her going and its name was revenge.

At that time Al wanted a baby more than anything in the world, Jonny's child. She knew, rationally, that she was in no fit state to care for another human being. She knew that Jonny was rarely sober enough to engage in the necessary preliminaries to pregnancy – one of the things she liked about him normally – but the craving would not be denied and, night after night, she would caress his tired body on their leaking mattress by candlelight in an attempt to gain his seed.

Nothing happened. A visit to a terse doctor at a genito-urinary clinic in the Elephant and Castle showed that she had an untreated infection in her fallopian tubes, legacy of the years in Kennington, which had rendered her infertile. IVF was the only hope but she knew that no doctor was going to treat her, not with her record and in her circumstances.

It was barely two weeks later, while she was still trying to digest this news, that Jonny broke into a loft flat in Waterloo, intending to steal cash and small valuables to feed his habit. To his surprise and glee he found a stash of heroin in what passed for a sugar jar in the chrome and ebony kitchen. Two hours later he was dead on arrival at hospital.

The doctor in Accident and Emergency broke the news to Al with a tired pity in his eyes, a sense that he had seen it all before but that it still had the gift to move him. 'I don't know what that heroin was cut with,' he told her, 'but it was lethal. I have to call the police now.'

Al made her escape before they could arrive, as he had intended. Three days later she was picked up by the River Police, half-naked and gibbering in the Thames at Wapping, standing up to her waist in icy water, her hands raised to the heavens. Like the brother-in-law she'd never met, she'd suffered a mental collapse that put her into a psychiatric ward at the age of twenty-two.

Al had brains, even if she didn't have a degree from Cambridge. They ran in the family. As the months passed and she pieced her shattered self together, she realised that she had a stark choice to make: she could spend the rest of her life drifting, taking an escalating cocktail of drugs, prostituting herself, checking in and out of prison and mental facilities, probably following Jonny into an early grave. Or she could take her life by the scruff of the neck and shake it.

She chose the latter course. She knew it wouldn't be easy but she was determined.

She rather liked the ward: the quiet, the peace; the single, inviolable bed. Nobody bothered her there except once when an orderly tried to put his hand down her T-shirt and she bit him. She made no complaint and nor did he but, later, when she was on Edith Austin Ward, she kept a suspicious eye on Brian, the male nurse. Edith Austin was an all-male ward but she knew that the possession of male genitalia did not keep you safe from sexual predators. Jonny had had some tales to tell of his stepfather, his stepfather's friends.

After six months the ward had been closed to save money, part of the 'cuts'. The worst cases were moved to other hospitals but Al, as a patient who was improving fast, was sent to a hostel in Hackney. She was supposed to report in regularly, attend a group session twice a week, but soon she stopped going and nobody seemed bothered.

The six months she spent in a psychiatric ward were to stand her in good stead. By the time she lied to Dr Peach at the Kennet Hospital about her credentials she knew the routine, the jargon, the bustling, cheerful demeanour of the nurses. She knew the names of the drugs and what they did and their side effects. She could put together a

307

convincing CV, based in hospitals in the north of England, most of which had been closed as part of those same 'cuts'.

Even the drama therapy that she'd been gently pushed into had come in useful, as she'd shown herself to be no mean actress. Perhaps she shouldn't be surprised by that, she thought cynically, remembering all the acting she had done in Kennington: the squeals of pleasure, the girlish giggling.

Greg entered Alice Mason's name on the Police National Computer database and watched the details flow onto his screen.

Petty stuff, he thought, that told a sad tale, all in central London a few years ago. There were numerous arrests for soliciting, resulting in fines; convictions for petty theft including a time when she'd stolen a client's wallet and he'd made a complaint to the police. Prostitutes usually worked on the assumption that a punter would be too ashamed and embarrassed and let it go.

Alice had been unlucky, which was probably the story of her life.

Early entries gave an address in south London; later they varied with each conviction and one telling case stated that she was of no fixed abode. She had been sixteen at the time of the first arrest, just too old to be deemed a child at risk and taken into care.

Even now, he realised with a jolt, she was so very young. Tomorrow was her birthday and she would be twenty-six.

He rang an inspector he knew at West End Central, Ed Morrison, a man who'd spent three years in Vice in the late 90s before transferring to Fraud, worn out by the sordid nights in Soho. After the ritual exchange of greetings and enquiries after health, he mentioned Alice's name to him and Morrison thought hard.

'It rings a bell, though they often have lots of names, of course. There were so many of them: girls, runaways, ending up on the game, into drugs and petty crime. The story seldom varies, alas. What's she look like? Not that that's much help; even their hair colour changes overnight.'

'Blonde, and she wears it short now. Blue eyes. Average height, slim build. That's not much help, is it?'

'Not much.' He could hear Ed's fingers tapping at a keyboard at the other end. 'Hold on. Got her. Alice Mason. South London mostly, not my territory. Wait. I remember now. I busted her once at a flat in Old Compton Street where she was making a porn film, hardcore, nasty stuff, animals. *Day at the Zoo*, it was called. Doesn't that sound innocuous?'

'Poor kid.'

'Mmm, that was my first reaction. Trouble

was; she seemed to be having a whale of a time. What's your interest, sir, if I may ask.'

'Abduction and murder,' Greg said succinctly.

The inspector whistled. 'That's a hell of a leap to make.'

'Not so much the usual story,' Greg agreed.

'There was a history of mental illness, now I come to think about it.'

'I was afraid of that,' Greg said.

A year after leaving the psychiatric ward, Al joined a training course as a computer operator and found a job working for a company in Croydon on the night shift. She told them she was twenty and fresh out of college to explain why she had no National Insurance number and they fixed her up and she was legal at last.

She liked to work nights, gazing out of the high-rise windows over the forlorn and sprawling lights of London, and the pay was better. For a while she felt as if she had a real life, although she steered clear of relationships with men.

It was during that time that she became Alice again.

It was another two years before she became obsessed, once more, with her family in Leicester. She blamed them, for everything that had gone wrong in her life.

Above all, she blamed Joanna.

One of her colleagues showed her how to use the Internet to search for people and she was surprised to find no trace of her mother and father at the old address, or anywhere in the county. Widening the search, she found Nigel Masons and Judith Masons but never at the same address and the idea that her tedious parents would have done anything so exciting as separating was beyond her imagining.

That there was no sign of Joanna was less unexpected: she knew as a given fact that Joanna would have married some handsome, brilliant young man and changed her name. She would have a big house in the country, maybe a couple of kids by now, a nanny and a cleaning woman, a four-wheel drive in the triple garage.

She took a fortnight's leave and headed for Leicester, confident that no one would recognise her from the old days. It wasn't that her appearance had changed that much – she was a little thinner than in her puppy-fat days and wore her hair shorter and blonder – but no one would be expecting to see Alice Mason who had vanished, unmourned, from the face of the earth.

She would be rendered, thus, invisible.

Alice is going home, she told herself, with a cold feeling in her heart. She often thought of herself in the third person,

311

especially when anything reminded her of her childhood.

She started at the offices of the *Leicester Mercury* in St George Street. She was there for two days, examining the back editions on microfiche, sure that she was not wasting her time since her parents were the sort of people who announced family events to the world, as if anybody cared.

Sure enough, her patience was rewarded. She found the announcement of Joanna's engagement eight years ago, to Roger, only son of Dr and Mrs Alfred Troy of Cirencester. Six months later there was a photo of her sister standing outside their parents' parish church, beautiful in a white silk, calf-length dress, a bouquet of lilies in her fist.

She was laughing into the camera.

The announcements of the deaths of her parents saddened her. She didn't mourn them but regretted that they were no longer alive, that they were beyond revenge. But it didn't matter because Joanna was the one she hated. She noted with amusement that her father's death was announced with a sentimental little verse, while her mother's, five months later, was plain and tasteful: Joanna's work.

In both cases they were the much-loved father/mother of Joanna. She, Alice, had been erased from the family tree which she saw as a dying willow, drooping its branches to the earth, digging its roots deep in a desperate search for water, under-mining the foundations of any structure within reach.

She almost stopped then, satisfied with the data she had accumulated, but she had no wish to see the sights of Leicester and little to occupy her time till dinner at her hotel, so she read on. An hour later other researchers turned to stare at the young blonde woman screaming hysterically:

'No! Not her too. It's not fair!'

The phone rang before Greg had finished shaving on Friday morning. It was Whit-taker.

'Got a call first thing,' he said, 'from a bloke in Slough who recognised Salem's picture in the paper. He sold him a car last Saturday, for cash. He gave his name as Harrison, John Harrison, and an address in Reading, but the bloke was certain it was him in the photo. I checked the address, too, and it doesn't exist.'

'Brilliant!'

'Bit of an old banger, F-reg Peugeot 205, dark green.' Whittaker read out the regis-tration number.

'Get it circulated to every police force in the country,' Greg said.

'Have done.'

'Good boy.'

'But, sir... who's driving it?'

'Most likely a woman called Alice Mason,' Greg said.

She had been cheated.

She obtained a copy of her sister's marriage certificate from St Catherine's House in London. It gave the address in Swindon where Roger and Joanna had been living at the time of their marriage. She searched for Roger on the Internet but he was no longer in Wiltshire. Troy was an uncommon name and she soon located him in Newbury.

Flat eight, Beaumont House, Peabody Green. She typed it carefully into her Psion organiser.

'Beloved wife of Roger and mother of Emilia,' the Mercury had said, announcing Joanna's death. There had even been a little 'human interest' story: the golden girl of suburban Leicester, struck down in her prime by cruel fate. The reporter had milked it for all it was worth and the wedding photo had been dug out of the archives, just shoulders and smug, smiling head.

But there was another Troy on the electoral register at that address with Roger. It seemed that the loving husband had wasted no time in replacing Joanna. Perhaps there were more children by now.

In which case, she thought, they won't miss one.

'Dr Peach has done us a computer image of Alice Mason,' Greg told his troops. 'The chances are that she's got out of the Newbury area as fast as she can, but I'm issuing a copy to all our uniformed officers. Everybody is on the look-out for the car Salem bought last Saturday too. She may have abandoned it but there's a chance she's hung onto it.'

'She's clearly a clever woman,' Megan added, 'and with luck she'll think she's too smart for us stupid plods and get careless.'

'Can the little girl still be alive?' Nicolaides gave voice to all their fears.

'We can only hope,' Greg said. 'Alice Mason's motive for taking her is obscure. We won't know what it is till we find her.'

'She may just have wanted custody of her sister's child,' Megan said.

'Or she may want the ultimate revenge on the family that cast her out. Barbara, I'd like you to take a copy of the picture over to Peabody Green. That old man you mentioned...'

'Digby Mercer.'

'See if he recognises her as Salem's girl. And show it to the Troys. Mrs Troy can confirm how good a likeness it is.'

Newbury: Alice didn't know it although it was barely fifty miles from London. Like

315

many Londoners, by birth or adoption, she had seldom ventured beyond the confines of the capital these past ten years, imagining a desert land marked 'Here be dragons' on the far side of the M25.

She never went back to Croydon, simply did not return from her holiday, sent no message, gave no notice. Let them think what they liked. Her employer had known her, in any case, as Alice Baird. She had taken Jonny's name partly as a tribute to him and partly so that no employer would see her criminal record. She had even obtained a birth certificate in that name from the ever-obliging St Catherine, not caring that she was stealing another woman's identity. Now she reverted to Mason. It seemed only fitting if she was the last of the family.

The one who had survived.

She needed all her brains and guile and it took her six months to find out everything she needed to know and get herself into a position to do something about it. Alice didn't mind; she had all the time in the world.

She got a job cleaning offices since there was no danger of anyone seeing her as there might have been had she worked in a café or at McDonalds, remembering her later, wondering how an office cleaner had become a skilled nurse overnight. She worked from six till eight each morning and from seven till ten each night and earned enough to keep herself. The days were spent on research.

It was a stroke of luck that Concepta Troy was a psychiatric nurse, because Alice had useful experience of that trade, albeit from the other side of the counter. There were always vacancies for psychiatric nurses as the burn-out rate was high. Pretty and personable, neatly and smartly dressed, she presented herself at a nursing agency with her superb references and her relevant experience.

People were gullible, she had found, credulous; they had only themselves to blame for their trust. She explained away the fact that her NI number was in a different name by claiming a brief marriage followed by reversion to her maiden name. She asked for this sad business to be kept confidential and Dr Peach had respected that.

A week later she was introduced to Concepta Troy by Sarah Peach, eyeing with surprise the lumpen creature who had replaced her immaculate sister in her brother-in-law's affections.

Although it was not, as she soon discovered, as simple as that.

Digby Mercer examined the photo with great care, producing a pair of spectacles from his breast pocket for the purpose.

After several minutes scrutiny he shook his head. 'I would be doing you no favours if I tried to say yay or nay, Miss Carey. It was dark and the truth is that I don't know.'

Concepta sat staring into her cup of tea at the breakfast bar. It was half past eleven and she was due at work at noon but she couldn't rouse herself. She heard Roger come in behind her. He laid a hand on her shoulder and she overlaid it with hers without looking up. He sat on the stool next to her and poked his face in front of her so she couldn't help but look at him.

'Are you going to tell me what's eating you?' he asked. She mumbled something and he had to ask her to repeat it.

'I thought she was my friend,' she said more clearly, 'but she was using me.'

'Ah!'

She had been suspicious at first of Alice's overtures of friendship, treating them with coldness, almost hostility, but Alice did not give up and soon Concepta began to think that her friendship must be something worth the winning if her new colleague was so determined. Alice had a warmth of manner, a way about her that made her easy to be with. Soon Concepta was meeting her for a glass of wine after work, practising saying, 'My husband this' and 'My husband that.'

By the end of January she had woken one morning, looking forward to going to work, and said to herself, 'I have a friend.'

'You told her about me and Millie?' Roger asked.

'You, Joanna, Millie, Joshua Salem. I told her every last thing that she needed to know.'

'It's not your fault.'

'Then whose fault is it?'

'Alice's.'

'I'll not make that mistake again.'

He put his arm round her and nuzzled her cheek with his dry lips. 'Don't do that, Concepta, don't close yourself away. You can make friends, real friends. After all, you've got the knack now – you've had some practice.'

She moved clumsily out of his embrace, slipping off her stool and heading for her bedroom. 'I must get ready for work.'

He would have followed her had the doorbell not rung. Exasperated, he flung the front door open with a vigour he had not owned in three years. He took Barbara Carey into the sitting room and examined the picture she showed him with care.

'I haven't seen her before,' he concluded, 'only pictures of her as a child, but by God she looks like Jo. The face is the same shape, the mouth, the nose.' He heard his wife in the hall. 'Concepta, come and see if this a good likeness of Alice Mason.'

Concepta did no more than glance at the picture.

'That's her,' she said and went out.

Chapter 18

Joshua Salem had been easy meat to Alice; she knew that he would be from Concepta's frequent complaints about him. She knew his type. She knew all types of men. Joshua was the charmless dork who couldn't get a girlfriend, the man who called himself a loner because no one wanted to be his friend.

In her Kennington days, they had been more interested in talk than sex, pathetically eager to know that you liked them, that you welcomed their visit, handing the money over in a brown envelope, discreetly, so they could fool themselves that it was not a business transaction.

She trusted Concepta's assessment of the man because she had found the Irish woman to be a shrewd judge of character, in general, the unbiased observer of humanity that those who stand on its fringes often are. She hadn't seen through Alice, of course, but then Alice was special.

By the end of January she had tracked him down. It was a simple matter of waiting invisibly in the café opposite his office to see where he went after work. She hit lucky on the third day as he came across to the café and ordered a dish of lasagne with chips and a mug of milky coffee. The woman behind the counter greeted him as a regular but not with any enthusiasm.

Not a big tipper, Alice concluded. She sat with a pot of tea and a book open in front of her, a dry work of sociology. She caught his eye as he took his table, looking immediately away like a bashful virgin.

A few minutes later she looked up again. He'd demolished his stodgy meal and was drinking his coffee and watching her, flecks of tomato sauce in his moustache. She smiled a faint encouragement. He was two tables away and called over, 'Interested in family dynamics?'

'Oh, yes.'

Was she ever.

He got up, making his way clumsily toward her, pushing aside a chair that was in the way with a harsh grating sound on the linoleum. He gestured to the empty seat across from her. 'May I?'

'Please do.' She let her hand rise to her throat in a classic gesture of happy confusion.

'I'm Josh, by the way. Joshua Salem.'

'Alice Mason.'

'Are you a social worker too?'

'I'm a psychiatric nurse,' she told him. 'At the Kennet Hospital.'

And now she had his full attention.

If there was one thing Alice knew, it was how to manipulate men and Josh Salem was only too ready to give himself into her hands. He was grateful to have a girlfriend at last, especially such a pretty, dainty blonde. So undemanding was he in his sexual desires, that she had no need of her more esoteric tricks to keep his interest.

Roll on, roll off, like those channel ferries, with a couple of minutes grunting in between.

If anything, he seemed more appreciative of her companionship than of the sex, to have a girl whose hand he could proudly take in the street, whose shoulder he could put his arm round in ownership.

Above all he loved to hear her talk, weaving her fantasies of life on Edith Austin Ward, of Concepta Troy. She wondered sometimes if there was anything she couldn't make him believe. If she were to tell him earnestly that Concepta practised black magic at the full moon and was preparing to sacrifice a human child, the better to seal her pact with the devil, the chances were he would listen with wide-eyed credulity.

She would shake her head sometimes when he asked after her day, bite her lip, make him coax it out of her. 'I'm worried,' she would admit finally, 'about that little girl. Concepta seems to resent her so, to feel that she comes between her and Roger. She was telling me all about her...'

She had to be careful not to go too far, though, like the time he went rampaging off to a magistrate in search of a Place of Safety Order. If he were to be suspended from his job, or taken off the Troy case, it would make things harder for her.

She came to his house only after dark, slipping out of his bed again in the dawn while the world was still asleep with a last, lingering look of contempt at his flaccid male body. He was a rambler but he was pudgy; the walking didn't make up for the beer and the smoky bacon crisps. Once she'd been seen by the nosy old fool at number six but the streetlamp had been out and she was sure he'd seen little more than a shadow.

There were days when she thought that a shadow was all Alice was.

She didn't let him come to her place, wouldn't even tell him where she was living. 'I'm sleeping on a girlfriend's floor till I get fixed up. She doesn't like me to have visitors.' He immediately suggested that she move in with him, of course, but she said

323

coyly that she didn't think they were ready for that yet. She lovingly stroked his brow and said that maybe this was it, the real thing, and that they mustn't spoil it by rushing their fences.

She had a nasty vision of him producing a diamond ring and talking white nylon dresses and a slap-up reception, prawn cocktail and rubber chicken, a honeymoon in Marbella.

He hadn't got her home phone number and she didn't ring him. She knew from her years in the computer business how easy it was to trace calls these days. Two or three times he called her at work, late, when she was on the night shift and it was quiet. She got rid of him quickly.

People thought she was stupid, especially compared to Joanna, but she wasn't stupid. She had it all worked out.

He had an obsessive personality, she thought dispassionately, a residue of the long months of therapy in the hospital after Jonny's death. With most men it would be drink or football or motor cars; for Josh it was his work and one case in particular.

She made herself a cup of tea, strong, milky and sweet. She raised the mug to herself in a toast.

'Happy birthday, Alice.'

'Thank you, Alice.'

'You're welcome.'

She began to laugh.

She started to drop hints after a month or so, letting slip that there was more to her than he knew, that she had secrets she could not yet trust him with. Only when she was completely sure of his love could she tell him what had truly brought her to this unremarkable Berkshire town. He swore that same love, undying love.

To be fair, she thought, he had loved her unto death.

She waited till the beginning of March before stammering out her secret. He had stared at her with a disbelief that rapidly became a wild hope.

'Emilia is your niece?' He repeated it three times. 'You're her aunt?'

'Now you understand why I've been so worried about her. She's the only family I have. As if it wasn't enough to lose my sister in that awful way, I have to listen every day to that evil woman and her hate for little Emilia.'

If Salem had bothered to check his files he would have been reminded that Joanna's sister had run away from home at the age of fifteen, but this was his beloved Alice, his soulmate, who would not lie to him.

'You could apply for custody,' he said.

She shook her head sadly. 'Why would they give custody to an aunt rather than a father? The Troys are so plausible when there's anyone in authority around. You know that.'

She changed the subject, but two days later she repeated some cruel remark that Concepta had supposedly made to her and said, 'If only I could just take her and run away. I know she'd be happy with me. Besides...'

She feigned reluctance to go on but he pressed her.

'I lived with Roger and Joanna when they were first married, you see,' she said at last.

'I didn't know.'

'Our parents had just died and Jo offered me a home. We'd always been very close. I was a few years younger than her–' she'd lied to Josh about her age, knocking off a couple of years, just as she had with the men in Brixton '–I was sixteen.'

'Sweet sixteen.'

'I like to think so, except that it all went sour only too quickly.' Her face took on a distant look and she wouldn't meet his eyes. Pause, she thought, a disinterested observer of her own performance, gaze off stage left. Alice mustn't overdo it. 'No, I can't tell you. I'm too ashamed.'

'Alice, darling. Please.'

'You'd think with them just being married ... the perfect couple, that's what everyone called them. Jo was only twenty-two but that was already too old for him.'

She felt him go very still next to her, his body tensing. 'You mean... You don't mean...'

'Yes, Josh.' She turned to him with a desolate sigh. 'That's exactly what I mean. As far as Roger is concerned, the younger the better.'

'What happened,' he asked after a pause.

She examined her hands as minutely as Lady Macbeth. 'He attacked me one night while she was out, just leaped on me. I fought him. I bit and scratched, but he was stronger than you'd think and it would have been no good if Jo hadn't come home unexpectedly at that moment.'

'My God! What did she do?'

'She chose to believe him.'

'But couldn't she see the state you were in?'

'Oh, yes, and the state *he* was in, with the marks of my nails across his cheek, but she didn't want to see. She said I must have led him on, that I must have instigated it.'

'Oh, that's so typical: the blame the victim mentality. I see it all the time in my work.'

'She called me a few choice names and told me to get out of her house. Since then I've found it so difficult to trust a man, till now.' She wound her arms round his neck. 'So that's why I'm worried about my niece,' she concluded, burying her soft lips in his neck, her eyes fixed stonily on the far wall, on a tedious landscape of his mother's. 'Of what he might do to little Emilia. But no one will believe my story.'

Except a fool like you.

It was enough, more than enough to sow the seed in Salem's uncomplicated brain. Soon he brought the plan to her as his own, offering it to her as a present, as the proof of his love. She demurred, evincing a respect for the law which would have surprised many officers of the Metropolitan Police's vice squad. Alice Mason was a nurse, an upstanding member of the community. It wouldn't be right.

Would it?

'We could start a new life together; you, me and Emilia, a real family. I know I can be a true father to her. I love her and she already thinks of me as Uncle Josh.'

'I have to think about this. It's a big step.'

Joshua worked on his plan, wanting to present her with something so detailed that it almost constituted a *fait accompli*. He had long booked his fortnight's holiday for just before Easter. It would be the ideal opportunity.

Alice reluctantly allowed herself to be persuaded, not for her own sake, of course, but for the health and wellbeing of the little niece who reminded her so vividly of the big sister she had worshipped.

'Auntie Alice?'

'What?' Alice snapped. She had little experience of caring for children, had thought it was enough to stick them in front of the telly and give them sweets if they whinged, but the little brat would not stop asking questions.

'When is Daddy coming?'

'Soon. I told you. I told you twice. So just shut up.'

Emilia looked at her with surprise. She was used to patience from her father, to having her questions answered in a considered and adult manner. She was beginning to think that this excursion with her auntie wasn't such a big adventure after all.

Uncle Josh had told her they were going on holiday, just the three of them, to give Daddy and Mummy a rest, that it would be fun, but it was days now since she had seen Uncle Josh and Auntie Alice had said that Daddy would be coming to join them, after all. But when?

Her small lip began to quiver. 'I want Desmond.'

'What?'

'Desmond, my hamster.'

'Oh, for God's sake!'

'I miss him. We should have brought him.'

'I'll get you another hamster. Soon.'

'I don't want another hamster.' The lip quivered harder and tears sprang from her eyes. 'I want Desmond.'

She had waited for Josh in the car, tucked away in the car park behind Peabody Green, ducking down if anybody walked past in case it was someone from the hospital who knew her. It wasn't Josh's work car; that would be too easy to trace. She had made him buy one, answering an ad in the paper and paying cash, giving a false name and address.

He would never have thought of that.

He had the money. He had plenty of money although he didn't like to spend it. He was a miser, a trait she particularly despised in men. They had all the power and most of the money and yet they were cheapskates.

She knew it might take time. Concepta had told her how Roger dozed off if he was having one of his bad days but today might not be such a day. Josh might have to go back tomorrow, and the next day. She could be patient. She had waited a long time for this revenge on Joanna and a few days made no difference.

They had been lucky.

Josh had rented the flat, also using his savings, again in a false name, so he had assured her: a cosy nest for the two of them and their little girl, or so he thought. She filled it with supplies, tins enough to last out a siege so she wouldn't have to go out. She thought she'd be safer there than on the move, on the run. They would be expecting her to run, even to leave the country, so she would bluff them by staying right here in Newbury.

True, the police would be looking for a man and a girl child, but somebody might recognise Emilia.

Monday lunchtime, once the three of them were safely installed in the flat, she went out to a call box on the other side of town to ring in sick.

She lavished love on the child all Monday afternoon, doting on her in front of Josh. In secret, she watched the little girl without feeling, with emptiness. She tried to see in her face the contours of her sister's, but there was nothing.

They had her in bed by seven, the two of them gazing down at her as she lay in her cot in the new pink pyjamas Josh had bought for her, smiling a little uncertainly. Josh read her a story, then placed a gentle kiss on her forehead, saying, 'Goodnight, Darling.'

'Sleep tight,' Alice trilled. 'Don't let the bedbugs bite.'

They ate bacon and beans and boiled

potatoes from a tin. Neither of them had learned to cook. The previous night, at his house, she had sent him out for a Chinese takeaway while she used a program she'd brought with her on floppy disc to clear the hard disc on his computer, erasing beyond retrieval any incriminating files he might once have had there.

She knew him for a fool, the sort of man who would leave a trail for the police, concocting some mawkish diary full of his love and his plans for the future.

They looked in on Emilia, like real parents, as they went to bed and she submitted to his embraces for the last time. There had been no real need to do that but it pleased her to snuff him out at the height of his pleasure. She had the hypo, ready primed, in the bedside drawer and as his groans reached their crescendo she stuck it into his thigh.

She had relished the startled look in his eyes as he felt the needle jam into his vein – she hadn't bothered with finesse, with sparing him pain – the clouding over as his mind lost control of his body in the space of ten or fifteen seconds.

She felt him go limp inside her and pushed him off in disgust, rolling him onto his back.

She straddled him, as she often had for his pleasure, placing her hands carefully on each side of his neck, pressing her thumbs into the arteries to stop the flow of oxygen to the brain. She had had customers in the Kennington years who liked to be half throttled during sex and she knew exactly when to stop; it was just that today there would be no stopping.

She could have used enough of the drug to kill him outright; she could have stifled him with a pillow; but this was the fulfilment of a long-held dream. His eyes were open and wide with panic. He was not unconscious; nor was he free of pain.

That was one of the best things about Thiopental – that it was not an analgesic, merely something that calmed or disabled a patient before the main anaesthetic was administered – and Salem felt every moment of his death. He knew what was happening to him but was powerless to prevent it, his arms not responding to the frantic commands of his brain, struggling to comprehend.

His fleshy Adam's apple bobbed between her thumbs. He was breathing hard at first, then his mouth opened and closed, grabbing at oxygen but not getting it into his lungs. Then he was not breathing at all and the only sound was her own gasps as a thrill of excitement that was almost sexual pulsed through her.

'Well, Josh,' she said softly, 'if you'd only

given me such pleasure while you were alive.'

She checked on Emilia who was sleeping soundly, helped by a very mild sedative in her suppertime orange juice, then made a quick but thorough reconnaissance outside. She had chosen an area of mostly young professionals, people who were at their desks by eight and in bed by midnight, people who treated their neighbours with indifference.

Returning to the body, she was struck by its resemblance to the corpse of Jonny Baird, lying in a hospital bed all those years ago, so small and damaged, yet invulnerable.

She realised with a flash of anger that Joshua had scored some sort of deranged victory over her by passing beyond pain or care.

'Bastard!'

She thwacked the body hard, pushing it to the floor and delivering a series of kicks to the head and abdomen and groin.

'Bastard!'

The car was parked immediately in front of the small block. Shortly before one o'clock she wrapped Josh's body in the bedspread, slung the bundle over her shoulder and stowed him in the boot.

Alice is strong, she thought.

She tossed a mental coin and drove south

on empty roads, beyond the town boundaries, till she came to a country lane bordered by fields, dead ending in woods.

Pulling up in a passing place by a stile, she humped the corpse over the gate, fetched the spade she'd picked up from a garden on Sunday morning when the householder had carelessly gone in for his elevenses, and dug as small a hole as she needed. It had taken an hour but no car had passed in that time and even the sheep ignored her.

With farmers operating a siege mentality, it could be weeks – months – before the body came to light.

If ever.

Alice used porn videos the way she used romantic fiction on the night shift: to pass the time and give her a good laugh. Even hardcore porn was about as realistic as the best efforts of Mills & Boon in its depiction of the relationship between men and women.

She'd acquired the taste in Kennington. Iqbal was her special friend in those days. He had found her in a cheap coffee bar off Piccadilly the afternoon of her arrival in London when she'd been wondering where she was going to sleep that night and what she was going to do. He'd struck up a conversation with her and listened with sympathy to her story, buying her more coffee, then a burger and fries. She was too young to drink alcohol in public but he'd had a bottle of vodka in his car and had urged her to help herself.

It was the real stuff – Polish – like an oily acid in her throat.

He'd been her saviour, offering her a place to live and a job, when so many runaways ended up on the streets with a sleeping bag and a whiny cur on a string. He came round on Fridays to collect the money she'd earned and spend a few minutes being nice to her. He had casually thrown a tape at her one day as he was leaving.

'Take a look at this, pretty baby. See what you think.'

She might have been disgusted or appalled. Instead she was intrigued and amused. When Iqbal suggested on his next visit that she might like to be a film star, since she was every bit as gorgeous as Michelle Pfeiffer, she had understood his meaning perfectly and accepted with eager grace.

The empty flats and derelict warehouses where filming took place had been cold, often deliberately so, the better to emphasise her nipples. Bored men stood around, incapable of anything but the most basic conversation, and so much the better. She had almost enjoyed herself and the presence of an audience had enhanced the fun.

At least the men were young and fit, not old and fat and gross like the ones who came to the flat.

They liked her and asked for her again and Iqbal had been pleased. She had been a film star for two years until, almost overnight, they'd said she was getting too old, that her face – or whatever part of her anatomy it was that interested the punters – was too familiar. It wasn't long after that that Iqbal had turfed her out of the flat, explaining that he specialised in 'chickens' – very young girls – and that she was past her use-by date.

She had gone quietly. She'd been half expecting it. It wasn't as if she hadn't seen other girls go the same way over the years and she knew Iqbal was lying when he told her she was special to him. She wasn't going to make a fool of herself, as some of them had done, wailing, 'but I thought you loved me,' as he threw their belongings into the street, flinging their arms round his neck, weeping and clinging, until he had to threaten them with his Alsatian, Ajax.

No, she had offered him her hand and he shook it in surprise. She asked him for a tenner for a taxi and he gave it to her. As she drove away, he called, 'Good luck, Al,' after her.

She examined her collection and slipped a cassette from its cover which bore the label,

337

'Nursing Training'. Naughty nurses, these, and night nurses. Not one of hers but quite good all the same.

She put it in the VCR and pressed the play button, fast forwarding till the film started. It was good quality – she was a connoisseur – not the grainy rubbish they sold you from under the counter in Soho, rip-off city. She watched the first few minutes with a small smile on her face, then turned to Emilia.

'Just watch this while I heat us up some beans, eh?'

Emilia, surprised by the film but not old enough to be disturbed by it, nodded. She had learned already that Auntie Alice didn't encourage redundant chatter. She snuggled down in the cushions of the sofa, put her thumb in her mouth, and watched the colours flash past.

The thumb-sucking had been a baby habit, discarded for the last year or so. The faint sensation that something was not quite right with her little world had sent her reaching for its tactile comfort these last three days.

Chapter 19

Megan watched without irritation as Gregory Summers paced up and down his office thinking, too absorbed in her own thoughts to care.

Philip had driven down the previous evening to collect Gareth, demurring at his travelling all the way to Newcastle by train on his own, especially in these days of unreliable service following the Hatfield derailment, dismissing her suggestion that she could put him on a plane. He had brushed aside her fulsome apologies.

'He'll be fine. It's almost the Easter hols and I'll give him a programme of reading that'll do him far more good than that national curriculum.'

They both knew that their son might be better off at boarding school in the circumstances but it was against both their principles and neither could be the first to suggest it, so it would hang in the air between them, forever unspoken.

Philip had kissed her chastely on the cheek on leaving and she'd felt wretched. He had always been supportive of her work, never reproached her when she seemed to put it before husband and child, and no word of censure passed his lips now.

Barbara was also watching Greg pace, sympathising. There was a helplessness in their position as they waited for a break.

Another break, she should say, since the car which Salem had bought for cash had been unearthed in a road in Stroud Green at noon that day when a resident had reported it as abandoned. It had been left there some time during Tuesday night, the retired accountant complained indignantly, and not moved since. It didn't belong to any of his neighbours and it had no business there.

'I rang the council yesterday,' he concluded, 'but do they take any notice? So I called the police.'

'So,' Greg said. 'That suggests that Alice disposed of Salem within a few hours of the abduction and buried his body that same night. Tuesday she firebombed his cottage, got rid of his mobile and dumped the car.'

'Ruthless,' Megan said, 'and she doesn't hang about.'

They were agreed that Alice Mason had not gone to ground in Stroud Green. 'It's a residential area,' Barbara explained to Megan. 'Crescents, Drives and Closes, single-family houses, all owner-occupied. People know each other, insofar as people

340

know each other at all in towns these days.'

'Alice would stick out like a sore thumb,' Greg concluded, unoriginally. 'She's somewhere else, not far away, assuming she walked back after dumping the car, in a rented flat or a rooming house, a B&B.'

'Rented flat,' Barbara said. 'She won't want anyone talking to Emilia or taking too much interest in them.'

'If she still has Emilia with her,' Megan said, silencing them.

'I think we must assume that they're still together,' Greg said eventually, since he didn't want to contemplate the alternative. The field at Halfacre Farm had been searched extensively, as had the neighbouring pastures, but there was no sign of a second grave, however small.

Every police officer in Newbury had a copy of the computer-generated image of Alice provided by Dr Peach, along with the information, belatedly recalled by the psychiatrist, that she had also been known to use the surname Baird. Greg and Barbara had drawn up a list of the most likely districts of town and every available man and woman had been dispatched to show the picture round to newsagents and grocers, to the proprietors of takeaway restaurants and video rental stores.

If Alice was still in Newbury then somebody, surely, must have caught a glimpse of her these last few days.

Meanwhile the car had been recovered from Stroud Green and was being examined. If it had been used to transport a dead body, then there would be proof of some kind, evidence, too, that Alice had been in there, as driver or passenger, proof that would be vital in a trial.

They had debated for half the afternoon the pros and cons of releasing Alice's name and picture to the press until Greg had finally decided against it. At all costs, she must not be panicked. So long as she didn't know that Salem's body had been found and that the police knew who she was, Emilia might yet be safe.

It was Friday and Susan Habib went home at five sharp on Fridays, switching the phone through to Greg's office as she departed. At 6.15 it rang and he answered it.

'Superintendent Summers.'

'Gregory.' A man's voice, youngish, suave. He didn't immediately recognise it but the owner swiftly identified himself. 'Adam Chaucer speaking.'

Gregory! As if they were friends when, if anything, they were deadly enemies. Chaucer worked for the local television news programme and they had clashed brutally during the Jordan Abbot investigation. He was a vain, ambitious, unscrupulous hack who cared nothing for the sensibilities of the

342

people who were his stories.

Greg said, 'What do you want?' and Megan looked in mild surprise at the belligerence in his tone. She raised her eyebrows at Barbara, who shrugged ignorance.

'I heard you found a dead body yesterday lunchtime–'

'Who told you that?'

'Now, now, Gregory. I have to protect my sources, as you know. My information is that it's a social worker named Joshua Salem and I thought you might like to comment.'

'No comment.' Greg went to hang up but Chaucer was speaking again.

'Only I have my main slot after the local news on Friday night in which I feature a big breaking story – well, I don't have to tell you; I'm sure you're an avid viewer – and I thought I'd cover the murder of this Salem bloke tonight. I'm told he abducted a child, one of his cases. Is that correct?'

It took Greg a moment to recover the use of his voice. 'You can't run this story, Chaucer.'

Barbara said, 'Oh!' as enlightenment dawned. She mouthed 'Journalist, complete pig' at the DCI.

'Oh?' Chaucer said, 'And there was me thinking it was a free country.'

'You might endanger the life of a child.'

'So it is true. All of it. And the girl is still missing. I thought so. Well, it'd have bee

nice if you'd agreed to co-operate, Gregory
– you could have taken part in the programme, telegenic chap like you – but watch
out for the story. Around 10.20 tonight.'

Greg was almost shouting. 'You can't use
it, man.'

'Public interest.'

'There's no public interest aspect.'

'You think the public aren't interested in a
missing toddler?' There was laughter in the
man's voice. 'Shame on you.'

'That's not the same thing as public
interest and you know it.'

'All right. I happen to think that there *is* a
public interest angle in the fact that a
member of Newbury Social Services apparently kidnapped a child that was supposed
to be under his care. Local people have a
right to know that their municipal
employees aren't suddenly going to run
amok in this way.'

'If you have an ounce of common decency
in you, Chaucer–'

He laughed. 'Oh, I think we both know
that I haven't. Any more than you have.
Which reminds me: how's that little daughter-in-law of yours? You had any further
thoughts about giving me an interview on
that?'

Greg slammed the receiver down. He was
breathing hard and the two women looked in
concern at how pale he had gone, his anger

the white heat of a fire that has burned beyond red.

'Adam Chaucer?' Barbara asked.

'He knows.'

'Bugger.'

'Did Deirdre Washowski blab?' Megan asked.

'I can't believe it,' Greg said, 'not Deirdre.'

'Nor do I,' Barbara said.

'Too many people knew,' Greg said, 'The Troys, the Fergussons, Barry Chitty, Digby Mercer, Mrs Halfacre. It could have leaked from any of them, maybe quite by accident.'

'Only I sometimes wonder if he doesn't have some sort of mole in the station,' Barbara said. 'This isn't the first time...'

One day Greg would have to look into that, one day when he hadn't got a child's life to save and only hours in which to do it. He had handled it badly. He felt a blazing hatred for Chaucer; if ever it was he who wound up dead in a ditch then Greg wouldn't be busting a gut to find the murderer.

Who was he kidding? – of course he would.

The phone rang again almost immediately. He took a deep breath and picked up the receiver. 'Look here,' he began in a more conciliatory tone. Even Adam Chaucer couldn't be beyond the reach of reason, surely.

'Mr Summers?' A woman's voice, husky

and quite sexy, he had heard it recently. 'It's Emma Bacon. We met on Wednesday when my son, Jack–'

'Yes, Mrs Bacon. What can I do for you?' He knew that he sounded brusque but now was not the time for her to pester him about selling his house.

She didn't seem to mind his tone, or even notice it. 'Only when I got back to the office yesterday and was telling the troops about the boys' little adventure, one of them mentioned that your people had been on to us just the day before, asking about holiday lets that we might have handled – Lake District, Cornwall, that sort of thing.'

'Yes, we contacted all letting agencies.'

'My people told your constable, quite correctly, that we don't deal with that sort of thing. Only, having met you like that and you being so kind to Jack and Tim, I wanted to do anything I could to help, so I told them to double-check the sort of lettings that we do handle – assured shortholds, six months minimum – just on the off-chance.'

She had Greg's full attention now.

'And, to cut a long story short, Dennis Harris has just come to tell me that we did a letting in the name of Salem less than a month ago. Here, in Newbury.'

'Hold on!' Greg put the phone on speaker and signalled to Barbara, miming pen and paper. 'Where!'

'It's in Halifax Road, number five Per-
simmon Court.' Barbara scribbled frantically.
'Only thing is, it was in the name of G.
Salem, not J. Salem.'

'Grace!' Megan exclaimed. 'His mother's
name.'

'Did your employee see the tenant?' Greg
asked.

'He's a bit vague – I sometimes think he
only notices the pretty girls. He remembers
that it was a youngish man who said the
tenancy was for his elderly mother. As she
was retired we couldn't take up employer
references but we did get some from her
bank.'

'She's not been dead that long,' Megan
said. 'I bet he never closed her bank
account.'

'Is that any help?' Emma asked.

'Mrs Bacon... I feel almost inclined to let
you sell my house out of sheer gratitude.'

She laughed. 'I shall hold you to that.
Goodbye ... for now.'

They hung up. Greg said, 'Persimmon
Court? I don't know it.'

'It's a new block of flats,' Barbara said,
'singles and childless couples, expensive, all
mod cons.'

Greg's mouth felt dry. 'Is this it?'

'I think so.'

'Barbara, help me round up every available
man. Megan, get on to HQ at Kidlington.

347

Tell them I want a hostage negotiator. If Chaucer goes ahead with his story then Mason will know very soon that we've found Salem's body If it comes to that then Emilia will make the perfect hostage.'

He strode towards the door. 'Give him the address and tell him to meet us there. We've got less than four hours before Chaucer splashes Joshua Salem's murder all over the television news.'

It was quiet for a Friday, Alice thought. She had watched all her videos and had no desire for live television which would give her a link to the outside world. She had rejected that world as it had rejected her; she would remove Emilia from that world, too, into another and more deadly dimension.

She thought, Alice is bored.

She went to the bedroom window and drew the curtain back cautiously on a cold, clear twilight. Rush hour was over and the stream of passing cars was steady, heading both in and out of town. Street lamps flickered on, one by one, ochre, then yellow, then white. There were no pedestrians.

Emilia, half drowsing on the sofa, roused herself and asked for food. Auntie Alice could get cross, she thought, but Auntie Alice is hungry too.

She went into the kitchen and opened another tin of beans. She poured them into a mug and put it in the microwave. She took two slices of white bread from the freezer and put them in the toaster. While she waited she lit a cigarette. She had forty packets in a cardboard box with the rest of the supplies, enough to last her a month.

Alice thinks of everything, she thought.

The toast popped up, startling her. It was pale on one side, blackened on the other. She took two plates from the sink, still with the crumbs and tomato smears of lunch, and served supper.

There had been other possible routes for her revenge on Joanna. When she had first heard the full story of her marriage and death she had toyed with the idea of taking her place, of becoming the perfect Joanna by marrying Roger Troy. It was what everybody had asked of her as a child, after all: that she should be more like Joanna, that she should be a facsimile of her, her shadow.

But she soon discovered that Roger Troy was no longer much of a catch. The fine young man with the hopeful future, the brilliant scientist who might one day win the Nobel prize; both were gone forever.

Besides, what glory was there in taking a man away from a woman like Concepta? It would be easy, baby-candy-takingly easy.

Where was the triumph in that?

She stroked her finger along Emilia's

plump cheek.

'You're a pretty little thing,' she said.

The child, baffled by her aunt's constant changes of mood, dared no reply.

Hole up here for a month, Alice thought, then head for London. She knew plenty of places where she could get a good price for the girl.

'How would you like to be a film star?' she asked dreamily.

She had ventured out of the flat only once since burying Josh's body, on Tuesday night. She had waited till darkness fell and used the same mild sedative which would keep Emilia sleeping during her absence. Dressed in black from head to toe she had disposed of Salem's mobile phone on the ring road, then left the car in a dark corner of the Kennet car park and made her way on foot to Peabody Green.

A glass bottle, some petrol, a wad of cotton wool: that was all it took. It had been the work of a minute on the deserted footpath, before she sprinted away towards the grounds of the Kennet. She knew that the hateful chintzes would catch and burn, flaring up in a cloud of fumes to lick curtains and ceilings.

Alice is destroying evidence, she told herself, but she knew that the real object of destruction was all that remained of Joshua Salem.

Around midnight she had ventured out again and dumped the car in a suburban close on the southern fringes of Newbury. That had meant a walk back of about two miles, nothing to Alice who had often walked the hard pavements of London for days at a time: restlessly pacing through fancy streets and rough ones; past shops where women spent twenty thousand pounds on a dress and Oxfam where they paid a pound; glancing through the windows of happy family houses with pianos and paintings, and derelict buildings where men slept rough.

'It's getting dark,' Greg said, as his car sped through the Friday-night streets of Newbury. It had been a drizzly day and, although it had dried up now, there was no sunlight to linger and eke out the day. In residential streets householders were drawing their curtains. On the pavements of the town centre younger people were heading purposefully for pubs and restaurants before moving on to clubs.

He had Megan beside him. Barbara had taken a detour via Bacon, Travis, Maxton to acquire a spare key and was following in her own car. In theory they could walk straight in and take Alice, but she had shown that she wouldn't hesitate to kill and it was the work of a moment to stifle a three-year-old girl or cut her throat. The sound of their key in the lock might be enough.

'She may have bolted the door on the inside,' Megan pointed out.

Greg's mobile rang. He didn't stop but reached for it in the inside pocket of his jacket and handed it to Megan who answered it. 'The hostage negotiator is on his way,' she reported, 'but he won't be here for at least an hour.'

'No, well we don't need him till Chaucer's piece has gone out. If it turns into a siege then it can easily escalate out of control. We've got a couple of hours' grace while Mason doesn't know that we know Salem is dead. Even then, she won't know that we know her whereabouts. With luck, she'll be relaxing, letting down her guard.'

Greg had spent the last hour and a half mobilising the considerable resources of the Newbury police and had set up a surveillance van on the street. Halifax Road was half a mile long, mostly blocks of flats of every vintage from Edwardian to last week. He slowed down, not sure which one was Persimmon Court, but then he spotted the nondescript white van.

Andy Whittaker, dressed in overalls, had taken up a manhole cover and was pretending to examine the cavity beneath, while Nicolaides hefted a tool box onto the pavement then paused to swig some red liquid from a plastic bottle, glancing casually about him as he did so.

Greg drew round the nearest corner and parked, switching off his lights. He had a good view of the back of the building from here: it was a modern block, five storeys high with two flats to each floor, each running the full depth of the building. There was a locked street door but no porterage. Each flat had a narrow, wrought iron balcony overlooking the functional gardens and a fire escape was accessible from each one.

He rang Andy's mobile. 'That was quick work. Which flat is it?'

'Second floor, on the right as you face the building.'

'I'll be with you in a minute.'

He took out his binoculars and trained them on the flat identified, the second-floor left from his point of view. Either the french door that led onto the balcony was uncurtained or Alice Mason had not yet bothered to draw them. Light spilled out onto the space, delineating a ferny plant in an oversized pot, drooping for lack of care, a round metal table and two matching chairs, both heavy with raindrops. He could see part of the wall inside and a splash of ceiling, painted cream, what looked like a teak wall unit, shelves and cupboards, empty.

A possible point of entry, he thought, but

the glass would be toughened in a new flat like that. Not that they couldn't break in if they had to, but they would lose the crucial seconds that might save a child's life.

A few feet to the left of the french door was a window shaded by a blind with a scalloped edge, an inch or two short of being fully pulled down. Kitchen, he thought, in darkness. She was in the living room – he was certain of it – with Emilia, watching TV.

So near and yet beyond his reach.

Alice stared at the phone in horror as it began to trill, its rhythmic double pulse shatteringly loud in the room.

'Nobody knows Alice is here,' she muttered.

Emilia looked at the slim cream-coloured handset, then back at her aunt. She knew that when phones rang people leaped to answer them.

Even Alice found a ringing telephone hard to ignore. She picked up the cordless receiver, examined it and pressed a button with the word YES written on it.

She took her cue and said tonelessly, 'Yes?'

'Mrs Hutton?' A woman's voice, oozing niceness.

'No. No Mrs Hutton here.'

She went to hang up but the woman was

already speaking again. Alice could hear the rustle of paper, a script.

'This is Maureen from Berkshire Kitchens in Reading. We're looking for three flats in your area where we can display our new range of–'

'Sodoffsodoffsodoffsodoffsodoff.'

Alice slammed the receiver down. Then she picked it up again to press the NO button. She could hear the woman's twittering like a distant bird.

'Half price... Special offer...'

She ripped the phone jack out of its socket and slumped into the nearest armchair, breathing deeply. She was sweating, the wool of her grey jersey damp and clammy under her arms. She went back into the bedroom, showered and changed into her nurse's uniform. She found it calming, almost as if she were, in truth, a nurse and a custodian of people's sanity.

She hadn't changed the sheets since Monday night and the room smelled of Josh, of a cheap cologne that he affected.

She felt suddenly sick.

'All right, Maureen?' Greg said to Barbara.

'It's got to be her. You heard her reaction.'

'I heard a woman who's fed up of being disturbed by telephone salesmen when she's watching *Brookside*.'

'She was hysterical.'

'Yes,' Greg said soberly, 'and that's not good.'

They were all in the surveillance van now, crammed in the rear with their equipment, hot despite the unseasonable cold.

'She may not even answer the phone if we ring again,' Megan said. 'We may have cut off our sole point of contact.'

The back door of the van opened and Andy Whittaker climbed in. He had entered Persimmon Court and listened at the door of flat five, any noise he might make covered by the distraction of the phone call.

Greg merely looked at him and cocked his head.

'Two locks,' Andy said, 'latch and mortice. We have keys to both of those but the mortice has a key in it on the inside, so our key won't work, or not in any sort of hurry.'

'Chains? Bolts?'

'Impossible to say. Stout, solid door, fireproof, conforming to modern building regulations.'

Damn those modern building regulations, Greg thought.

'So what now?' Barbara said.

Greg looked at his watch. It was half-past eight. He had less than two hours and it was time for his brain to work overtime. He sat in silence for a few minutes, holding up his hand to stop any member of his team who tried to speak. He could not afford to lose his train of thought.

'We'll trick her out,' he said at last. 'A simple piece of subterfuge. Find me a number for the gas board.'

Forty minutes later a group of cross-looking people were gathering in the car park at the front of Persimmon Court as two vans from the local gas board waited ominously at the entrance.

'I can't smell anything,' one man complained, stamping and flapping his arms against the cold. 'Who reported this gas leak, anyway?'

'One of your neighbours, sir,' Greg said blandly.

'Well, shouldn't we get ... I dunno–' He gestured in no particular direction. '–out of the vicinity altogether. I mean, if there's going to be an explosion...'

'With luck, there'll be no explosion,' Greg said, 'and I agree that you should all remove to a safe distance, just as soon as we're sure we've vacated all the flats. If you have friends or family nearby you might like to go there, otherwise the gas board has made arrangements with the Ramada hotel up by the motorway.'

'Oh, no,' the man said firmly. 'If my home's going up in flames then I want to be here when it happens.'

357

'You own your flat, Mr...'

'Rigsby. Yes. Number four.'

'Not a tenant?'

'No.'

'So, do you know the other residents?'

'Mostly.' He glanced round, pointing. 'Mary Renwick from number one. Mr and Mrs Cheeseby from number eight. The blonde woman from number seven.'

'What about flat five?'

Rigsby thought about it. 'That's a buy-to-let, mostly short lets, six months, a year. It was empty last I knew but someone may have moved in in the past week or so. I've been away.'

Alice, disturbed by the bubbling up of noise from outside, went into the bedroom and pushed back the curtain, forming a gap an inch wide through which she could peer. Then she lifted it higher and scrutinised the scene below, baffled and suspicious. Why were half the occupants of the building gathered in the car park at this time of night? Why were they milling around, talking to each other in that un-English way, laughing in a release of tension.

It looked like a fire drill.

As she thought this a siren became audible and a fire engine drew up on the road, stopping alongside the ambulance and two marked police cars that she'd just noticed.

As she spotted the gas vans, she heard a gentle but insistent knocking at the front door and spun round on her heel.

She looked back out of the window, then at the front door, at a loss. Emilia's piping voice called, 'Auntie Alice?'

'Quiet.' She sidled up to the door. 'Yes? What is it?'

'Gas board, madam.' A man's voice, Berkshire accent, working class, reassuring. 'We have a suspected leak in this building. I'm afraid I'm going to have to ask you to evacuate while we investigate the source.'

'It's ... not convenient.'

'I'm sorry, madam, but I must insist. We do have the authority to make a forcible entry if we deem it necessary.'

Alice took a deep breath, collecting herself like an actress preparing for her big scene. 'Just a minute.'

Standing on the landing, out of the sightline of the door, Greg heard two bolts being drawn back.

Their keys would have been useless.

He tensed himself as he heard the lock released from the inside. The gas board official, better known at Newbury police station as DC Andy Whittaker, stood in his hard hat and fluorescent jacket with a bland look – not quite a smile – that gave nothing away. He would be the first thing the woman saw when she opened the door and he wasn't about to scare her back into the flat.

Barbara and Megan were behind Greg. On the other side of the door, he had Nicolaides and two uniformed men waiting, pressed against the wall.

The latch turned and the door opened a couple of inches, catching against the extent of a stout security chain.

A good-looking boy, Alice thought, if you liked that sort of thing. Late twenties, tall, obviously took care of himself, stayed in shape. She smoothed down her hair and was glad that she'd put her uniform on.

It's her, Andy thought. No doubt about it. Behind his back he raised his thumbs to his colleagues. 'Awfully sorry about this, madam,' he said, 'but you can't be too careful with gas.'

'Yes. I mean, no. One second.' The door shut and they heard the rattle of the chain being removed. She opened the door wider now so that he would see she was a nurse. 'I'm sorry if I don't seem quite on the ball but I've been asleep. On the night shift, you see. Bit groggy.'

'If we could just have you out of the building for a while. Please don't use the lift.' She could hear footsteps on the stairs at the end of the corridor, people making their way swiftly down, not panicking.

The gasman said, 'Is it just yourself?'

Her mind had been turning over frantically. 'Yes,' she said, 'I live alone.' Let the brat stay here, however real the danger.

'I don't want to hurry you, miss,' Andy said, and Greg could hear an edge of tension creeping into his voice.

'Can I just get–'

'Your keys and maybe your handbag, love. Grab a warm coat, if you've got one. Have to leave the rest, I'm afraid.'

She turned away towards the hall stand where her jacket lay, her wallet and keys in the pocket. For a few seconds, she had her back to the door and to Andy. He took one swift step forward, flinging the door wide, grabbed her by both arms and dragged her bodily out into the corridor.

He said, 'Alice Mason, I'm arresting you on suspicion of murder and child abduction–'

Alice was struggling and writhing as he completed the caution, trying to bite and kick him. Nicolaides joined in restraining her, producing a pair of handcuffs which he snapped on, anchoring her hands behind her back. As she continued to kick they forced her face-down on the floor, not bothering to be gentle, and Nicolaides pressed his full weight down on her flailing legs and feet.

She raised her head and began to scream.

'No! No! No! No!'

Inside the flat, Emilia whimpered. 'Auntie Alice?'

Her distress led them straight to her. Megan, the only mother present, swept the little girl up in her arms and hugged her. 'It's all right, Emilia.' She pressed her lips to the child's soft hair. 'It's okay, sweetheart. Everything's okay.'

Greg said, 'Thank God!'

He turned and stared at the flickering images on the television, curiosity turning to rapid disbelief. The nature of his work made him familiar with pornography but this sickened even him. He stepped forward and snapped the set off, ejected the cassette, ripped out the tape and slowly shredded it.

And he didn't care if he was destroying evidence.

As Megan comforted the child, Greg took out his mobile phone and dialled. 'It's Superintendent Summers. I want a SOCO team to flat five, Persimmon Court, Halifax Road, as soon as possible. Yes, Halifax, corner of Beverley Road. Okay. Thanks.'

Nicolaides came into the flat. 'Andy's taking the prisoner back to the station, sir,' he said.

'Okay. I'd like you to stay here, George, and organise SOCO. They're on their way.'

'Sir.'

Greg glanced at his watch – quarter to ten

– and dialled again. A female voice answered at once, young and with the rising inflection, apparently caused by watching too many Australian soaps, which turned every statement into a question. 'Newbury News Round? This is Kirsten speaking? How can I help you?'

'I want to speak to Adam Chaucer.'

'Mr Chaucer is preparing for his slot? He can't be disturbed at the moment? If you'd like to ring back after his programme...?'

'No, just give him a message. Tell him Superintendent Summers called. Tell him publish and be damned.'

'Pardon?'

He hung up.

Emilia had been sniffling into Megan's shoulder for a few minutes. Now she raised her head, summoned up her considerable courage and said, 'I'd like to go home please.'

As they carried the child downstairs, a short, plump man with a mass of grey hair bustled up to them.

'Superintendent Summers? I'm Dr Robin Kilkenny, the hostage negotiator. Sorry I took so long. Traffic was terrible on the A34.'

Chapter 20

'She's fine,' the doctor said. 'She's not been sleeping too well and she seems to have been living on tinned beans, by her own account. She's tired and pale but nothing that a few days rest, fresh air and healthy food won't put right. I'd like to keep her in for twenty-four hours for observation but then she can go home.'

'And ... any sign of abuse?'

'None,' the doctor said firmly. 'Either physical or sexual.'

'Should she see a psychologist?'

The doctor shook his head. 'I wouldn't, personally. She's young enough to forget the whole thing in a few days. She doesn't even understand that she was kidnapped – as far as she's concerned she's been staying with her auntie for a few days to give Mummy and Daddy a rest – so why make a trauma out of it?'

Greg briefly described the video that had been playing in the little girl's line of vision as he'd entered the flat. He spared no details. The doctor winced but stood firm. 'She won't have understood it and she'll have forgotten she ever saw it by next week.'

Barbara came into the ward at that moment, closely followed by the Troys. Greg had sent her to fetch them the moment they had Emilia safe.

'Where is she?' Concepta said.

Greg pointed into the private room behind him and both parents went in without further ado. He heard Emilia exclaim, 'Daddy!' then, with equal gusto, 'Mummy!'

'Can I leave this in your capable hands?' he asked Barbara.

'Yes, sir.'

'Don't worry,' the doctor said, 'we'll rig up camp beds for the parents overnight. We're used to it.'

'Come on then,' Greg said to Megan, 'let's do this.'

They drove back to the station in silence, but the doctor who had examined Alice on her arrival – not Tessa MacDonald who was still recuperating, but her locum – would not allow them to interview her that evening and they both went home to bed, a little relieved, arranging to meet for this necessary ordeal first thing in the morning.

Poor, pathetic Alice, Greg thought. Who knew what she had suffered during the years since she had so foolishly left the protection of her parents' home? Most runaways came back in a few weeks, persuaded of how much muddier the grass was the other side of the fence. Their parents were so relieved by their safe return that they usually found a compromise, a *modus vivendi*.

But for the ones who did not come back, the boys as well as the girls, an early death was often the least of the horrors they faced.

He got her a lawyer, although she hadn't asked for one. She hadn't spoken at all, according to the overnight custody sergeant, nor had she eaten any of the meals offered her.

The solicitor on call was a recent recruit to the job, a tall, gangly youth in a too-new suit, with a loud tie knotted beneath his prominent Adam's apple. He looked uncomfortable, as if he wished he were round the other side of the table, squashed safely between the two police officers, rather than seated next to the silent and immobile figure of his client. Every time he swallowed – and that was often – his Adam's apple bobbed up and down like a cork on the sea.

Greg repeated the caution Andy had given her the night before and reminded her of the two counts on which she was being questioned.

'You have been arrested on suspicion of the murder of Joshua Salem and the abduction and unlawful detention of Emilia Troy. Would you please confirm your name for the tape recorder. You are

Alice Louise Mason?'

She turned her cool blue eyes on him without replying. He realised with a shock that she was a pretty woman with her blonde hair and her soft, fair skin, her trim figure, her wide mouth. He thought he saw a flash of amusement pass through her eyes as she noted his reaction. She bared her teeth at him in what might have been a smile or a snarl.

'Miss Mason?' he said.

'Alice is here but she cannot speak to you.'

Her voice was deeper than he had expected and the room seemed to turn cold as if they were at a seance and a spirit voice was speaking through her teasing lips.

He said, 'Cannot or will not?'

She merely repeated her answer.

'Did you know Joshua Salem?'

'Alice is here–'

'But she cannot speak to me. Yes, I heard you the first time but I can be stubborn too, Miss Mason. Did you know Joshua Salem?'

They sat in total silence for what seemed like an hour but was probably two or three minutes, the two tapes in the recorder churning relentlessly on, recording nothing. Then Alice spoke again.

'Alice has known many men.' Her lip curled in contempt. 'Men are all the same.'

Greg leaned back in his chair and crossed

his arms, perplexed. Before suspects had lost the right to silence it had been common to sit in this room and hear nothing but 'no comment', but this – this third-person distancing, these vague generalisations – was beyond his experience. She made him feel dirty. Her eyes said that he could hide from her none of the baseness of his animal nature. He licked his dry lips and glanced at Megan but she seemed no more able to deal with the suspect than he was.

'We'll take a break,' he said and they both left the room. Greg was not surprised to find the solicitor hard on their heels.

'Don't leave me alone in there with her,' he begged in an urgent whisper. Greg nodded to the uniformed officer in the corridor to go in and keep an eye on the prisoner.

He took Megan to one side. 'Is she faking it?'

'I don't think so.'

'Nor do I.'

Greg pondered. Normally he would have had her admitted to Edith Austin Ward for assessment but that was clearly impossible. He would have to arrange for her to go to another psychiatric facility in another town and that was likely to take all day.

Although Broadmoor wasn't far from here.

Meanwhile, if he wanted to hang on to her beyond the evening, he would have to charge her with something, and once he'd charged her he would be unable to question her further about that crime. The thought of not having to be alone in a room with those icy eyes was a welcome one. Not that he would be alone, he reminded himself; it just felt that way.

Sergeant Dick Maybey accosted him at that moment, unexpectedly looming along the corridor. 'Excuse me, sir. Dee Washowski's here, says to tell you Dr Troy called her first thing and asked if she'd represent his sister-in-law. Does that make any sense?'

'Yes,' Greg said. From what he had seen of Roger Troy's noble nature it made perfect sense. 'Bring her through.'

Deirdre Washowski sailed up to them a moment later, wearing what appeared to be a velvet gown in purple and gold. She ran a sardonic eye over the young solicitor. 'Sorry to steal your client, Adrian.'

'Oh!' The young man had finally grasped what was happening. His Adam's apple did a grateful little dance. 'You're very welcome, Ms Washowski. See you.'

And he was gone.

'What's the matter with him?' Deirdre wondered aloud.

'Bad hangover?' Greg suggested guilelessly. 'Now. Alice Mason. What charges is she facing?'

'She's been arrested on suspicion of the

murder of Joshua Salem and the kidnapping and unlawful detention of Emilia Troy.'

'Then I'd like a few words alone with her.'

Greg gestured to the door of the interview room. 'Be my guest.'

Deirdre went in and the young constable immediately came out, pulling an eloquent face. 'Bet you a tenner she's in there less than five minutes,' Megan murmured.

'Deirdre's made of stern stuff. You're on.'

They both stood staring at the second hands of their watches. After four and a half minutes the door opened and the solicitor came out. Greg tutted with annoyance and nodded to the constable who sighed, braced himself and went back in.

'It's not often I find myself at a loss,' Deirdre admitted. 'I think she needs psychiatric assessment.'

'I couldn't agree more,' Greg said. 'All right, here's a plan. We charge her with the abduction. That's pretty incontrovertible since she was taken red-handed with the little girl without her parents' knowledge or consent. Then we put her up before the magistrates this afternoon and get her remanded in custody for psychiatric reports. That way we can question her about the murder at a later date.'

'She's not exactly going to impress the magistrates,' Megan agreed.

'Can I rely on you not to argue for bail, Deirdre?'

'It goes against the grain ... but, yes, I think it's in my client's best interest in this case. Give me a call on my mobile when you're ready and I'll meet you in court.'

She made to leave but Greg detained her with a hand on her velvet arm. 'Dee, you know I asked you to keep the fact that we'd found Salem's body under your hat?'

'Which I did.'

'Okay.'

She gave him a brief, questioning look, and was gone.

'You believe her?' Megan asked.

'Implicitly. Now, I wonder if we'll ever get anything useful out of Alice about the murder.'

'We have plenty of evidence against her,' Megan pointed out. 'Her prints are on the car Salem bought. There's forensic to prove that his body was in the boot. She had access to the drug he was sedated with and SOCO have found another phial of it at Persimmon Court.'

She was right, Greg thought. They hardly needed an admission of guilt and he already had the feeling that she would not be found fit to stand trial.

'Can I leave you to deal with the paper-work, Megan, charge her, get her remande and find her a place in a secure unit.'

'Yes, sir.' Greg turned away and she cleared her throat. 'Ahem, aren't we forgetting something?'

'Sorry!' He took a ten pound note from his wallet and gave it to her. 'I pay my debts.'

'Pleasure doing business with you, sir. You off home?'

'Not yet. I want to pop back to the hospital to see how the Troys are getting on.' He felt guilty and ashamed of his own hostility to Concepta, prompted by nothing but her plainness and her lack of charm.

Emilia's joyful, welcoming 'Mummy!' still echoed in his brain.

He wished them luck. He liked to envisage Roger Troy solving the problem of cold fusion and becoming a billionaire overnight, moving his wife and daughter to a beautiful house in the country, knighted by the Queen and honoured by the Nobel committee.

But he wasn't holding his breath.

Megan went methodically about her tasks. It was Saturday but she had nothing to rush home for, a single mother without her child. By the time she had got Alice remanded and transferred to a hospital in Oxford it was 3pm and she was wondering what to do with the rest of the day.

Damn! She had promised to go shopping 'th her mother for Tim and Pat's golden wedding party tonight. She rang her parents' number and Matilda answered, swiftly dismissing Megan's apologies and explanations.

'It's not worth getting anything new, darling. I'll wear my blue. And my pearls. Be the belle of the ball.'

'Have a great time,' Megan said, 'and ring me tomorrow. Tell me all about it.'

'I'll try.'

Roger and Concepta got off the bus a few hours later and walked into the Peabody Estate with Emilia between them, holding both their hands. Superintendent Summers had offered them a lift but they preferred to take the bus. It was a fine evening and shafts of late sunlight lit up the houses and flats, making them beautiful.

As they reached the Green, Digby Mercer was sitting outside his cottage in a striped deckchair, nursing a gin and tonic. He waved to them. They waved back, their eyes sliding across the boarded-up front of Josh Salem's cottage, refusing to see it.

They had no room to pity him.

Emilia had been unusually silent and they were concerned as to how traumatised she had been by her ordeal, but as Beaumont House came in sight she yelled, 'Home! Home. DESMOND!' and, loosing their hands, ran laughing away across the lush grass which was overdue for the first cut of the year.

'Superintendent Summers told me you tried to confess to murdering Salem in order to protect me,' Roger said as they followed at a more sedate pace. 'Now why would you do a stupid thing like that?' She didn't answer and he pursued the matter. 'Did you think that I had harmed Millie?'

'Of course not!'

'Then I can make no sense of it, dear girl.'

'I just wanted them to let you go,' she muttered. 'I thought being locked up in a police cell might be too much for you.'

'Foolish woman!' He shook his head. 'What are we to do with you? Why are you so determined to keep me a sad invalid when I'm getting better every day? I'll be able to look for a job before long. I'm sure of it.'

'What about the search for the Holy Grail?'

'I can work on that too, in my spare time. Are you afraid that if I don't *need* you any more then I won't *want* you any more?' She hung her head, not answering. '...Concepta? Look at me.'

She seemed unable to comply and he put his arm round her. 'I've been thinking about what you were saying a few months ago.'

'What?' she sniffed.

'About having a baby of our own, a little

374

brother or sister for Emilia.'

She stopped stock still.

A moment later, Digby Mercer picked up his G&T and escaped into his cottage, his face pink with embarrassment.

It was a bizarre sight: a plain, shapeless woman, standing in the middle of Peabody Green, unashamedly weeping.

Chapter 21

Angie was wearing a pair of very short shorts with braces over a cropped top and Greg wanted to tell her that she'd catch her death. Her bare legs ended in trainers and she'd dyed her hair bright red and clipped it into bunches. Apparently she was a character called Misty from Pokémon. She should have looked stupid but Greg found the outfit oddly arousing.

Cracking legs, he thought.

Fancy dress was definitely for the young. What were you supposed to go as when you were pushing fifty? The Emperor Tiberius? Henry the Eighth? How come all the famous old people in history were monsters?

Because the good died young, obviously.

Del picked her up at 9.30, also dressed as a Pokémon character named Gary, as he explained, or rather Gawy, since his speech impediment seemed to be worsening. He wore a blue tunic over lighter blue trousers ending in ski boots. A pendant hung round his neck and he'd also dyed his hair red and gelled it into spikes.

Now, he did look stupid, Greg thought spitefully, although he'd at least made sure he'd be warm enough.

They looked at each other warily, then Greg decided on joviality. 'Lucky, things worked out in time for your party.'

'Yes.' Del visibly relaxed. 'Emilia is safely home and Annie's decided to put the past behind her and make a fwesh start in the States. So evewyone's fine.'

Except Joshua Salem and Alice Mason, Greg thought, and nobody cared about them; they'd been alone in the world. A shiver ran down his spine because Angie was all that kept him from being alone in the world.

'Even better,' Del added, 'they can't decide whether to sell the house or went it out so I'm going to stay there housesitting for the foreseeable.'

Greg had a mental image of Del putting off would-be buyers or tenants with tales of dwy wot, wising damp and the ghost in the chimney bweast. The Fergussons must be out of their minds.

'Good,' he said. 'Well.'

He wanted to add, 'Wun along now.'

Del took the hint. He was, as on his previous visit, very polite. 'Don't wowwy, Mr Summers. I'll take good care of Ange.'

'No drinking and driving – and that goes for dope too.'

'No, sir!'

As they were leaving they met Piers Hamilton on the doorstep, wielding a bottle of Chianti. He looked Angie up and down in the porch light and whistled. 'Misty from Pokémon, right? Almost enough to turn me straight.'

'See you, Piers.' She gave him a smacking kiss on the cheek and wagged her finger at him. 'Don't get Greg into mischief.'

'Spoilsport,' he yelled after her as the two youngsters scampered off to Del's car singing, 'I'll teach you and you'll teach me, Po-ké-mon!'

Piers let himself in, shut the door behind him and handed the wine to Greg who was standing gloomily in the hall, a half-drunk glass in his hand. He looked affectionately at his young friend whose handsome features were hardly marred by the faint scar above his lip, the only testament to a savage beating he had taken the previous summer.

'You know your outside painting needs doing?' Piers remarked.

'You offering?'

'No, but I'll take a photo of it for you.'

'That's a great help.'

'We eating?' Piers asked.

'I've phoned out for pizza. Should be here in half an hour.'

'Pudding?'

'Mississippi mud pie,' Greg said proudly.

'Ooh, you know how to spoil a boy! Who's Angie's friend?'

'Kid from college.'

'That's a flash car he's got there.'

'He's rich.'

'That *is* annoying. Well look on the bright side. They could be going dressed as Tinky Winky and Dipsy.'

'I'm sure I didn't watch kids' TV when I was that age,' Greg grumbled.

'No? Never rushed home from the sixth form to catch *The Magic Roundabout?* "Bed, said Zebedee." Boing!'

'Now you come to mention it...'

'*Plus ça change.*'

Greg led the way into the kitchen where a bottle of claret stood already open, a third missing. He topped up his own glass and filled one for Piers. 'Thanks for coming over.'

'You all right, mate? You seem a bit down.'

'I don't like the way that boy talks to me,' Greg blurted out.

'Not sufficiently respectful to the great panjandrum?'

'On the contrary! He talks to me as if I

were Angie's father – *Sir*, this and *Mr Summers* that – and I can't help wondering if she's actually told him that we're living together, that I'm her *partner*, or if he thinks I'm some elderly relative.'

'Mmm.' Piers took a long sip of his wine.

'Maybe she's embarrassed, Piers, ashamed of being shacked up with an old geezer like me.'

'Well, you've still got all your own teeth.'

'They all *belong* to me legally,' Greg agreed, 'but I had to buy three of them from the dentist. Not cheap either.'

'Look, Greg, one thing that struck me about Angie, first time I met her, was how grown-up she was, how mature.'

'Which is why she's now dressed as a cartoon character? A *Japanese* cartoon character.'

'Keeping in touch with her inner child, *Sensei.*'

'But most of her classmates haven't yet hit twenty. I'm older than their parents. And it's all a bit sordid. She's my daughter-in-law.'

'From what I know of the younger generation, they would not give it a second thought. I think you fret about it far more than anybody else does.'

But Greg could picture it, the first weeks of term at Reading the previous autumn, as the young people got to know each other, exchanged personal details, hopes and dreams. Angelica hesitating when she was asked about her home situation, then finding that the moment to tell the truth had passed.

He realised that Piers had said something. 'Sorry?'

'I said, Have you asked her?'

'Er, no.'

'Duh!'

It was gone midnight by the time Piers left, and no sign of Angie. He undressed, bathed and cleaned his teeth with unaccustomed slowness, then slipped into bed, leaving the door open, the better to hear her return. He assumed that he wouldn't sleep, lying with one ear cocked for the noise of a car outside, the inconsiderate slamming of its doors, but was dozing almost at once.

A rough tongue licking his face wakened him and he reached out in the darkness to encounter, not Angie's soft skin, as he might have hoped, but a furry pelt. He realised that the mouth that was licking him was not as fresh as he expected Angie's to be, even after a hard night's partying. Nor did she tend to snort like that. Nor did she have a beard.

He clicked on the light.

'Bellini, you know you're not allowed on the bed.'

The dog panted and snuggled into his

neck, one paw across his upper arm. He sighed, switched the light off again and settled down, soothed by her warmth. When he woke again a few minutes later, she had gone.

Typical woman, he thought.

He woke up for the third time when Angie slipped into bed beside him, her naked body slightly cold next to one that had been rolled up in a duvet for a good two hours.

'What time is it?' he grunted.

'Gone two. Go back to sleep.'

'Ugh!' He turned over and stared at the readout on his radio-alarm: 2:33.

'I'd have been home ages ago,' Angie whispered, 'but there was one hell of a smash on the Bath Road just the other side of Froxfield.'

He whispered back, 'Yeah?'

'Yeah.' She shuddered. 'Don't see how anybody could have survived it.'

'Why are we whispering?'

'I have no idea.'

In a normal voice, he asked, 'How many cars?'

'Only one that I could make out but it was pulverised. Oh, and there was a lorry but I couldn't see any damage on that. All your lot were there: three uniform cars, ambulance, fire engine.' Greg could picture the scene: the blue lights flashing silently, the sombre faces. 'The road was completely blocked for

381

a time,' Angie went on, 'so even though it was the middle of the night there was quite a hold up.'

He was no longer sleepy. He rolled over and she nestled happily into his arms. He kissed her hair which tasted funny with the dye.

'How long will your hair stay red?' he asked.

'It'll wash out next time I shampoo it.'

'Oh... Angie?'

'Mmm?'

'Does Del know that you and I live together, that we're ... that I'm your boyfriend?'

Sleepily, she said, 'Course.'

'Oh.'

'What?' He felt her raise her head in the darkness. 'You're not jealous?'

'Well...'

She burst out laughing. 'He's just a mate, a pal. Didn't you have women friends when you were young?'

'Not really. You didn't so much in those days. Well, Elise, but I was younger then, before puberty.'

Angie said dismissively, 'He's just a kid. He's nineteen, for God's sake. He's a fwiend.' They both giggled cruelly at Del's speech impediment.

Nineteen was young, he remembered, when you were twenty-four.

She said, 'I had a whotsit tonight, an epiphany.'

'An epiphany? Crikey.'

'I was standing propping up the wall, thinking how I was too old for this sort of party, watching Del dancing with some seventeen-year-old in a catsuit, when I saw why you asked if he reminded me of someone.'

'Ah!'

'You think he looks like Fred, don't you?'

'There's a superficial resemblance,' he admitted. 'Fred was better looking.'

'And that's what this burst of jealousy has been about, hasn't it?'

'I suppose.'

'You think because my first love was a well-built blond, then that's what I'm on the lookout for. I'm not that shallow, Greg.'

'We all have a *type*,' he said lamely.

'I'm nothing like Diana,' she pointed out, referring to his ex-wife, Fred's mother.

'One of your greatest charms!'

He resumed kissing her hair and soon her hands began to move down his body, causing goosebumps where they touched.

Chapter 22

'No DCI Davies?' Greg asked when he reached the station on Monday morning and looked into the CID room.

Barbara, Whittaker and Nicolaides exchanged glances.

Greg said, 'Just tell me.'

'DCI Davies won't be in today, sir,' Barbara said. 'Her father and mother were killed in a car smash on the A4 outside Froxfield. Saturday night – early hours of Sunday morning.'

'My God!'

Greg sat down abruptly on the nearest chair. He remembered Angie's description of the scene: the car pulverised beyond hope of survivors.

Megan opened the door to his knock. There were shadows of sleeplessness under her eyes, emphasised by the pallor of her face.

'I only just heard,' he said. 'I came round to see if there was anything I can do.'

She stood back to let him in and he went into the house which had the anonymity of the rental. Instinct led him to the sitting room on his left, an oblong space running the depth of the house with a square bay at the front. Patio doors at the back led into a small garden with a child's swing.

The walls were painted cream, a darker shade on the woodwork. A beige carpet covered the floor, matching beige curtains with tiny flowers. The sofa and armchairs were plain, pale blue, grouped around the television. A display cabinet in blond wood stood empty against the farther wall behind a dining table and four chairs. There were no ornaments, books or family photographs.

It looked as if no one lived here.

'We haven't really had time to settle in,' she explained, as if reading his thoughts.

She stood in the doorway, her arms wrapped loosely round her torso. She was in mufti: a short, black corduroy skirt, a fluffy pink sweater which looked almost in-decently cheerful, bare legs ending in mules. He didn't know whether to offer a hug, feeling again the initial awkwardness of their first meeting in ten years.

It had been less than a week ago.

'What's happening?' he asked, knowing the need for action in these circumstances, for the feeling that something was being done.

'PM went down yesterday afternoon, but they didn't find anything. I mean, there was a theory that Mum had been drinking but she hardly drank at all and she was well below the limit.'

'She was driving?'

'Yes.'

Megan pulled a string of pearls out of her skirt pocket and looked at them. Her mother's only good piece of jewellery, handed to her by a sympathetic uniform who knew that they might otherwise disappear somewhere along the line of the investigation. She turned them over, admiring their lustre in the light.

'Pearls have to be worn regularly,' she said.

'Yes, I think I've heard that.'

'Without the warmth of human contact, they sicken and die.'

'Like us?'

'Yes.' She took a deep breath and, not raising her eyes from the pinky-white baubles, blurted out, 'I think she did it on purpose, Greg.'

'What!'

'No! Forget I said that.'

'But why would she do such a thing?'

Realising that she had gone too far to turn back and that he would wait for an explanation, she went on. 'They'd been to a golden wedding, two of their oldest friends, Tim and Pat Machin. I went to see them yesterday afternoon. They were shocked and horrified, of course, but I could tell there was something they didn't want to say and I dragged it out of them.

'They'd been embarrassed by Dad's behaviour and so had Mum. They said they knew he'd been ill but they barely recognised him as the same person. He was crude, aggressive, loud. Some of the people there were old friends of Dad's who knew about his stroke and made allowances, but there were plenty of strangers there, people who were shocked by him or – worse – laughing.

'Mum was mortified and tried to leave early but he wasn't having any of it. He was drinking heavily too. Finally he almost got into a fight with a man whose wife he insulted and Mum dragged him away.'

'So she was upset,' Greg said, 'not concentrating on the road. Perhaps she wasn't used to night driving. Or she wasn't used to being up so late and dozed off at the wheel.'

Megan shook her head. 'She was a very careful driver. We used to joke about it. Here's what I think happened. She was brooding. She realised that she couldn't stand it any more. I think she saw that lorry coming on the other carriageway and that it was the work of a moment to steer the car straight into its path; she wouldn't even have to think about it. She knew the lorry driver wouldn't be hurt – she would never knowingly have risked the life of a third party – but to end the pain there and then. I think it was too tempting.'

They were both silent for a moment. Eventually, Greg said, 'What does the lorry driver say?'

'That she shot across the road towards him, that he didn't stand a chance of avoiding her. Uniform are talking about the fell-asleep-at-the-wheel scenario.'

'Then let them,' he said firmly.

'Oh, don't worry.' She slipped the necklace back into her pocket, knowing that she would never wear it, that it would die slowly in a drawer. 'I'm not going to say all this at the Coroner's Court. I'm not going to paint my own mother as a murderer and a suicide.'

'Maybe it was him,' Greg suggested. 'Perhaps he seized the wheel at the crucial moment and twisted it out of her hands.'

Megan shook her head, not as a negative but as a way of saying that they would never know. 'If only I hadn't told Mum about his visit to Halfacre farm. He begged me not to.'

'I don't see how you could have kept it from her.'

'What if that was the last straw?'

'It sounds like this party was the last straw. And if he hadn't gone on that ramble then Salem's body might have lain undiscovered for months and Emilia might still be missing and in who knows what state.'

'True. He was due to see his GP today as well.'

'Could he have done much to help?'

'...I don't suppose so. I went to their house yesterday afternoon, make sure everything was locked up and switched off. I can hardly bear to think, at the moment, about clearing it out, going through all their stuff, though it'll have to be done, and soon. I was looking at the family photograph albums, the mementoes – the vases and ornaments they brought back from family holidays. They'd been married forty-seven years, you know.'

'It's a long time.'

'And they were engaged for four. They were "saving up to get married". People don't do that any more. It wasn't perfect but they both knew their role in the relationship: he made the big decisions; she fed us both and looked after us. Even if they hadn't suited each other so well, it would never have occurred to them to split up. That generation didn't. They made the best of it.'

He laid a comradely hand on her shoulder and she overlaid it with one of hers, accepting the uncomplicated affection which he was offering.

'I can only guess what you're going through,' he said.

'As I can only guess what you went through when your son died.'

Point taken: it was a lucky man or woman who got through life without some personal devastation. They picked up the pieces and they went on.

'And there's the guilt,' she added, 'because I'm also relieved.'

Greg understood about the guilt too.

She glanced at her watch. 'My husband and son will be here any minute to pick me up. Philip has been marvellous. When I rang him last night to tell him the news we were on the phone for hours. He'd have driven straight down through the night if Gareth hadn't already been in bed. I think I'd forgotten, these last few years, what a thoroughly decent man he is and I'm starting to wonder if we couldn't have tried harder...'

'You think there might be a chance of reconciliation?'

'Oh, I don't know! It could be a dead-cat bounce, as they say in the City, but lately I've been reminded of what somebody said once about the deep peace of the marital bed. Who was it?'

'Search me.'

'We've a holiday cottage on the Northumberland Coast we didn't get round to selling yet. A few days there will be restful. Maybe the view of Lindisfarne by sunset will help put things in perspective.'

'Of course,' he said. 'Take a few days compassionate leave, as much as you need.'

She shook her head. 'I have plenty of leave owing.' She was suddenly awkward. 'The thing is, sir, now that Mum and Dad are dead I have nothing to keep me in Newbury.'

'Oh!'

'I'm sorry, but I'll be applying to transfer back to my old patch as soon as may be. My boss told me when I left that the door would be open if he had anything to do with it.'

'I'm sure.'

'I'm letting you down, aren't I?'

'We'll manage. We're used to it.'

He could hear Jim Barkiss's raucous laugh in his mind's ear. 'To lose one DCI, my dear Gregory, may be regarded as a misfortune; to lose two looks like carelessness; but to lose *three*...'

'It's not as if I've exactly covered myself with glory here,' Megan was saying as he turned his mind back to listening to her. 'With the Troy case. I didn't check out their garage till you pointed it out... You never really trusted me with the investigation–'

'That's not–'

'And you were right. After all, it was my fault Salem's house got gutted.'

'Your fault?'

'Babs wanted to leave someone on guard overnight. I overrode that.'

'I see. I didn't realise.' He owed Barbara an apology, but it wouldn't be the first time. She was a gracious acceptor of apologies. 'You had a lot on your mind.'

'Well...'

She glanced at her weekend bag where it stood, propping open the sitting room door, and he recognised his dismissal.

'I'll get off then.'

As they stood together at the front door, each wondering what form of farewell was appropriate, a navy blue BMW pulled up in the drive with one short blast of its horn. The passenger door opened and a boy of nine scrambled out, trying not to smile too hard at his mother as he recalled that his granny and grandpa were dead.

Greg looked at Megan's son with interest and a little surprise: he was tall for his age, thin; intense dark eyes gleamed intelligence out of a brown face; he had the high brow and cheekbones of an African prince.

'Mum!' He hugged her unselfconsciously as she stroked his wiry curls.

The driver of the car stood a little awkwardly half in, half out of his door. He was an ebony-coloured man in expensively casual clothes. In the resonant tones of the better type of English boarding school he said one word.

'Megan.'

It was enough. She said, 'Philip!' He slammed the car door shut and joined the tableau in the porch.

Their business was far from finished, Greg thought.

'I'm ready,' Megan said. 'Greg this is my

husband, Philip Adelakum, and our son Gareth. My boss, Superintendent Summers.'

The two men shook hands in acknowledgement of the introduction, not needing speech. Adelakum picked up his wife's bag and slung it in the boot of the BMW. Megan turned to Greg and shook his hand in her turn.

'I expect we'll run into each other again,' she said, 'maybe at some training course or conference.'

He thought that she winked at him, but he couldn't be sure.

He got into his car and drove off, but after five minutes he swerved into a handy lay-by and switched off the engine. He sat slumped in his seat for a while, oblivious to the coming and going of other vehicles, to the van that offered tea and fetid burgers, to desperate drivers sneaking into the shelter of the bushes to relieve themselves.

He was mulling over the crazy notions that had been going through his head since Megan had told him that her son was nine years old, born, therefore, some months after their brief liaison.

Of course her son was not also his; why had such a ludicrous idea ever entered his mind? When you'd lost one son, you didn't get another as painlessly as that, bypassing the sleepless nights and the teething and the toddler tantrums.

He couldn't face going back to the office. He would take the rest of the day off. He'd been putting in the hours this last week and they owed it to him. It was Monday and Angie worked at home on Mondays and he had a strong need to be with her.

He was at the end of a phone if a crisis arose.

Superintendent Gregory Summers drove home to the deep peace of the non-marital bed, feeling a little sad.

The publishers hope that this book has given you enjoyable reading. Large Print Books are especially designed to be as easy to see and hold as possible. If you wish a complete list of our books please ask at your local library or write directly to:

Magna Large Print Books
Magna House, Long Preston,
Skipton, North Yorkshire.
BD23 4ND

This Large Print Book, for people
who cannot read normal print,
is published under the auspices of

THE ULVERSCROFT FOUNDATION

Other MAGNA Titles
In Large Print

ANNE BAKER
Merseyside Girls

JESSICA BLAIR
The Long Way Home

W. J. BURLEY
The House Of Care

MEG HUTCHINSON
No Place For A Woman

JOAN JONKER
Many A Tear Has To Fall

LYNDA PAGE
All Or Nothing

NICHOLAS RHEA
Constable Over The Bridge

MARGARET THORNTON
Beyond The Sunset